UNDER THE STARS

USA *TODAY* BESTSELLING AUTHOR

TIA LOUISE

This book is a work of fiction. Names, characters, places, and incidents are products of the author's imagination or are used fictitiously. Any resemblance to actual events or locales or persons, living or dead, is entirely coincidental.

For the survivors.

CONTENTS

PROLOGUE

"What value is life if we are not together?"
–Jane Austen

Five years, seven months after **Under the Lights.**

Lara

The sunrise paints the early morning clouds in gold, salmon, orange, and yellow, burning stripes above the emerald green and deep blue waters of the Mediterranean Sea.

I walk on sugar-white sands down a grassy hill from Freddie's villa in Nice, the one he allows us to live in since Molly stopped being able to sleep.

Since she became obsessed with revenge.

My chest is heavy, and my mind is filled with images of our last errand…

A cold white night.

A beautiful man with beautiful eyes and a beautiful soul.

An urgent knock on the door blasting it all to hell.

The salty breeze whips around me, twisting my dark hair into a rope where it's tied at my neck. Catching the sides of my oversized white shirt, I pull it closer around my body, covering the thin tank underneath.

"Lara!" The high voice catches my attention, and I look up to the top of the hill.

Molly waves and starts down the weathered wooden staircase leading from the top of the berm to the shore where I stand. Every morning I'm here. I'm easy to find… for anyone who's looking.

The salt water washes over my feet, cold and shocking. I watch as the watery sand surrounds them and they slowly disappear.

Tiny splashes, and a Yorkshire terrier joins me in the surf. I bend down to pat his little head. "Hi, Pierre."

"Hey!" Molly bends down to scoop up her little dog. "It's time to talk about what's next."

My lips press into a sad smile, and I stand, placing my arm around her waist. She allows me this small token of affection as we resume my stroll down the shoreline.

"We have at least four months before we can do anything," I say, hoping to placate her.

Her body stiffens, but the fight has left me. I understood before. She needed to finish a job no one else could be trusted to do, but now I'm tired. I'm sad, and I'm ready to be done with it. No matter how much we've accomplished, how much justice is served, I can't help feeling like it cost me everything.

Almost everything.

My mind skips across the miles to that night seven months ago…

I stood in the doorway, and our eyes locked over the evidence of what she'd done.

Only minutes before, I'd been surrounded by Mark's strong arms, secure and happy, in a cocoon of love and protection. I'd looked ahead, into a future of all the beautiful things that might be mine.

The faintest knock on the door changed it.

"It's over," I said looking down at the dead body.

Molly stood looking at her handiwork, lips tight and body stiff.

No tremors.

No fear.

No regrets.

"They're all gone," I said.

Reaching out, I tried to touch her, to comfort her, but she pulled away, anger lining her young face.

"There's still one more."

My brow furrowed as I recalled her list of names. "That was the last one."

"There's one more. The biggest one of all."

My reticence makes her angry, and my arm is awkward around her stiff body. Vigilante justice is the path she chose, but my wounds have lost their power. They're not worth the fresh ones I've acquired.

"Four months, tops," she argues, blue eyes slicing into mine.

Barely contained rage bubbles behind those eyes. She's got the taste for blood, and whether it's to avenge her or me, she wants more. She wants it all. She hasn't lost anything. For her it's been only gain, and she won't stop until they're all dead.

"You understand in four months, I'll barely be out of recovery?"

"I understand no one would ever suspect the three of us in four months."

Exhaling a deep breath, I try. If I've already lost everything, what does it matter? Anyway, she's probably right. In four months, we'll be even less suspicious.

We stop walking and turn to face the emerald waters. The briny air pushes her hair back and around her shoulders. Tendrils spin around my face, and the inescapable sorrow filters through my chest.

"I can't do this anymore."

"Yes, you can." Her voice is flat, and she bends to put Pierre on the dry sand. "I'm going up. How much longer will you be out here? Celeste is making Quiche Lorraine for breakfast."

Another sigh. "I'll be up in a bit. I'm finishing my exercise."

"Don't stay out too long or I'll eat all the food! Come, Pierre!"

I watch her run up the tall staircase, her little dog at her heels, thinking of the reasons she has to run. I remember her as a small girl on the street, in the dark alley behind the theater. She was thin and starving and hunched in the corner waiting to die.

She was so malnourished, I thought she was younger than her actual age, which was twelve. I remember carrying her inside and fighting with Rosa. I remember Rosa boxing my ears and telling me the first time that kid cried, she'd throw us both in the alley with the rats. I remember the terror I felt that night and Molly falling asleep so quietly with her head on my chest.

She needed me. She loved me, and I loved her fiercely in return.

I remember her running around the theater, a sweet and innocent kid never suspecting the hawk was circling above, watching her, closing in to steal her soul and warp her future. I'll never forgive myself for what happened to her. I'll never forgive myself for not being there to protect her.

A flash of pain moves through my stomach, and I remember someone saying the same words to me not so long ago…

Walking to the edge of the water, I look out at the surf, at the waves rushing in and out. I think about how nothing bad can happen here. The sins of the past are far, far away from this beautiful place.

Only it's a lie.

The sins of the past are never far away.

We carry them with us in our hearts wherever we go.

No matter how far we run, we can never outrun ourselves.

Tears are in my eyes, and I blink them away. My emotions are so close to the surface these days. I squat and wrap my arms around my knees, holding my insides together and wishing...

My wishes never come true.

"Lara!" A strong male voice cuts through the breeze.

For a moment I don't believe it. It's a wish caught on the wind and carried away out to sea.

"Lara!" It's louder this time, closer.

Nervous anticipation floods my chest. I stand and look up and over my shoulder. The staircase where Molly descended is empty. The one ahead of it is empty as well.

Was it a dream?

Another shout, and I realize it's coming from behind me. Turning, I see a tall figure jogging down the steps. He's alone, and he's moving fast. I look around, and no one is here. I have nowhere to run, nowhere to hide.

My heart alternates between beating out of my chest and dying. I'm back on that train, seeing him for the first time out of the blue, completely caught off-guard, alternately panicking and rejoicing... *He's alive!*

He's wearing faded jeans and a plain white t-shirt. His caramel hair is a little longer, but not much. It moves in the breeze as he approaches me.

He's strong and pure and gorgeous as ever, and the way we touched, our glorious reunion is stronger and hotter in my memory than the sun climbing higher in the sky.

I want to cry. I want to sing. I want to hold him…

But now everything has changed.

He only pauses a moment at the bottom before dipping his head and starting forward, heading to me at a steady clip. I'm standing in the surf defenseless against reality racing closer by the second.

Catching the sides of my blouse, I pull the thin cotton around my body. I wrap my arms over my stomach just in case. The wide straw hat is on my head, and it flaps and bows in the sea breeze.

I'm barefoot, so at six foot two, he towers over my tiny frame. I wait, watching the play of the wind on the fabric of his clothes, knowing I have nothing to say, no excuses to give. My heart beats painfully hard at the thought of everything he has the right to say. I'm utterly defenseless.

Still, he's so blindingly sexy. He's standing here, looking down on me, clenching and unclenching his fists. His full lips press together then relax as if he doesn't know where to begin. I can't take the pressure, so I say the first thing I think.

"You shaved your beard."

He reaches up and passes a hand over his cheek and chin. "It's coming back."

"Five o'clock shadow." I nod, swallowing my nerves. "It looks good on you."

So much emotion swirls in his blue eyes, so much pain.

My heart aches at the way he looks at me. He'll never know how much I wanted to stay with him that ice-cold morning on the train.

The wind hits me hard in the face, and I reach up to keep my hat from blowing away, unintentionally releasing the large shirt covering the knit tank stretched over my growing stomach. His eyes dart down and widen. They fly back to mine, and everything changes.

"When were you going to tell me?" His voice is sharp, somewhere on the edge of anger and need.

"I-I don't know." I'm ashamed but elated. I want him here, but I know it can never be possible. "I didn't know how I could tell you… How we could make it work."

In a sweep, he steps forward, gripping my arms and giving me a light shake. "Dammit—you don't get to decide things like that on your own. You don't get to tell me what can and can't work when it comes to this."

It's too much. My chin drops, and the tears flood my eyes.

I'm standing on my favorite beach, in the place where we ran to for safety years ago. We're here because it's still safe, and we're hiding, hoping to start a new life…

I am starting a new life.

A new life is starting inside of me.

"How did you find me?" I look up at his ocean blue eyes.

They're grey like the waves during a storm, and I know his storm is the same one battering my insides. It's elation at seeing each other again. It's devastation at knowing anything between us is impossible.

"I've done nothing but search for you since the

day you left." He takes a few steps toward the berm the turns and strides back to me. "I searched all over the U.S. and Canada, Alaska... then I remembered what you said about France."

"It's a big country."

"It took me six months to find you."

"What happens now?"

Looking down, he clears his throat before blinking up to me again. "Didn't it mean anything to you?"

The tears are back, sneaky bastards, and I have to cough to keep them away. He has no idea how much all of it meant to me.

"You weren't supposed to be on that train." I touch the corners of my eyes.

The waves hiss and sizzle behind us. He steps closer, gripping my upper arms in tight fists. "I was on that train."

"Yes..." My next words hurt like the devil. "And did it not occur to you that my job was to keep the attractive detective occupied while she did what she needed to do?"

Blue eyes flash as if I struck him. He processes that statement only as long as it takes for his eyes to return to my pregnant stomach. "You didn't use protection."

"Neither did you."

His jaw is tight. "I don't want protection. I've only ever wanted you, to keep you safe from the demons."

"They weren't my demons on that trip."

Two more breaths. He looks out at the waves, and I watch as he's thinking, as his face melt from rage to reality. His gaze returns to me, and he seems to have reached a conclusion.

"No." He grabs me by the waist and pulls me to him, pausing only to angle my body to allow for my small baby bump. "You're not pushing me away again. I won't let you."

I'm surrounded by his strong arms, and in spite of it all, a surge of joy floods my veins. *I love you I love you I love you...* Every cell in my body sings his name, sings the joy burning in my chest.

It's all fucked up and wrong, but for six months, all I've dreamed of is being right here, never leaving again. My hand slides up, and my fingers clutch his shirt. I hold him in a way I have no right to do.

"You're a cop," I say quietly. "You can't let us get away with murder."

He straightens, catching my chin and lifting it. "Did you commit the crime?"

"No." *Not that one.*

He hugs me closer, and I tuck my face against him cherishing this moment of pure joy, listening to his heart beating strong in his chest.

When he speaks, his voice is low and grave, sorting through the facts. "I knew Esterhaus from my days as Gavin's doorman. I had no evidence, no way to arrest him for anything, so I watched him, waiting. We made yearly trips across country. We smoked. We drank scotch. We played cards." He pauses before continuing. "I knew he did wrong, but he never gave me any reason to suspect he hurt a child."

Clearing the tightness in my throat, I take a step back, out of his arms. Our eyes meet, and I can see he's waiting for me to give him a reason.

"When the theater changed, a handful of men became regular visitors." An involuntary shaking breaks out from my chest as I begin to travel down this dark path. The memory sickens me. Saying the words out loud makes my lips tremble with fear.

Still… If Molly survived it, I can say it.

"As you know, he wasn't a baron back then. He was only a businessman who visited the city."

"I remember your question the first night."

Sorrow radiates through my chest on every breath. It grips my shoulders as the memories punish me. No matter how many times I try to exorcise these demons, they always come back to bury me in guilt.

Mark pulls me close. He wraps one strong arm around my waist. The other he uses to smooth my hair back, to wipe the tears away with gentle hands.

"You tried to take her place?" His voice is rich with understanding.

"I never even knew when she was taken." My voice breaks. The floodgates in my chest open as the storms of grief rain down. "They took turns with her. She was only thirteen. She was just a little girl, and when she came back…"

I can't say it.

I exhale a violent sob.

I can still see her limp body.

I can still see the blood on her clothes.

Before she was so happy and full of life.

After, she was never the same again.

He holds me as I weep, sliding his hand up and down my back, kissing my head, my temple, my cheek.

"He was one of the men who raped her." Mark's voice is calm, resolute.

My cheeks are wet with tears, but I push them aside. I use my sleeve to dry my face, resentment giving me strength.

"The system is broken. For her to get justice… it would be impossible. It was so long ago and nothing was recorded. We have no physical evidence. It would be her word against his, a baron."

The muscle moves in his jaw, and he stares out to sea. His expression is stony, but when he turns back to me, his eyes soften.

"So you ran from me."

Dropping my chin again, I nod. "You can't be a part of this. I would never ask you to violate your oath or betray your honor that way."

He's quiet, but he puts his arm around my waist, pulling me to him again. "You're carrying my baby. You're the mother of my child, and you need to be with me."

My eyes squeeze closed as a pulse of emotion echoes in my chest. I want to be with him, with everything in my body.

But I made a promise, too.

"What else?" he asks as if reading my mind.

"I promised to help her find them all."

"How many are left?"

Resting my cheek against him, I inhale his faint citrus mixed with sea breeze scent. "One."

Briefly, I allow myself to remember that one. I consider how Mark has changed and how he would react if he knew the whole story of the last one. Mark isn't a weak young boy anymore. He would take the fight out of our hands if he knew it included me.

He would do something dangerous…

"You're not going after anyone while you're carrying our baby." His words distract me from my dark thoughts.

"No." I shake my head, holding onto his shirt. "I told her at least four months."

His expression changes to warmth, pride, and he places both hands on my stomach, smoothing them over the rounded swell of our baby growing inside. I place my hands on top of his, and we hold them, the three of us together at last.

"I dreamed of you carrying my child." His gaze remains on our hands. "You were always so beautiful. Now you're even more beautiful."

Fresh tears flood my eyes, and I can't help a smile. It's all so horrible and yet at the same time, it's so perfect.

"I'm more emotional now."

He catches my hands, holding them tightly in his. "You're going to marry me. We'll arrange everything here. We'll have a ceremony on this beach, and when the baby comes, he'll… she'll…" Curious eyes rise to mine.

A touch of nerves hits me.

We've never talked about this. I don't know what he wants.

"It's a girl," I say, waiting… holding my breath.

His eyes gleam and the smile brightens his face. "She."

He cups my cheeks and covers my mouth with his. It's hungry and passionate and… happy.

I reach up to hold him, and all of it is back, every emotion we've ever shared. Our lips chase, our tongues collide and curl together. Heat floods my panties, and desire rushes in like the waves. I want his shirt off. I want him inside me.

"I want to make love to you," he says, and I laugh. "What?" He grins.

"It's the only thing I can think about."

Joy bursts in my chest like a tiny plant pushing through the darkness of the soil. It won't be kept down. It radiates from the center of my being, stretching toward him like the sun.

"Look at me." His hands hold my cheeks. "We're going to figure this out. We're going to get married, the baby will come, and we will make it work." My fingers tighten on the soft fabric of his shirt as he speaks. "But before any of that, you have to know one thing: I love you, Lara. I love you more than any of this, with everything I have."

"Oh, Mark…" The swell of joy in my chest explodes into a burst of flowers. Butterflies take flight, and it's like spring has come.

"I love you," I answer quickly. "I love you so much."

Strong arms surround me, and we're lost in another passionate kiss. What's coming is too much for me to think about, but I'm holding onto the happiest ever after I never dreamed I could possibly have.

CHAPTER 1

"The murderer shall hang by the neck until dead..."
-Napoleonic Code

Six years after Under the Lights.

Mark

She's gone.

After only four weeks together, I roll over this morning to find her side of the bed cold and empty.

No warning.

No reason.

All she left behind is the shortest "Dear John" note in history.

Dear Mark,

I love you more than I can ever say, but I can't pull you any further into this. I can't ruin your life. I'm so sorry. Please don't try to find me.

Love,
Lara

Don't try to find me, my ass.

I'm out of bed, tearing through the large house, going from room to room searching for any clues to where they went. All I get is the same sickening *déjà vu* from the last time she ran.

The room we've been sharing is clean except for my things. Molly's room is pristine, like no one has ever been in it. Not even a trace of her little dog. Racing downstairs, the living room looks like the showroom of a furniture store. The kitchen could be featured in fucking Pottery Barn.

Whipping out my phone, I call her number. It rings once, and her voicemail picks up. My voice is strained as I leave a message, unconvinced she'll even hear it. I know how call-blocking works.

"Don't do this, Lara. Call me back."

Dropping onto a barstool, I put my face in my hands.

"Lara." The force of anger and frustration coursing through my body changes my voice to a growl.

When I ran into her on the White Pass-Yukon Route, the first time I'd seen her in five years, she left behind a dead body and me with my dick in my hands trying to figure out what happened.

I finally found her here, in a villa in Nice owned by Freddie Lovel, the rich guy who used to visit her after her Pussycat Angels performances.

For three weeks, we've been the only people living in this elaborate home.

Returning to our bedroom, I stand in the open doorway of the balcony. Overhead is an awning covered in wisteria, and in front of me is a panoramic view of the Mediterranean Sea.

My jaw tightens as memories of the nights we sat out here listening to the ocean, drinking wine, making love, and making plans for our wedding, for our daughter, flood my mind.

We planned to name her Jillian after my mother, who died when I was only ten. She'd been the only good thing in my life when I was a boy, and when I lost her, it felt like everything unraveled.

I'd wanted to give that name a fresh beginning, welcome its grace back into our home, and Lara had agreed.

She'd sat there and fucking agreed to everything.

Now she leaves me flat, like I'm some kind of one-night stand.

Anger burns in my chest as I storm into the bedroom and start stuffing my things into my bag. I'm out the door and headed to the train station in less than ten minutes.

Destination, Paris, the seventh arrondissement.

When I arrive at the white building with black shutters and antique metal accents, he's coming out the front door.

"*Excusez-moi.*" With a nod, he attempts to pass me at the front steps.

"Excuse me." I put my hand on his shoulder and hold up my badge. "Detective Mark Fitzhugh. I need to speak with you about Lara or Larissa Hale."

He steps back, assessing me with slate-gray eyes. "I'm sorry, is there a problem?"

"May we step inside?"

"Of course." We enter his elegant townhome in the most expensive neighborhood in Paris.

I spent the six-hour train ride from Nice researching this man and his millions. His father is an exporter who works with several businesses in New Orleans, from food to coffee to liquor. The Lovels own several houses, ranging from Paris to the villa in Nice to a condo in New Orleans.

"May I offer you a drink?" Freddie looks like he hasn't worked a day in his life.

He's dressed in faded dark gray trousers with brown shoes, a crisp white long-sleeved shirt with a black blazer, and a scarf tied at his neck.

"No thanks." I take out my phone as if I'm reading notes. "How long did Lara Hale live here with you?"

It's not really pertinent to my investigation, but fuck it. I want to know.

"I'm sorry, you seem to be mistaken. Miss Hale never lived with me. She stayed with my sister Annemarie."

The fist in my chest unclenches slightly. He wasn't her lover. "Is your sister's house nearby?"

"She has a three-bedroom apartment on the rue Bonaparte."

I have no idea where that is. "That's close to here?"

"It's about three blocks away."

The anger returns. "So she stayed with you overnight?"

His eyes narrow, and a small smile curls his lips. "I didn't have that kind of relationship with Lara. She came to Paris hoping for a better life. I merely offered her a place to stay."

"With your sister."

"I confess, I had hoped eventually it would be with me, but *c'est la vie*. It never happened."

For a moment, we quietly assess each other. Until he cocks his head. "Do we know one another? You seem familiar…"

"We've never met." It's true — we've never been formally introduced.

"So what's this about? Is Lara in trouble?"

Not so fast. "How long has she lived in your villa in Nice?"

His eyebrows jump. "She moved there shortly after arriving in Paris. She stayed here barely a month when her sister began having... issues."

"What type of issues?"

A small table holding several crystal bottles of different shades of liquor sits in front of a large, arched window. He walks to it, and for a moment seems lost in thought.

"Paris can be difficult. It's like New Orleans... but about ten times bigger and ten times less forgiving. Add the language barrier, and some might feel overwhelmed."

"What happened to Molly?"

He faces me. "She had trouble sleeping. Night terrors, I think you call it. Screaming in the night, dreaming of someone chasing her, hurting her. We tried getting her a little dog—"

"Did she ever say any names?" I realize I'm leaning forward, anxious for anything.

"I was never there when it happened. Annemarie told me later." He exhales deeply, studying his fingers. "But they were both miserable here. My sister said she would find Lara crying all the time. I finally suggested they might be happier in Nice."

"You sent them to your villa?"

"If you're going to mourn, you should at least have beautiful scenery."

I rock back on my heels, my feelings toward this man conflicted. He seems to genuinely care about them, and I should be thankful.

"So you have no idea where they might be now?"

"I wish I did. I still believe Lara could have a fantastic career as a singer if only..." Turning his arm, he checks the heavy silver watch. "I do need to get to my lunch date, so if that's all?"

Reaching into my breast pocket, I take out my business card. "If you hear from either one, please let me know."

He studies it a moment. "I'll let them know you're looking for them, Mr. Fitzhugh."

"I'd rather you didn't."

His smile grows wider. "My loyalty is to the ladies. Not you."

"And if they committed a crime?"

Gray eyes move up and down my less-fashionable attire. "You're not a French policeman."

"I don't want to arrest them. I want to help them."

"Then they will be pleased to hear you're looking for them."

My room in the Hotel Saint Germaine is small and functional, and once I'm inside, I sit on the bed and book the next flight leaving Paris. I'm no closer to knowing where they went than I was this morning, but I do know they're both struggling with some emotional turmoil.

Frustration twists in my chest as I wait for my laptop to boot. Why would she do this? Why wouldn't she let me in? What about my baby girl?

Again I take out my phone, but this time I send a text.

"Lara." My jaw is clenched. "Where are you?"

Tossing the device on the bed, I rub my temples. This morning, I didn't even stop to consider how her leaving affected me. I hopped on a train for the city and spent the ride learning all I could about the man who brought her here... only to discover he's not an asshole and is actually more interested in her singing career. Unexpected.

In New Orleans, Molly was just a kid who wanted me to teach her to draw. Five years later, on the train to Canada, I didn't even recognize her. She was the femme fatale, and Esterhaus fell right into her hands. She pretended to be an innocent doll, when in reality, she was a cold-blooded killer with an agenda.

I scroll through my emails with Freddie's words about night terrors lingering in my thoughts. Why do they keep running? Who is left?

I'll head back to Juneau and search from my office. Hopefully I can get to Lara before they go further down this rabbit hole.

Before someone else dies.

CHAPTER 2

"Heads inside a dream." -Lorde

Three months later.

Lara

Mark's soft lips cover mine.

My fingers curl in his light brown hair, and I inhale deeply, relaxing in his strong arms. He's never been timid with his kisses. He's never been timid with his love-making. Warm breath whispers on my neck, and the tiny hairs on my body rise as his lips trace my ribs, moving lower to my waist.

A soft moan comes from my throat as he loops his fingers around my panties and tugs them aside. He's always been forceful, and I love it. An aching pulse rises from the center of my body up through my arms and down to the arches of my feet as his lips close over my clit, giving it a gentle pull before circling it with his tongue.

"Mark!" I gasp, my orgasm rising fast.

Circling, pulling, stroking—my eyes squeeze shut, my back rises off the bed. My fists clench in the soft sheets as the irresistible tightness grows stronger in my belly.

"Oh, God!" I cry out as the crash of orgasm breaks through me, leaving me shuddering in its wake.

He's up fast, kissing his way up my body. He stops at my left breast, giving the nipple a gentle pull before kissing a trail across to the other. Every touch sends another spark of pleasure to my tingling core.

Until finally our mouths meet, and I'm lost in his deep kiss, tongues entwining, tasting, pulling. So long I've waited for this, but it's my turn to take the lead.

Like a playful kitten, I rise up and push him into the pillows, kissing his smiling lips, then his eyes. I taste salty tears, and my own eyes heat. He's never been sentimental, but being separated has been overwhelmingly cruel.

I close my eyes and slide my face down to his bare chest. His heart beats as fast as mine, and a flutter of happiness fills me. I trace my finger over the lines of his stomach and the few coarse hairs scattered there, pressing my lips to his hot skin.

I feel his erection against my stomach, and slide my hand down to grip it, tugging gently. I move slowly, letting the tension build, but he's impatient.

With a low growl he says my name and flips me under him again, searching for my mouth and pushing it open, pushing my thighs apart as he reaches between us to line his tip at my entrance.

With a sharp thrust, he fills me to the hilt.

"Mark!" My head tips back, and I gasp at the sensation.

Peppermint is on my tongue. He holds my hair back and kisses my neck, thrusting rapidly, sending me higher with every invasion. My second orgasm is building, and his mouth is on my throat, my cheek, my temple.

Another sizzle of desire pulses through me, and I wrap my legs around his waist, sending him even deeper.

"Lara," he groans, driving faster until he holds, pulsing and filling me.

An excited sigh slips from my throat. His arms circle my waist, and he holds me in the secure embrace I love. My hands grip his shoulders as the waves of bliss flow over me, over both of us.

"I love you," I whisper, and my eyes flutter open.

The room is pitch black and cold.

Silence presses against my inner ears so hard they ache.

My heart beats fast and my body is hot from the fading orgasm, but it's only a dream. I'm alone here, lying on my stomach in the soft bed piled high with pillows and duvets. My arms are stretched out, searching to hold him, but no one is there.

I close my eyes and try to get back into the dream. It was so real. I can still feel him, still hear his voice. I press my face into the pillow, searching for his scent, but I only smell fresh detergent on a cool pillow.

In that instant, an ache twists deep in my stomach. My knees rise and my pillow muffles the low moan I can't hold inside as I begin to weep. I'm throbbing, the physical frustration as painful as my emptiness. I wrap my arms around my legs and hold them, fighting for control. I have to hold on.

Several minutes pass, and I'm finally able to calm my breathing. I roll to the side and sit up carefully, reaching for a tissue from the box by my bed. I'm dressed in a long tee, and I go to the door, quietly crossing the hall to Jillian's room.

It's a tiny room Roland said he's sure was meant to be a pantry. We've put her portable crib in it and a cute little Tree of Life lamp complete with animals circling it, and she's snug and warm in the little space.

But when I approach, I see her crib is empty.

"What?" A jolt of fear seizes my chest, and I search, feeling around in the blankets.

Her baby scent is still there, and the mattress is warm.

Dashing out of the room, I run into the living area, when I stop in my tracks. Sitting on the leather couch, his feet on the coffee table and a Kindle in his hand, Roland has my little girl swaddled and sleeping on his chest.

The sight eases the pressure, calms the fears, and I go to them, quietly padding across the wood floor.

Worried eyes flicker to mine. "Another dream?"

I sit on the couch right beside him, and rest my head on my hand. Jillian's eyes are closed, but her little rosebud lips move in a sucking motion.

I smile and place my hand on her back. "She's going to want her bottle soon."

"You didn't answer my question." His voice is low and soothing.

Shifting in my seat, I look straight ahead at the French doors lining the front of his house. "I miss him so much."

"He needs to know his daughter. It's cruel to keep her from him."

Guilt floods my chest. "It's the hardest thing I've ever done," I whisper. "But I couldn't leave her behind, and I couldn't pull him deeper into this."

"He's going to find you, and when he does, I hope he takes a riding crop to your ass. If it were me, you wouldn't sit comfortably for a week, possibly a month."

My watery eyes roll. "You've been watching *Fifty Shades of Grey* again."

"Damn straight. Jamie Dornan is fine."

I manage to exhale a short laugh, but I'm still miserable. "And why do you have Jilly out of her crib?"

"I thought I heard her cry." My eyes narrow, and he chuckles. "Okay, I wanted to hold her."

"She's pretty amazing." I slide my hand over her back. "Are you sure you don't mind keeping her for me?"

"She can stay with Uncle Roland as long as she wants. Just let me know when you're ready to give her to me."

His words help me smile through the pain, but it's never far away. "What about your work?"

"Evie can't wait to be over here spoiling her rotten the nights I have to play."

"You like the piano bar?"

"It's fun." He exhales, shifting in his seat. "I don't know if I'll stay there forever, but the pay is excellent, no stress—"

"And you stopped smoking."

"God, that was the worst part," he groans. "I'm not sure which I hate more, the patch or the gum."

I put my head on his shoulder, stroking my daughter's back again. "I'm glad you had to quit. It's much healthier."

"No smoking in bars. Who would've believed something like that would happen? Still, I'm through the worst of it." His slim hand covers mine. "Funny how they grandfathered in the Pussycat club... then it burned to the ground."

"Good riddance." The very thought of that place provokes a visceral response in me. Despite it all, I made some lifelong friends there. "How is Evie?"

"Very happy. She loves her boys. It's one of my better matches, if I do say so myself."

"You say that like it's a real relationship."

His brow furrows. "What do you mean? They've been together almost six years."

33

"Phillip and Armand are gay…" My voice drops. "What does Evie get out of it?"

"A very nice home, clothes, excellent food, and from what I've heard, pretty mind-blowing orgasms."

I pull back, thinking about that. "Who does she…"

Roland's dark eyes slide to mine. "How can you possibly be so innocent after everything that happened? For starters, Armand is bisexual."

Sitting back, I try to imagine. "I didn't think that was a thing."

"Time to evolve, dear."

"Okay, so Armand goes both ways, but Phillip doesn't."

"From what I've heard, they liked to switch up which piggy's in the middle."

"As in Evie…" My forehead wrinkles. "But that hurts. Bad."

"Darling, being forced is very different from having someone you love carefully filling all your holes."

A cringe involuntarily moves through me. "Can we leave bad memories buried? The best part is not remembering any of it. Still, it took so much therapy to get over."

"I'm sorry." His warm hand covers mine, and he gives it a squeeze. "You brought it up."

"I did not."

Jillian starts to squirm, and we both stop talking. He mouths "you did" to me, and I narrow my eyes.

Once it's clear my daughter isn't waking up, I sigh and shake my head. "To each his own," I whisper.

"Speaking of, how's your own?"

I put my face on my hand again. "He's so good."

"I'm sure he is." I get a naughty wink for that.

"No, I mean... Well, yes, he is, but I mean in every way. He's so good. He really is a hero." The light through the windows is growing slowly brighter, and I push off the couch to start Jillian's bottle.

"You're really good," Roland says, catching my hand. "You're beautiful and talented and loyal to a fault. And when you make a promise, you damn well keep it."

"This one is going to be better than all of us," I say, leaning down to kiss my baby's head, her chestnut hair soft against my lips.

She starts to move, and I know she'll be awake soon.

Roland rubs his hand up and down her back. "You've done enough for her."

It takes me a moment to realize he means Molly. "I made a promise."

"And she's taking advantage of it. With all that therapy, why didn't she take part?"

"Confronting these men is her version of therapy."

"You said she found Esterhaus in Canada. He's the last one. So why the trip to Seattle?"

Standing in the kitchen doorway, I look down at my feet, turning the truth over in my mind before speaking it. "We're going after Gavin."

Anger flashes across his face. "No."

"He harbored Guy. He protected the monsters. He used all of us so they could pocket hundreds of thousands of—"

"I said *no*." His voice is stern. "Let sleeping dogs lie."

"I can't do that."

"*You* can't? You?" His dark brow lowers, and he leans forward. "I thought all this was because of your promise to Molly. Instead it's about you?"

"He's the last one Molly wanted to go after."

"But you're clearly onboard."

Tears sting in my eyes. "How could he give away a little girl like she was nothing?"

"Because to him, she was nothing."

"That better not be all." My teeth clench, and I shake my head. "He'd better come up with a better reason than that."

"Or what? You'll kill him?"

I can't answer that question. I'm not planning to do anything like that ever again. At the same time, I can't make any promises on how I might respond to seeing him after everything that's happened.

"Lara." Warning is in his voice.

"I just want to know why."

"You need Mark. Gavin is dangerous. He'll do whatever it takes to protect himself."

"Mark is a cop, Roland. If he knows what we've done… What I've done…" Pain burns in my heart, pain mingled with fear, because while I know I'm right, I know what Roland is saying is the truth. Gavin has always been powerful and unpredictable.

Still, how can I ask Mark to choose between helping us and breaking his oath to uphold the law? Our justice falls in the gray zone laws haven't been able to sort out yet.

"How will you find him? He went underground shortly after the fire, and no one's seen or heard from him in years."

"Molly will find him."

He exhales deeply and shakes his head. "Let the past go and learn to live with it."

"After I find Gavin." I go into the small kitchen and prepare Jillian's formula.

Shaking the bottle, I return to find her big blue eyes open and her small hands reaching for Roland's face. She's smiling, and every time her little palm makes contact with his lips, he gives it a kiss. For a minute I stand and watch them, wishing it could all be this simple.

"I don't know how I'm going to leave her tomorrow." My chest tightens, and I'm afraid I might cry again. "Three days feels like a lifetime."

"I'll take good care of her."

"I know." I hand him the bottle and sit beside them on the couch. As soon as I sit, she fusses for me, and he hands her over. This dark topic is wearing me down, and I can't think about it. I can't analyze it. I just have to do it.

"So tell me about Rosa and the other girls," I say, hoping for a distraction. "What are they doing?"

"Oh, they're scattered around town. Rosa's working at another show. Vanessa's still stripping. Badly. Bea's on the school board—"

"You've got to be kidding me."

"I wish I were."

I'm out of words, so I look at my sweet baby's face. She smiles, tangling her tiny fingers in my hair, and my chest relaxes. She's only three months old, but she's so alert and happy. Her world is bright and full of hope, and I'll do everything in my power to keep it that way.

I glance up at my friend and think about us here now, outside that prison. "We never used to talk like this."

He nods. "It's true. It was hard to think of much else besides survival in those days."

My eyes return to Jillian. "I can't imagine her being trapped in a place like that."

Roland scoots forward and untangles her fingers from my hair. "Do you ever sing anymore?"

"It's been a long time."

"Here." He takes my hand. "Sing it with me."

My nose wrinkles. "I don't want to. It's been too long."

"Just the main chorus." He hums the first note, but I don't think I can do it.

Still, when he begins, I join him on the harmony.

You're in my arms, and it feels so right...
But it's simply aaahhhn illusion.

"You know, sometimes I wondered if you wrote those words for Mark and me."

"It was some of my best work." He leans back on the couch, sliding his hands down his thighs. "I don't miss the pressure or the darkness, but I do miss the creative freedom."

"You can't do what you want now?"

"I can. I just don't have anyone to do it with."

Jillian finishes her bottle, and I put it on the table, positioning her on my shoulder so I can burp her. He watches, and I can tell what he's thinking.

"Sing with me tonight."

I'm shaking my head no before he even finishes speaking. "I have to pack, and I want to spend my last night with her."

"Jilly will be asleep before I even leave for the bar." He takes her out of my arms. "We'll do the old songs. I've missed your voice."

"Give her back to me."

"You're not burping her right." He puts her on his shoulder and starts patting her little back. She burps immediately. "See?"

"No!" I start to laugh. "I got her warmed up for you."

"She just loves Uncle Roland best."

It feels good to laugh, to be here with him fussing over my daughter. "Let me hold her now."

"She's very comfortable."

"Here." I hold out my hands.

"You're going to make her cry."

Shaking my head, I get off the couch and carry the bottle to the kitchen. "I'll text Molly later and let her know. She'll probably want to join us."

"I'll buy her a drink."

"We'll stay until Jilly starts to cry."

"Baby in a bar. Welcome home, *cher*."

Cutting my eyes at him, I gaze out the window at the rising sun. "Nobody says *cher* anymore. And it's not a bar. It's a musical venue."

"So you'll do it?" He watches me calmly, knowing I'll say yes.

"I'll do it, but it doesn't change anything."

"I never expected it would."

Tomorrow we leave here on the quest for the last old man who thinks he got away with it. Maybe I do care too much about this one.

CHAPTER 3

Never look back to what broke you.

Mark

Is this your girl?

The message pops up on my computer screen as I'm sitting at my desk in Juneau, sliding a pencil up and down.

Leaning forward, I tap my middle finger on the mouse pad, and, "What the fuck?" I shout, sitting forward in my chair.

It's been three months. Three fucking months. Ninety days of searching, scouring the dark web for any signs of "Doll-Baby," the username I read over Molly's shoulder in Nice. I found old queries on Silk Road connecting Esterhaus to the White Pass line where they found him, and I know it's how she's finding her victims.

What I don't have are two important pieces of information—where they are now and who's next. Since the old theater in New Orleans burned to the ground, everyone associated with the place has scattered. One by one, the five members of the sex club are dead or missing.

Esterhaus was the last one I could find alive.

Guy has completely vanished.

My eyes fly around the browser window. The entertainment section of NOLA.com has a hazy candid photograph of Lara in profile. She's standing in a bar beside a piano. The pianist's back is turned, but I'd recognize that guy anywhere.

"Of course she's with Roland," I say, wondering why the fuck I didn't track down that guy first.

How did you find this? I message back.

Check the headline, is the reply.

It reads "Dark Angel Returns."

Resurfaces, is more like it.

Snatching up my phone, I book a plane ticket to New Orleans as I'm walking to my supervisor's office. She has more guts than I thought going back to New Orleans, but where else would she go? Roland has always had her back.

Donovan Lee is sitting at his desk, studying an open folder. He's classic native Alaskan, with straight dark hair and bronze skin.

"Knock knock," I say, taking a chair in front of him.

"Fitz." He looks up and smiles briefly before looking down again. "What's on your mind?"

"I need to take a few days off, sir."

That gets his full attention. He rocks back in the chair and studies me. "What for this time?"

"Personal matter. I found my daughter."

He nods, looking grave. "Nothing hits you like family."

If only he knew.

"It's a slow month." He glances at the file in front of him. "I suppose we could do without you for a personal matter. If it's *only* about a personal matter."

Clearing my throat, I scoot back in the chair. I consider how much I can tell him without revealing my motives. Legally, I can't do anything about Lara's past or mine in New Orleans. Still, I can try and get some answers. I can get my family back.

"It's possible Esterhaus was part of a sex trafficking ring that extended from New Orleans to the Pacific Northwest to the Yukon Territory."

"Pacific Northwest…" Donovan puts a hand over his mouth, thinking. "The chief in Seattle is one of my oldest friends. He might appreciate a tip like that. How much evidence do you have?"

"When I lived in New Orleans, I worked at a theater in the French Quarter. A burlesque show."

His eyebrows rise. "Good for you. What capacity?"

"I started on the set crew, but after a few weeks, I became a sort of everything guy for the owner. I ran errands, oversaw deliveries, and verified IDs and stood guard outside a room where… sex parties took place."

"Nothing illegal about that if it's not in a private home and they have the proper licensing."

"Unless the female participants were there against their will." My jaw tightens. "Unless the men paid to have sex with minors. In that case, it goes from a group of kinky consenting adults to sex trafficking."

Donovan's brow lowers, and he leans back in his chair. "You were a part of that?"

"At the time, I didn't have hard evidence of what was happening. As I've studied further since I left that place, I've learned more."

"It's going to be hard to prove a bunch of strippers weren't consensual participants in a sex club."

"With all due respect, sir, burlesque dancers are not strippers, and exotic dancers are not automatically prostitutes."

He arches an eyebrow. "Sounds like you have a personal interest in this matter."

I look at my hands, thinking about my response. From the start, I've done everything in my power to keep the girls off the radar. It's getting harder the deeper we get, the more they run.

Donovan interrupts my thoughts. "So this Esterhaus was a member?"

"I saw him there a few times. He claimed he got out because he didn't like the way things were being handled."

"And now he's dead."

"Yes, sir."

On the train, Esterhaus told Lara he'd divested his interest in the New Orleans club because he didn't agree with the decisions, but Molly hunted him down and killed him anyway. The level of violence indicated rage, revenge.

I'm willing to bet Esterhaus didn't get out before they molested a thirteen-year-old girl, who's now on the trail of every man involved in her abuse.

Guy. They have to be searching for Guy. He's the only one I haven't been able to find, and he was arguably the leader. He had more power than Gavin. He was the one who hurt Lara, who had me beaten almost to death when I tried to save her. A wince passes through me at the memory.

"Fitz?" I blink up to see Donovan leaning forward on his desk. "You still with me?"

"Yes, I was just remembering some information. I'm sorry."

He grins and nods. "I like it when my men are passionate about the cases they work on. It means they're more likely to get results."

"So you'll approve the trip?"

He nods. "Keep in touch, keep your expenses to a minimum. Let me know what you find but don't cross any jurisdictional lines. You're officially traveling to see your kid. This isn't your case down there."

"Yes, sir."

Roland plays at a popular piano bar a few blocks northwest of where the theater used to be. He's halfway through a raucous version of "Piano Man" with the entire drunken crowd singing along when I enter the dim-lit room.

It's a smaller bar off the main building with dark-wood paneling on the walls and vintage furnishings. Small tables are scattered throughout with the piano on an elevated stage in the center.

An enormous fishbowl is placed at the side of the piano, and patrons walk forward and drop napkins in it constantly. I check my watch. It's five minutes until two a.m., which makes this the last song of the night.

All the tables are full, so I stroll across the red-brick breezeway separating the smaller bar from the open-air patio out back. A large fountain is in the center, and the tone is quieter, more relaxed.

"May I take your order?" A waitress wearing a uniform of dark green shorts and a white shirt with a green bow tie waits expectantly.

"I'm just meeting someone, thanks."

She nods and continues on, and I realize this part of the establishment is open all night. Leaning against the black wrought-iron fence, I wait for the final strains of the Billy Joel classic to end and the cheering to die down.

Twenty more minutes pass before the place has almost completely cleared out, and I step inside to see Roland disappearing through a side door.

"Shit," I hiss, pushing aside chairs to cross the room before the door slams shut.

I'm too late. It closes in my face, and I have to run through the brick courtyard again, pushing my way through a mob of drunk tourists milling about.

"Watch it!" A man shouts, but I keep going, down the half-block to Toulouse Street.

I skid around the corner, my shoes slipping on the damp flagstone, but I see him far ahead, walking fast. My heart pounds. I'm sure he didn't see me in the bar — it was too dark and crowded — and I know I can find him tomorrow, but I can't help believing he's leading me to Lara. My desire to see her drives me forward.

He walks two more blocks north before stopping abruptly in front of an older home. It's nicely renovated, and as he passes through the wrought iron gate, I realize it's a duplex.

Voices erupt from inside the moment he opens the door, but he quickly shuts it behind him. I walk down to the corner to wait, unsure if this is his home or someone else's.

Another half-hour passes before a silver Accord with a pink Lyft sticker in the window pulls up to the curb. The door of the house opens, and Roland steps out with a girl I recognize. It's Evie. I'm more convinced than ever Lara has to be inside.

"See you tomorrow," she calls, and they embrace briefly before she trots down to the waiting vehicle.

Once she's gone, I'm through the gate and up the steps to his narrow front porch in record time. My insides hum, and I take a few steadying breaths before I knock. They're here. Lara, my daughter…

Swallowing the knot in my throat, I raise my hand and bang on the solid wood. The noise of footsteps from inside approaches the door.

"Did you forget something?" He calls, opening the door and freezing. "Mark."

All the rage I've suppressed for ninety long days breaks to the surface, and it takes an indescribable force of will not to grab him by the neck. When I was here before, we were the same size. Now I'm quite a bit larger than this guy who's been helping hide my wife and child from me. A baby I've never even seen.

"Where is she?" It comes out as more of a growl than a question.

To my surprise, he doesn't even hesitate. Stepping back, he waves his hand in a sweeping motion, allowing me entrance. "Right this way."

I'm on his heels as he leads me through the narrow house. He stops at a door, which he opens slowly, carefully. I push him aside and step into the closet-sized room.

A lamp in the shape of a large tree with little animals circling at the bottom casts a soft yellow light, and I have to duck slightly to avoid banging my head on the doorjamb.

"What is this?" I'm confused until I see the crib against the wall. My mouth goes dry, and my heart beats painfully harder with each step.

The scent of baby powder is in the air, and when I look over the white rail, my breath disappears. Inside is a tiny body wrapped tightly in a pink blanket. Her head is covered in a halo of light brown hair. My sight goes blurry, and I reach up to push the wetness aside.

"You can pick her up if you'd like," Roland says from where he's waiting at the door. "She's a pretty solid sleeper."

The anger, the driving desperation, all of it melts as I stand looking down at my baby girl's sleeping body.

"I don't know how." My voice is quiet.

A shuffling behind me, and Roland is at the side of the crib reaching in to lift her gently. Her little face scrunches in a frown, but he puts her on my chest, her forehead touching my neck, and the last shred of my fight disappears.

"Mark Fitzhugh, meet your daughter, Jillian."

I cup her body in my hands, and hold her against my heart. My eyes close, listening to her breathing, feeling her warmth through my shirt. She's here... soft, angelic, tiny, and so real.

When I can speak again, I blink over to see Roland touching his eyes. He smiles, and I wonder why I hated this guy so much all those years ago.

"She's so little," I whisper.

"She's actually right at the seventieth percentile for size and weight."

"I don't know what that means." Her face moves, and she makes a little grunting noise. Another piece of my heart melts.

Roland's eyes are soft as he touches her back. "It means she's perfect."

Fuck, he didn't have to tell me that. My hand cradles the back of her head, and I lower her gently. I want to study her little face and see all the ways she looks like me, all the ways she looks like her mother.

"I never knew babies could be so small." Smiling down, I look at her pixie nose, her rosebud lips... I want her to open her eyes so I can see if they're blue.

"She's grown quite a bit," he says. "You're coming in at the good part. She's making eye contact and smiling. Three months is the magic time."

The magic time was all of it. The pregnancy itself, when she was born. I'd wanted to be there for every moment stolen from me. From us. My stomach tightens, and I glance up at him. "Where's Lara?"

"Come into the living room." He ducks out the door, and I follow him, walking slowly as if my footsteps might disturb Jillian.

I scan the wood-paneled room. Leather furnishings are arranged in a way that divides the living area from a compact dining area. The kitchen is through a wide, open doorway in the back. Two doors are to my left, and I assume they lead to bedrooms.

"Is she here?"

Roland sits on the edge of a leather armchair, leaning forward. "Sit on the couch, and we can talk."

I stop in the center of the room and study him. The house is quiet, and I don't understand. "Where is she?"

"She left this morning."

"Left? Where did she go? Why did she leave the baby with you?" The questions pour out, but as quickly as they form, I know the answers. "She's doing it again."

"Sit." He motions to the couch, but I can't sit down. My pulse is racing, and holding my daughter has changed everything.

"Okay, don't sit." Roland clears his throat and looks at his hands. "I need to fill in the blanks so you'll understand what's happening."

"I think I know what you're going to say." Lifting Jilly so her head is against my chest, something shifts inside me in a way I never expected. "Molly was raped, and now Lara feels it's her duty to help her pursue this vigilante justice."

His eyebrows rise. "She told you that?"

"I was with her on the train when they found their last... victim." I'm not even sure what to call those bastards anymore.

Jilly's head moves, and she emits another little baby sound. I'm already imagining her saying her first words, learning to walk, ride a bike... I remember when Molly was just a sweet kid. I accused Lara of treating her as if she were her daughter.

Putting to words, speaking out loud what happened to Molly provokes a desire for vengeance in me I didn't have ten minutes ago. I can't even think of someone hurting Jillian the way Molly was hurt. I don't know the level of brutality I would inflict upon the man who tried. And in Molly's case, it was four men.

"They're going after Guy." As I say it, my muscles tense. "It's why she left the baby with you. Molly found him... You have to tell me where they went. It's not safe."

"They're not going after Guy."

His words pull me up short. "What?"

He shifts in the chair, and I can tell by his body language there's more to the story I don't know. "Guy is dead. He died in the fire."

"There's no record of his death. I searched all the reports. I searched everywhere—"

"You worked for Gavin. You know he could keep things out of the news."

"Still, there would have been a police report..."

Dark eyes meet mine, and he shakes his head slowly. "He called in a favor."

Landry. Gavin had that corrupt cop in his pocket. "But why?"

Roland shrugs. "He didn't want the publicity. Didn't want the investigation..."

"So it was foul play." I'm not surprised by this. "Perhaps he was able to keep the official record sealed, but there is still a record that should include cause of death."

"Maybe... I never looked."

My brow furrows, and I sit down on the couch. Jillian snuggles against my chest, and I smooth my hand over her little back as I recall the list of names. "If Guy is dead, Esterhaus should have been the last one."

"He should have been."

"I don't understand."

When Roland's eyes mine, they're serious. "They're going after Gavin."

I'm on my feet before he's even finished speaking. "We have to go after them. Now."

Holding Jillian in one hand, I dig for my phone with the other. She starts to fuss, and Roland stands to take her from me.

"How long ago did they leave? Where are they?"

"Seattle. They left this morning. She texted me her hotel and the room number in case I needed to reach her."

His words hurt more than all the kicks to the stomach I took that night so long ago when I tried to save her. "She won't reply to any of my calls or texts."

Roland's chin drops. "She blocked your number."

Shit, I take it back. That hurts more.

Clearing my throat, I continue typing on my phone. "I'm getting two plane tickets from New Orleans to Seattle. Grab your things. You're coming with me."

"I have to work. Besides, Lara would kill me if I brought Jillian out there."

"And I'm not leaving the two of you here like sitting ducks." Our eyes clash and for a moment, I think he's going to argue. Instead, he exhales and starts down the hall.

"I didn't want her going alone in the first place."

"I'm calling a Lyft. We leave in ten minutes."

CHAPTER 4

Never water yourself down because someone can't handle you at 100 proof.

Lara

Capitol Hill reminds me of uptown New Orleans at night.

Molly walks beside me on Pine Street, dressed in opaque black tights and a bright, royal-blue mini-dress. Her long hair, normally bleached white these days, is dyed silver, and she's wearing a black cardigan zipped closed.

By contrast, I'm in dark jeans, a black tee, and a modified khaki trench coat. True to its reputation, Seattle started out sunny and warm when we arrived this morning at noon. Now it's chilly and drizzling.

"He'll recognize me right away," I say under my breath as we approach the bar on Thomas Street.

"I told you to cut your hair. Or at least change the color." She's impatient. She's always impatient now, and it's gotten worse since Jilly was born.

"I want him to recognize me." I want him to know it's me confronting him.

We weave through the young people dressed in ripped tights or bold, black and white striped blazers. A fellow in a maroon jacket with black lapels coasts up beside Molly.

"You're new around here," he says, and I press my lips together, waiting for the backlash.

Molly stops walking at once and turns to him.

"What makes you say that?"

The fellow grins, and his eyes roam up and down her slender frame. I give him credit—he only hesitates a moment on her full bosom.

"I know all the beautiful girls in Cap Hill," he continues. "I've never seen you before."

"Maybe you have, and you don't remember." She's flirting, which puts me on guard.

Normally she shuts men down immediately with a biting insult. The fact she's toying with him makes me wonder what she's up to.

"I'd remember."

We continue walking. His hands are shoved in the front pockets of his tight black jeans, and he scuffs beside her in a pair of enormous combat boots.

She pushes a long silver curl behind her ear and blinks at him. "What's your name?"

"Joshua."

Hearts are in his eyes, and I pull out my phone. I pretend to check my messages, but the truth is, I only message Roland and Evie. I had to block Mark's number, which broke my heart, but not nearly as much as the texts he kept sending.

Don't do this…
Come back to me…
I love you…

My eyes squeeze shut against the pain.

"Joshua." Molly says his name as if testing it on her tongue. "I'm Maggie and this is my cousin Lucy."

"Maggie May," he spreads his arms wide.

"Umm, sure." Molly's brow lowers, and I know she doesn't get the reference. "So you've always lived in Cap Hill?"

He nods his bright orange head. "Born and raised."

"Do you know the guy who owns the bar Montage?"

"Brisbee?" Josh scrubs long fingers through his sparse beard.

"I-I'm not sure…" Molly and I exchange a glance. "Is he a big guy with sort of reddish hair?"

"That's him." Joshua brightens with recognition. "He moved here about eight years ago? Dates Kevin—"

"Wait," I cut him off. "You said he dates Kevin. Is Kevin a guy?"

"That's right, beautiful." Joshua turns his charm on me. "I can take you to meet him if you want."

We both stop, and the young man stops with us. "We're just looking for the owner of Montage," Molly says. "I thought he was named something different. Do you know where he moved here from?"

"New Orleans. It's the theme of the bar. Everybody knows Brisbee."

"Why is that?" she asks.

Josh shrugs. "He takes in runaways, helps them find jobs."

Molly and I exchange a look. I'm not sure what to make of this new information. "Is he there every night?" I ask.

Joshua frowns at me, and I can tell our questions are making him suspicious.

"What are you? Bill collectors?"

I shake my head. "No."

"Long lost wife?"

Another no.

"Long lost kid?"

Negative.

"Undercover cops?"

"We're just old friends," Molly interrupts us. "We're from New Orleans, and we need to tell him... his brother died."

We're walking, and I frown at her behind our jovial guide's back. Gavin already knows that. She dismisses me.

Joshua's voice turns solemn. "That's too bad. I'm not close friends with the guy, but nobody needs to hear that. I'll introduce you if he's there."

We follow Joshua up the semi-crowded street, past brightly lit cafes where hipsters are eating corn dogs.

"I want a corn dog," Molly says almost if from a dream.

"Unicorn has the best corn dogs," Joshua says. "I recommend the poutine dog."

She blinks up at him and smiles. "You're nice."

"Don't fall for it, kid." He elbows her arm. "I'm just trying to get in your pants."

I'm surprised when she bursts out laughing. Molly's smiles have all but disappeared since we left the theater, her laughter is even more scarce. Whoever this guy is, he's doing something right.

"Here we are!" We stop in front of a storefront painted like a carnival.

The exterior is a mixture of Pepto-Bismol pink, turquoise blue, and gold metallic fleur de lis, and the sign is a literal montage of bottle caps spelling out the name. It's jam-packed with patrons, and Molly's all set to charge inside.

"Wait." I grab her arm. My insides recoil, and I'm not sure I'm ready to confront Gavin this way. All the memories of being in that theater, being one step above a prisoner, doing what he said, being trapped...

"What?" Molly frowns at me, and Joshua steps up beside her.

"You look like you're going to be sick," he says.

I turn away from them, going to the corner of the building, then I lean against the brick wall. I'm having a hard time catching my breath, and I recognize this panic. It's happening too fast, I'm not prepared. Maybe I do need Mark here. Maybe I need him to hold my hand and tell me to breathe.

Molly grabs our guide's arm, pushing him toward the entrance to the club. "Josh, can you give us a second?"

"Sure thing." He trots to the door, and she storms to where I'm breaking down.

"What are we doing here?" I whisper half to myself, half to her.

"What are *you* doing?" she snaps. "I'm here to confront the asshole who turned me over to his fucking gang of rapists."

My insides cringe, and I can't stop shaking. She's right. She has every reason to be the sword of vengeance. My situation isn't as simple.

Gavin gave me a place to live. He knew my mother. He paid so I could stay on at the Catholic boarding school after she died. He tried to protect me from the monster.

The night he sent Roland in to save me drifts through my mind…

"Have you forgotten what he is?" I meet the cold blue eyes of the girl I thought I rescued.

Maybe I'm the monster… maybe we're all monsters.

"Josh said he's helping girls now. Maybe he's changed?"

"A snake can change its skin, but it's still a snake," she hisses. "Now get it together."

She's right. Maybe I only want him to have changed so we can walk away before this goes too far. If only…

I think about everything I said to Roland, why we're here and what I want. I want answers. We might all be monsters, but we don't all give little girls away like they're meaningless commodities.

Nodding, I push off the wall and do my best to calm my racing nerves. "It's different for me."

"No, it's not." She's walking ahead of me. "He gave you to Guy the same as he did me."

Not exactly the same… I went after him. I rolled those dice and lost.

Joshua is leaning against the glass window when we reappear, and he perks up when he sees us. "Right this way, ladies!"

Molly skips up to him and takes his arm, and I follow them through the narrow entrance. Her ability to play the part of the innocent amazes me. Once we're inside, I see what the place lacks in width is made up for in height.

A balcony overlooks the main floor, and along the back wall a staircase leads down to what I assume is a basement bar. A steady stream of patrons goes up and down the stairs carrying fluorescent red, blue, and yellow-colored drinks.

The inside of the bar is as brightly painted as the exterior, and rainbow Christmas lights are twined around all the banisters and skinny columns. The music blasting is early-1980s art rock.

We stand in a small circle on the black and white tiled floor. "They didn't card us," Molly shouts in the middle of our group.

"I'm friends with Jake," Joshua shouts back.

"Friends?" Molly looks from the stocky guy at the door to the skinny kid leading us around.

"Okay, he's my uncle."

"Where's Gavin?" I ask, but Joshua frowns at me. "I mean…" *Shit.*

"Brisbee," Molly shouts.

Joshua shakes his head. "Jake said he hasn't been in tonight. Probably doing something with Kevin. He might not come in after all."

"No…" The whisper is out before I can stop it, and Molly cuts her eyes to me.

"I'm getting a drink," I say, not really wanting one.

We're only supposed to be here two days. Losing tonight is a setback, and I don't want to extend this errand any longer than we have to. Molly is determined to confront Gavin. I have my own questions, but otherwise, this isn't the same as the other men. He never touched her. He never touched me. It's possible he's trying to make up for the sins of his past…

Molly appears at my arm. "You're doing it again."

Tilting my head to the side, I lean against the bar. Joshua is talking to a group sitting at one of the high tables.

"What do you want to do?" I ask. "Call it a night?"

"Nobody said we have to do this at night. Joshua can get us his address. We can go to his home tomorrow."

"Ambush him? Do you think that's smart?"

I lift the fluorescent blue drink in front of me and take a sip. It tastes like Malibu rum and pineapple juice. *Too sweet.*

"How would you suggest we do it?"

"You're actually asking for my input?" That's a first. She doesn't answer, only glares at me impatiently. "I think we should call and arrange a meeting at a public place. Some place he can't do anything."

"Where we can't do anything."

"What do you want to do, Molly?"

Her features are stony, and I know she's pulling away, going wherever she goes in her mind that allows her to do what she does.

"I want to do what I always do. Make him pay for what he did to me."

I shake my head. "It made sense to make the others pay, but Gavin never touched you."

"What do you want from him?"

My fingers are on the frosty glass, and I trace them up and down the sides. "I want to ask him why. I want him to tell me there's more to the story I don't know. I want him to give me a good reason for what he did."

Blue eyes flash. "You're saying there's a good reason for what he did?"

"No." My voice is barely above a whisper.

"Then how will you ever get what you want?"

"Maybe I won't," I say with a shrug. "See if Joshua knows how to reach him. I'll make the call."

I wait at the bar, watching as she goes to where he stands. If I didn't know her, she'd seem like any other Seattle kid, pretty, edgy, a touch of darkness. Joshua is clearly smitten. He takes out a pen and writes what she tells him on a napkin.

I take another sip of the blue beverage, and wince again at the intense sweetness. My eyes are heavy from jet lag, and the drink is making me feel buzzed. I can't remember the last time I had a cocktail—it was before Jillian was born.

Molly kisses her new friend on the cheek and walks back to where I'm standing.

"He gave me his number." She looks at the bar, her expression blank.

"Just like that?" I'm a little uncomfortable being acquainted with someone so ready to hand out other people's personal information. "I'm glad you didn't tell him our real names."

"Oh, I meant Joshua gave me his number—his own number. He's going to ask if it's okay for us to call. He'll let me know one way or the other."

"Tomorrow," I say under my breath. "We'll either be back here or somewhere else."

"And if we're back here, I'll be ready."

Leaning my head on my hand, the noise, the loud music, the crowd, and the flashing lights are starting to wear me down. "I'm ready to go back to the hotel."

Her full pink lips twist into a frown. "It's barely midnight."

"Midnight here is two a.m. in New Orleans, and I just got over Nice."

She shrugs. "I've never been a night owl. We can call it quits."

Outside, the clouds have moved away, and the dark sky is littered with stars. Our hotel is ten blocks away, so we walk. Molly is beside me, but we don't touch. I remember a time when she hung on my arm constantly.

"What will you do after this?" I'm not sure what to call what we've been doing. "Where will you go?"

"Maybe I'll stay here."

My eyebrows rise. "Because of Joshua?"

"No." Her tone is impatient. "I like the vibe here. It's mysterious but not sinister."

"Even with Gavin?"

Her eyes flicker to mine. "He might not be staying for long."

We walk several blocks in silence, only the noises of our shoes on the pavement and the passing cars surround us.

"I guess you'll go to Juneau," she finally says.

"I don't know. I might've damaged that bridge beyond repair."

"Doubtful. You have his child."

Jillian. An ache moves through my stomach, and I don't feel like arguing anymore. The hotel rises before us, and I follow Molly through the revolving door. A stone table holds an enormous dispenser of iced cucumber water, and she stops to pour a glass.

She's taking a sip when her phone lights up, and we both jump. "It's Joshua," she hisses, slamming the glass on the counter.

Turning the face so I can see it, his text reads, *Brisbee said he'll see you. Be at Café Solstice tomorrow noon.*

Again, I feel sick and anxious. Molly is excited. We go to the elevator, and she paces the small box as I watch the numbers count up to five. The door bings, and we get out, going quickly down the short maze to our rooms.

I stand at my door, waiting as she opens hers across the hall. "Want to meet for breakfast?"

"I'll probably sleep in," she says.

I have no idea if I'll sleep at all. "I'll call you when it's time to go."

"I'll meet you in the lobby at eleven-thirty."

She goes into her room, and the door slams shut.

I slide the card and enter mine. A large bed fills most of the space. No sheet, only a thick, white comforter is on top of a covered mattress. My mind swirls as I stand in the doorway trying to plan what could happen tomorrow. I have no idea what to expect from this meeting.

I'm startled when Molly's door across the hall slams again, and I dash to mine, only to see her disappearing through the stairwell exit at the end of the hall. She's practically sprinting, and by the time I get there, she's gone. I hurry back to my room and go to the window, straining my head to try and see the street below.

I don't see anything.

I don't know where she went or why.

Grabbing my phone, I text with trembling fingers. *What are you doing?*

Two seconds pass...

Five...

No reply.

I feel sick. Did she hear from Joshua? Is she going to confront Gavin alone? I'm nervous and anxious and worried, which is ridiculous at this late date. She's demonstrated over and over her ability to survive, to exact her justice and get away with it.

Still...

Gavin is a different matter altogether. He's as much of a survivor as she is, and while her previous victims were clueless and easily duped, Gavin is smart. He knows us, and he'll know why we're coming. He'll know what he has to lose.

Coming here, waking these demons has never been my plan.

Since I had Jillian, I've realized the choices that had to be made for our lives to turn out as they did, and I want to distance us from these nightmares. I thought getting out of there would set me free, but instead, I'm chained by this never-ending quest.

It might be freeing her, but Molly's relentless pursuit hasn't given me satisfaction. It has left me hollow and alone. I walk through the silent room to the window and look out into the night wondering what she's doing right now and why she feels like she needs me here.

Maybe Roland is right, and I've done enough. I've sacrificed more than I ever imagined for her. I have my own daughter now, my own family. Perhaps it's time to cut Molly loose and let her follow her dark path without me.

I prepare for bed with concrete in my stomach.

Before I shut off the light, I text her one more time. *Tell me what's happening*.

The only response is silence.

CHAPTER 5

Know your worth then add tax.

Lara

"Where did you go last night?" I'm angry when we meet in the lobby.

After not sleeping all night, I finally heard her door slam at four a.m. Instead of charging across the hall, I fell into a deep sleep as if my body had been waiting hours for that noise.

"I had to run some errands before today." Her voice is steady, not the least bit tired.

She's wearing a pair of dark, chunky glasses, and when she blinks up at me, I gasp involuntarily. "What did you do to your eyes?"

They've gone from clear blue to an uncanny dark brown. "Contacts. Would you recognize me if you hadn't seen me in seven years?"

"Probably not."

"I'm not sure how much he ever looked at me anyway," she adds under her breath.

Her long hair is still silver and styled in supermodel curls, but she's dressed in a knee-length form-fitted navy dress, and heels.

"You look very elegant." I feel under-dressed in my jeans and short-sleeved shirt with the same khaki trench from last night.

"I scouted the café where we're meeting. There's a balcony above the main floor. I want you to hang back, go up there and wait if you can."

My brow furrows. "What will you do?"

Her chin lifts, and I'm impressed by how professional she is. "I thought about what you said, and I decided I'm going to give him a test. I'll let you know if he passes."

"Will you at least tell me what the test will look like?"

"If it goes as I expect, it'll look like nothing more than a business lunch." A small leather clutch hangs from her slim shoulder by a thin strap. It's brown to match her shoes. "If it doesn't, I'll be out of there in less than ten minutes, and we'll be finished here."

I stop walking and catch her arm. "Finished?"

Solemn eyes meet mine. "If he answers correctly, I'm willing to let bygones be bygones."

We resume our walk, but the feelings warring in my chest and stomach range from relief to resentment, satisfaction to lack of fulfillment. I still want answers. I still want to know why... At the same time, if she's willing to walk, perhaps it's better to do as Roland says and let sleeping devils lie.

"This is all because of what I said?"

She shrugs. "If you're right, and he walked away from that place and is now doing good, I won't hold him to not caring what happened to me. I was worthless to him."

"You weren't worthless to me."

A sad smile crosses her lips. "In the end it didn't matter."

We're at the café, and I hesitate on the front steps. She grips my forearm.

"Go around the corner and use the alley entrance. Stay out of sight. If he sees you, he'll recognize you immediately, and we'll lose our advantage."

I take a step back, away from the front window. "I'll wait for you upstairs."

She doesn't acknowledge my words. She enters the café, and I jog around to the alley.

From the balcony above, I watch as Molly joins Gavin at a dark wood table. He's still tall and imposing, but he's lost weight. His hair is shorter and seems redder than before. He has a beard. She sits directly across from him, and they proceed to enjoy a full lunch, complete with a bottle of wine.

Hidden in the balcony above, I order a latte and drink it slowly, allowing the perfectly brewed beverage to warm my insides as I wait for any signs of hunger. My stomach has been in knots for two days, and their prolonged reunion is not a good sign, based on what Molly said.

She passes what looks like a business card across the table to him. He takes it and reads a moment. They resume chatting, faces mostly serious, occasionally smiling, and when my waiter returns again, I order a cup of tomato basil soup and a half-sized quinoa three-bean salad. I take two bites and push it away unfinished.

Finally, after more than an hour, they stand. Molly's smile is strictly business, and Gavin escorts her to the door. I stay in the balcony area above watching as he pulls out his phone and checks it. Then he nods, and they part, each walking in opposite directions.

The waiter returns, and I order another small latte. Dread moves through my stomach as I wait until finally Molly appears at the top of the balcony. Her expression is muted, and she walks straight to the table and sits.

"Well?" My voice is barely above a whisper.

"Nothing has changed." A note of bitterness is in her tone.

"What does that mean?"

"He takes in runaways, and sells the prettiest ones to the highest bidder. He's even worse than before. I'll meet him tonight at Montage to take pictures and set up my first encounter. He calls them *experiences.*"

"What does that mean? Runaways…" A painful knot swells in my throat. "How old are they?"

"I don't know."

"Then we can't be sure—"

"Are you seriously giving him the benefit of the doubt?" Her voice is a razor.

"No." Guilt is a lead weight in my stomach.

I have to know what might have happened if we'd left… Would more underage girls have been hurt? Would it have been my fault? Again?

"Will you let me talk to him first?" My voice is quiet.

"What's left to say?"

I don't know… My hands surround the small cup in front of me, and I try to think. "Did he recognize you?"

"If he did, it would've been a much shorter lunch."

Nodding, I take a sip of cold coffee, and it turns my stomach. I pull out my wallet and leave a twenty and a ten on the table.

"I'm going with you tonight." I have to know the truth.

* * *

Mark

Our flight to Seattle lasts six hours.

For six hours, the only thing keeping me sane is the warm body of my little daughter against my chest. Roland has bottles and diapers, and if she cries, he picks one of the two options to soothe her.

"How do you know all this shit?" I watch as he changes her diaper on the tray table like an expert.

"It's not rocket science," he says. "She's a small human. She gets hungry, you feed her. She soils her pants, you change them. She cries, you hold her. It's actually pretty basic human behaviors."

"I never had any siblings."

He hands my now-happy daughter to me. "Neither did I, but I have a brain."

"Nice," I grumble, but having spent the last eight hours with him, my confidence is growing in my own ability to figure out what's happening with Jilly and what to do about it.

He stretches his long legs into the aisle. "What I wouldn't give for a cigarette."

Turning, I get comfortable holding her as I look out the window at the enormous peak rising through the clouds.

"Look, Jilly. Mount Rainier." I tilt her little body so she can see out the window.

She's busy sucking a clear blue pacifier, which Roland says will keep her ears from popping. How he knows these things is beyond me, but I'm not in the mood for another crack about common sense.

We left New Orleans at eight a.m., but because of the time change it's only eleven when we touch down. It's noon by the time we arrive at the hotel.

"I'm sorry, sir." The front desk attendant shakes his head, giving Roland a worried look. "You're not on the guest list for Miss Hale's room."

"But... this is her husband and child." He points to me, and I shift Jillian in my arms, going along with his half-truth.

The man smiles at us and does a little wave to the baby before turning back to Roland. "I'm sorry, I can't give you a key to her room without her permission."

His eyes light, and he pulls out his phone. "Do you have her phone number listed on her reservation?"

"Of course."

"What if I call her, and she verbally agrees for you to give us a key?"

He frowns and looks down at the computer. "I suppose—"

Roland holds up a finger, and I see Evie's picture appear on his phone face. *He's going to have Evie pretend to be Lara?*

Catching his arm, I pull him to the side. "This is illegal. If she calls security, I can't—"

"Trust me," he says in a low voice.

Five minutes later, we're in Roland's private room waiting for maintenance to deliver a portable crib. The key to Lara's room is in my pocket, and I slide my hands inside my blazer to remove my shoulder holster and gun.

"You're trusting me with that?" He slants a smile at me, and I shake my head.

"I'm putting it in the safe." I put the holster and my gun in the room safe and program it. Then I turn back. "I'll leave Jilly with you for now."

My insides twist with all the feelings I've battled for months. I'm not entirely sure what will happen when Lara and I see each other again, and it's probably best the baby isn't present.

"We'll be here."

Touching her back one last time, I'm amazed at how my baby girl's mere presence, her warmth and adorable smiles, have managed to cool the burning anger in my chest. Roland's descriptions of Lara's tears and desire to protect my honor have further taken the edge off the betrayal I've felt since waking up alone in Nice…

But none of it unblocks my telephone number.

None of it puts me in the room when Jillian was born.

None of it restores my trust Lara won't do it again.

The bitterness in my chest is smoldering, not extinguished, and I can't deny my primitive need to take her by the arms and shake her until she tells me how she could do it. How she could walk away from everything we said, leaving me with only a note.

I'm not sure what it'll take to make up for those wounds.

Her room is neat. Her suitcase is open and several outfits are draped over the edge. Toiletries are scattered across the bathroom, and a pair of heels is on the floor at the foot of her large bed.

She left the "Do not disturb" sign on the door, so housekeeping hasn't made the bed, and the entire room smells of her soft, floral perfume. I go to the picture windows and look out at a white arched bridge with Mount Rainier a haze in the distance.

A sailboat slowly passes, and I'm still turning over these thoughts, battling the tension of my warring emotions, when the noise of the door card bleeps behind me.

Time is up.

She's here.

Turning to face her, I almost lose the fight when she enters the room.

She's still so fucking beautiful. I'm spellbound as she pauses to remove her trench coat and hang it in the closet. She holds the doorknob as she toes off her boots, bending down to slip off her white ankle socks. Her long hair falls around her arms in large curls, but when she stands, her expression is so sad, so broken.

On both the train to Canada and the beach in Nice, she still had a spark of determination. Now the light seems to have gone out, and it touches something inside of me.

All these observations occur in the half-second before she sees me. The moment she does, everything changes.

"Mark!" she gasps, blue eyes wide with shock.

I'm across the room in five steps, and she tries to back away, slamming against the closed door. Her eyes close, and her hands go up in a defensive pose.

Without hesitation, I clutch her upper arms in my fists, pulling her against my chest. The heat of her skin is against mine, and her warm breath skates across my neck.

"Surprised to see me?" It's a low, husky growl, and my insides hum with all the emotions swirling tightly into a ball of rage and relief and fucking love for this woman.

She's panting, and with every breath, her breasts strain against her thin shirt.

"What are you doing here?" she asks.

My face is close to hers, our noses nearly touching. "Did you think I'd ever stop looking for you? Did you think I wouldn't find my daughter?"

Her eyes blink up to mine, ocean blue touched with tears. We gaze deeply into each other's souls for the beat of two hearts, and in that space I feel my wall of anger start to crack.

With a groan, I lean down and take her lips. I push them apart and sweep my tongue inside. She's off her feet, her hands in the sides of my hair, and our mouths chase each other's. We're biting and pulling lips, tongues entwining, the flavors of mint and sugar mingling in our mouths.

I lift her ass and carry her to the large bed in the center of the room, tossing her roughly onto her back. She makes a little cry, moving to her side as she watches me wide-eyed. I rip off my blazer, followed quickly by my tie.

"What are you doing?" Her voice is thick with need.

"You know what I'm doing." My shirt is over my head, and her eyes darken as they slide down my bare torso.

"Take off your clothes," I say, and she immediately grasps the hem of her shirt, pulling it over her head in a sweep.

Dark hair cascades around her shoulders, around her bra, which is sheer black lace. I see her dark nipples straining through the fabric, and my dick is an iron rod in my pants.

"All of it." I grasp my belt, then the button on my slacks.

She unfastens her jeans and lifts her hips to shove them off. I take them from her, dragging the tight fabric down the length of her silky legs. Stepping back, I drop them on the floor and admire her new curves. My tongue passes over my bottom lip as my eyes zero in on the triangle of fabric covering her bare pussy.

She whimpers, and I put a knee on the bed, climbing toward her like a lion stalking its prey, claiming what's mine.

I grasp the tiny scrap of lace and rip it off her body. She emits a little cry, and I bend down, pushing her thighs apart and sliding my tongue up the sweet spot between her legs. Her body falls back and she moans loudly as I focus my efforts on her clit. Holding her down, I circle that sensitive bud as her fingers thread and pull my hair, her nails curling and scratching my shoulders.

"Mark… Mark…" She chants my name as her hips rotate in time with my tongue.

Her taste is in my mouth, and I feel as the tremors rise in her legs, moving higher into her belly, her moans growing louder.

"I'm coming," she gasps, trembling more.

With one last pull, I kiss my way up to her navel, to her breasts still covered in black lace. Shoving the cups down, I pull a tight nipple into my mouth.

"Yes," she hisses, holding my cheeks now, her elbows bent beside her body.

She's squirming beneath me, shimmering on the edge of orgasm, when I rise up and look into her eyes. She's desperate with desire, flushed and needy.

"What do you want?" I demand, holding her shoulders with my hands.

She blinks rapidly. "You," she whispers.

"What did you say?" My brow is lowered, and I let her see a bit of the rage that's tormented me for three months.

"You," her voice cracks as she says it louder.

I move higher and claim her mouth again, twining my tongue with hers, swallowing the moan that aches from her throat when I move her thighs apart with my knee. My erection hangs heavy and thick between us, and she rocks her hips up to mine, ready to meet me.

But I hold back.

Pulling away, our mouths part with a little smack.

"No," I growl. "I want to hear you say it. What. Do. You. Want?"

She closes her eyes and yells. "You! I want you! Please, Mark…" Her voice breaks in a sob as she says my name, and it's enough for me.

I cover her mouth again, thrusting my tongue to hers as I drive my cock to the hilt into her hot, slippery depths.

"Oh, God!" Her mouth breaks away with a loud cry, and her hips rock fast in time with mine.

We thrust and grip, arms circling and pulling in a primitive ritual, a union of need and long-delayed gratification. I catch her knee in my arm and lift it higher, allowing me to go even deeper. Her head falls back, pressing into the pillows.

"Mark… yes," she gasps, and I run my tongue up the length of her throat, kissing and pulling the delicate skin between my lips and teeth.

A bright red mark appears, and satisfaction blooms low in my stomach. Her inner muscles ripple and pull as her orgasm rises faster. It triggers mine, pulling and massaging my cock deep inside her. I groan again as my mind starts to blank.

White-hot pleasure snakes up my legs, pulsing in the place where our bodies are joined. She breaks with a loud moan, and I'm right there with her, holding steady as we lift off the ground, as we soar through the clouds, past the highest peak, our arms and legs entwined and our bodies sparkling together, blanketed in orgasmic reunion.

I hold her, and her eyes are still closed. She's under me, and I'm inside her. Our bodies float gently down, shimmering and relaxing together as we find our way to calm.

We're breathing fast. She slowly blinks her eyes open, blue clashing with blue, and for all the anger I've held, for all the words I still need to say, having her this way, feeling us skin against skin as everything around us melts, I realize I've only been this happy one other time in my life — when I first held my daughter in my arms.

"I'm so glad you're here," she says, and I kiss her again.

CHAPTER 6

"I've never met a strong person with an easy past."

Lara

My fading orgasm is like warm honey beneath my skin, and my lips are sealed to Mark's. Our tongues entwine, curling, tasting, still hungry after so long apart, desperate for more. He's like water and oxygen, a deep breath of fresh air at the top of a tall mountain.

"Mark," I whisper as his lips move to my cheek, my ear.

I'm in his arms, and it feels so right.

And it's *not* an illusion.

It's very, very real.

He pulls me closer, we're skin against skin, and we rotate to the side. I place my palm against his cheek and look into his eyes... an ache moves through my stomach. I see so much love there and so much hurt. I want to take it all away, atone for what I've done, but I don't know how.

"What do you see?" I ask.

He doesn't smile. "You're looking at me the same way you did in Nice."

Reaching up, I trace my finger along the line of his jaw, smiling, hoping he'll smile back. "Like I love you?"

"Like it's a lie. Like you're going to leave again."

My brow falls, and I take my hand away. "How did you find me?"

"You returned to the scene of the crime."

"What?" Panic briefly grips me.

"You did a concert with Roland at the piano bar. It was featured on a local website."

"Oh." I relax again. "I should have realized. Nothing's private anymore. Cameras are everywhere."

"Almost everywhere."

My lips press together briefly, and I dare to meet his angry eyes. "I'm so sorry, Mark."

"Stop." The blaze of anger burns hotter. "Don't say it if you don't mean it."

"I do mean it. More than you could ever know."

He pushes into a sitting position, the muscles in his torso flexing as he moves. I reach out to trace my finger down his side, and he catches my hand, holding it away from his body. It hurts that he doesn't want me to touch him now.

I move to sit up beside him, clutching the duvet around my naked body. "What can I do? Is there any way I can make this right?"

His square jaw moves, and I want to touch him. Having him again, then having him pull away so quickly makes the pain of loss even more unbearable. "You'll have to prove I can trust you."

"How?" I'm eager to do whatever it takes.

"Leave here with me now. Come to Alaska, bring the baby, bring Molly... We can get her the help she needs—"

With every word my chest grows tighter. "I want that... I want all of that. I'm just not sure I can convince Molly. And, well... Would you be willing to wait just a few more days?"

His eyes flash. "So you can go after Gavin?"

"Roland told you that?"

"He told me this time it's more than Molly. This time it's for you."

"Yes, but not in the way you think. I want answers. He knows so much of my past…"

"And if the answers only lead to more questions? When does it end, Lara?"

"I don't know." My eyes are on my twisting fingers, and I remember how I felt last night, longing for Mark. Feeling like I'm in over my head. I remember the panic of eminent confrontation, and wanting him to hold my hand, tell me to breathe.

Slowly, I lift my eyes to his. "Would you help me?"

The smallest crack appears in the tension between us; the door keeping me out opens slightly. "What do you want me to do?"

Taking a chance, I put my hand on the back of his hand. He doesn't pull away this time.

"I don't want to do this alone. I want you to help me get the answers I need." His hand turns over, and our fingers thread, our palms slide together. I lift my eyes to meet his. "Will you help me find the peace I need? Help me banish this last demon?"

"I've only ever wanted to help you." His brow is still furrowed, but he's softening. "I'll tell Roland we might be staying a little longer."

That makes me jump back. "Roland's here? But who's watching—"

"Jillian's with him. With us—she's down the hall in his room."

He's still speaking as I rip the duvet off me and run to the closet to grab one of the white robes. I hastily tie it around my naked body, and I'm out the door, trotting down the hall when I realize I don't know the room number. Stopping, I look back to see

Mark wearing only his slacks, following me with a smile on his face. A real smile that warms me to my toes.

"It's Room 522," he calls, and I let out a little squeal, scanning the doors.

It's right across the hall, and I tap soft and fast on the door. It opens almost at once, and I do another squeal when I see her on his shoulder, bright blue eyes round and curious. As soon as she sees me, she smiles and makes her cute little baby noises, and I take her in my arms.

"Oh, Jilly!" My eyes heat, and I kiss the side of her head repeatedly, inhaling her baby-powder scent. "My little sweet potato. Did you miss Mommy? Mommy missed you so much!"

She makes a noise and scrubs her face against my shoulder. She presses her head against me, and I hug her close, swaying gently as I hold her little body, kissing her over and over. She fills me with so much calm and joy.

"I know I'm a step above chopped liver these days, but I'm glad to see you, too," Roland says, a wry smile curling his lips.

"I'm glad you're here." I step forward to kiss his cheek.

"Are you?" A dark brow cocks. "I was afraid you'd be livid with me for all of this."

"I thought I would, too," I say in a soft baby-voice, rubbing my nose against Jillian's skin. "But I'm so happy to see my sweet girl."

She coos, and the warmth at my back tells me Mark has joined us. His hands cover my shoulders, and I lean my back against his chest as he circles us in his arms.

"She really is a beauty," he says at my ear, and she perks up at the sound of him. She smiles and blinks, and he takes her out of my arms. "She's daddy's girl," he says, and Jilly leans her head against his bare chest, a chubby finger in her mouth.

"Well, of all the things." I put my hands on my hips, pretending to be offended, but the truth is I'm thrilled. She already seems to know and love her daddy.

"He's getting better at helping with her," Roland observes, leaning against the doorjamb, arms crossed.

"Hey, I've never been around babies before."

"I told you it isn't rocket science."

"Oh, ignore him," I fuss, placing my face close to Jilly's, my hand on her back. "He thinks he's the baby whisperer because she rarely cries for him."

"She only cries when her needs are not properly met."

Lifting my chin, my eyes meet Mark's, and we both laugh. Jilly's eyes blink slowly, and her little ear is pressed right above her daddy's heart. I wonder if she can hear it beating.

"Let's go to our room," I say softly. "When was her last bottle?"

"A few minutes before I opened the door. She's burped and changed and ready for a nap."

"What's going on here?" The impatient female voice causes me to take a step back. "What are they doing here?"

"Well, hello, Molly," Roland says in his usual play-formal way. "It's great to see you, too. Isn't the weather nice for Seattle?"

"Why are you here? You're supposed to be in New Orleans with the baby."

"Molly." I go to her, reaching for her hand. "Mark brought Roland and Jillian to find us."

"We weren't lost," she snaps, giving Roland a stern look. "He knew we were here."

"I think Lara mis-phrased that," Roland continues, teasing her annoyance. "I would've said Roland and Jillian were dragged along with Mark to find us... or does that make it more confusing?"

Turning to Mark, I put my hand on his forearm. "Would you take Jilly to our room so I can talk to Molly?"

The expression on his face is different from earlier—more open, loving. It seems I'm not the only one susceptible to our daughter's healing powers.

"Sure." He moves his arm so our hands unite. "I'll put her down for a nap. Don't be too long."

I smile, and he leaves us for our room. For a moment, all I can do is watch him walking away, silhouetted in the light from the far window, broad shoulders, narrow waist, amazing ass in those tailored slacks, ripples of muscles holding our tiny infant so gently against his bare chest.

"You can pull your tongue in your mouth now," Molly snarks. My eyes cut to hers, and she's fuming.

"I'll leave you two alone. *Moulin Rouge* is on." Roland steps away from the door, and it closes behind him with a slam.

We walk the short distance to her room and go inside. It's immaculately clean, with her clothes arranged by type and color in her suitcase. Her dresses are hung neatly in the closet, and her toiletries are aligned in rows with morning items on the left and evening on the right.

She whisper-shouts as soon as the door closes. "Why are they here?"

"I told you—"

"They're going to ruin everything. It's already tricky enough with you here, and now them?"

I don't know what to say. "I didn't ask them to come."

"So tell them to go and take that baby with them!" She's pacing the room, arms crossed, silver hair fanning around her.

"You mean my daughter?" I've done my best to be patient with her version of sibling rivalry, but I've sacrificed a lot for this girl.

She spins on her high heel and faces me. "We have a meeting in thirty minutes with Joshua. He has Candi, a runaway teen who works as one of Gavin's hookers. She's willing to talk to us."

My brow lowers. "About what?"

"To prove to you he hasn't changed. He only changed locations, but he's doing the same thing here he always did there."

Pressing my lips together, I sit on the edge of her bed, holding the robe closed at my chest. "It's not exactly the same if she works for him willingly. It's not legal, but if he's her pimp, it mean he protects her."

"Until Guy shows up!" Her eyes flash to mine, and I swallow the nerves tightening my throat. She hasn't said that name in years. Where is this coming from?

"Guy is dead. I told you—"

"But you never saw his body. No one did, and then the theater conveniently burned to the ground."

My eyes are fixed on my trembling fingers. Only two people know what really happened to Guy, and neither of us has ever spoken of it. It could be very bad. For both of us.

"He's not going to show up again," I say a little sterner, my insides tight.

"Doesn't matter. I'll be ready when he does." She's pacing again, her jaw clenched. "I'm searching for him, and I will find him."

Standing fast, I tighten the belt on my robe. "What time are we meeting this Candi?"

"Half hour at the Redwood Bar."

I glance at the clock on her bedside table, tension hot in my chest. "I'll meet you in the lobby at four forty-five."

I have to knock on my door, and when Mark opens it, my fears magically subside. He leans on one arm over my head, causing the muscles in his bare torso to flex so attractively. I don't even enter the room, I lean against the doorjamb in front of him.

"Did I mention how happy I am you're here?"

A sexy grin curls his lips. "Even if it spoils your plans?"

"I'll tell you a secret," I say, leaning closer. "We didn't have a plan. We never really do."

His face tightens. "Maybe you don't have a plan, but after what happened to Esterhaus, I'm pretty sure Molly does."

I know he's right, and the happy feelings provoked by the sight of him begin to wilt. "Where's Jilly?" I ask, passing him to enter the room.

The door closes quietly, and I glance back to see him easing it shut. Turning to the bed, I see my tiny baby sleeping peacefully, surrounded by large pillows. Everything about this has demolished any hope for me keeping him out.

Standing at the edge of the bed, I look down at her. He stands behind me again, placing his hands on the tops of my shoulders.

"She's like this perfect, magical little thing," I whisper watching her sleep, then my jaw clenches. "I'll never let anything bad happen to her as long as I live."

"You're not alone this time." He circles my waist with his arms, his chin on my shoulder. "If you think I'm ever letting the two of you out of my sight again, you've got another thing coming."

It comforts me to hear him say the words. It's something I never had before, something I always longed for. "Molly, on the other hand, is going to be more difficult to convince."

Straightening, he turns me to face him. "What did she say?"

"We're meeting this young guy, Joshua. He's introducing us to a girl who supposedly works for Gavin."

"Okay?" Confusion lines his brow.

"She's a prostitute." That changes his expression, and I step out of his arms, going to my closet. "Molly's convinced Gavin is doing the same thing here he did in New Orleans, and she wants to expose him."

"Good," he says, sitting on the edge of the bed. "She can expose him, and I can have him arrested. We need fresh evidence. Everything in New Orleans is either burned or hearsay."

Scooping up my underwear, I carry my jeans and a fresh blouse into the bathroom, calling softly. "I'm not sure arresting him is what Molly has in mind."

He steps to the door, watching as I dress. The smile on his lips heats my insides, and I wish I didn't have to leave.

"I want to go with you," he says.

Slipping my shirt over my head, I touch his chest, rising on my toes to kiss his lips. "If it's just Joshua and Candi, we're okay to go alone."

We exit the bathroom, and he goes to the dresser where the large, flatscreen television sits silent and dark. "Unblock my number."

The tone in his voice stops me. It's laced with remnant anger, and I almost wonder if we've gone all the way back to the beginning.

"Hand it to me," I say. He stretches it out, and I take it with trembling fingers, touching the face quickly and finding his name. "I only did it because it hurt too much to see…"

My voice breaks off, and he holds my forearms. "Never do it again."

Lifting my chin, my eyes are serious when they meet his. "I'll never do it again."

"Here," he reaches out, and I hand him my phone again. "I'm going to turn on your tracker, connect your phone with mine so I know where you are. If anything feels wrong, text me, and I'll be there. Jilly will be safe here with Roland."

Nodding, I rise on my toes to kiss his lips once more. "I will."

Taking my clutch, I go to the door and pause, looking back. He's standing, watching me, with our baby sleeping peacefully on the bed.

It's everything I want in the world, right here in this room.

CHAPTER 7

I walk slowly, but I never walk backward.

Mark

The moment Lara steps out the door, I turn on my phone, switching over to the app and watching the green dot as she leaves the building. I hate letting them go alone, but I don't want her pushing me out again. I want her to know she can trust me to trust her.

So I have to let her do this.

I can't follow her like the overprotective lover I am.

My stomach cramps, and I step to the bed where our little daughter sleeps. Her soft lashes lightly touch her rosy cheeks, and her brown hair bends in tiny curls around her ears.

I pick up my phone again and see the dot has moved deeper into Capitol Hill. Opening the messenger app, I text Roland.

Come watch the baby while I get my shit out of your room.

When we checked in, he got me a key, but I wasn't sure if Lara would welcome me or push me away. I was angry and defensive, and so desperate to see her. Our reunion went differently, much better than I expected.

A light tap on the door, and Roland holds up the card for his room when I open it. We trade places, and I head down to where he's staying. My carry-on suitcase is in the corner, and I quickly type in the code for the safe.

Taking out my light brown holster, I sling it over my shoulder and fasten the small buckle across my chest before slipping the black .45 Glock pistol into its leather case under my arm at my ribcage.

It's loaded, and even though I hope I don't have to, I'm prepared to use it.

Back in the room, Roland is reclined on the bed with sleeping Jillian at his side. The television is on with the volume turned low, and a flashy musical fills the screen.

"Where did they go?" he asks, eyes fixed on the show.

"Meeting some kids who work with Gavin," I say, taking out my laptop and pulling up the New Orleans Police Department's website.

"What for? Research?"

"I'm not sure. Lara didn't think it was anything to worry about, so I let her go alone."

"That's very big of you." I glance up, and that skeptical grin is on his face again.

"Yeah, well, I'm trying not to give her reasons to lie to me. I don't want her running again."

"She ran because she wanted to protect you. You're a cop."

"That's right. I am." And if I have to I sit here and wait, I'm doing my own research.

I type in my badge ID and password, and once I'm connected, I type in the words *Guy Hudson* and the address for the old theater.

The record of the fire appears, but no photographs, which is strange. Another surprise, his cause of death is listed as blunt-force trauma to the head, not smoke inhalation or fire.

Not what I was expecting.

The report states a beam or some other structure must have fallen, delivering a fatal injury as the victim lay in bed. His body was only partially burned in the fire, due to its location in a suite of rooms below the stage.

Rooms I know well.

"There should be pictures," I say to myself.

"What are you doing?" Roland watches me.

His hand is on Jillian's chest, and she's awake, waving a tiny fist in the air and kicking both feet. Her little legs make shushing sounds in the soft duvet.

"Checking the police report for Guy's death. I found it, but you're right, a lot of the information I'd expect to see is missing."

Standing, I go to the bed where my baby girl is moving around. Kneeling at the side, I slide my finger along her tiny fist until she grasps it. She's so strong. Her blue eyes meet mine, she smiles, and even with my mind troubled, I smile back as I hold her little hand.

"I told you Gavin called in a favor," Roland says, lifting her off the bed. "She needs to be changed. What are you trying to find?"

"I don't know… anything." I filter through the reasons for a partial police report. "Looking at that, I'm convinced something's being hidden or covered up. Maybe it wasn't Guy's body they found—"

"It was Guy's body." My natural suspicion is piqued by his quick reply.

"What makes you so sure?"

He shrugs, but I can tell he's backpedaling. "I was there. I saw Gavin's face. I saw the clothes on the body… He was in his secret salon. It was clearly Guy."

Watching him go to the door, my brows furrow.

He leaves the room carrying Jillian, and I sit thinking. Would Roland help with a cover up? Why? Who is he most loyal to…

I think I know.

I return to the police database and enter *Roland Desjardin*. Nothing comes up. I try again using the theater as his address. Again, nothing comes up.

My throat tightens, but I type *Larissa Hale* and the theater address.

Nothing comes up, and I sit back, exhaling with relief.

I'm going crazy sitting around here waiting for her to come back. Grabbing my phone again, I study the little dot. It's still somewhere deep in Capitol Hill, but it's moving now.

Pushing off my knees, I go to the room phone and order a pizza and two beers from room service. I text Roland, letting him know to come back for food then I stop at the room safe to secure my gun.

If I plan to dig deeper into the Guy Hudson case, I'll have to wait until we return to New Orleans. In the meantime, I need to shower.

* * *

Lara

The Redwood is a dive bar clearly popular with the locals. Inside, it looks like an old hunting lodge with dark wood walls, floors, and exposed-beam ceilings. Matching wooden tables and chairs are scattered throughout, and red lights cast an amber glow throughout the interior.

The place is brightened a bit by white Christmas lights twined around the skinny columns lining the floor, and antlers from all sorts of animals — deer, moose, something I don't even recognize — are hung between the neon beer signs. The faintest scent of ancient cigarette smoke still lingers from before the ban, and at the far end of the room, an enormous television flickers to life with the start of the black and white movie *The Mummy*. This place is truly a relic.

Joshua sits across the small table from me beside a girl with shoulder-length neon-rainbow hair. It's too dark for me to tell if she's wearing a wig or if it's all hers.

"This is some place," I say to no one in particular.

Josh is busy shelling peanuts and eating them. He's wearing a tailored, vintage blazer over dark jeans, and a Guinness is in front of him. The rest of us are having soft drinks.

"It's classic Cap Hill," he says, grinning at me. His neon orange hair is covered with a gray beanie. "It closed for a little while, and protests were organized until it reopened."

"Really?" I look around wondering why.

"So what do you want anyway?" The girl I assume is Candi shifts in her chair.

"Is Candi your real name?" Molly leans forward, studying her intently, almost like she's looking for signs of herself in this person.

"No, I changed my name to Candi. That's Candi with an *I* and a star on top."

Molly immediately sits back roughly in her chair, seeming disgusted with that additional information. "Let me guess… No, you tell me, why Candi?" Her tone is sarcastic.

The girl flutters her eyes and spins a lock of hair. "Because I'm sweet like candy, but I don't rot your teeth."

"Real original," Molly mutters under her breath.

Candi's eyes flash and her tone turns harsh. "You're real original. Silver hair went out three years ago. What's your name, anyway?"

Molly's eyes flicker to mine, and she grins. With that outburst, Candi might have redeemed herself.

"I'm Maggie and this is my sister Lucy." She turns to Joshua. "She'll do."

"Do what?" Candi asks, and I look to the both of them wondering the same thing.

Joshua only continues eating peanuts, tilting his head toward my partner for the answer.

"Tell me about working for Brisbee," Molly says. "You've been with him since you ran away from home?"

The girl pulls what looks like a plastic cigarette from her pocket and puts it in her mouth.

"Uh, you can't vape in here," Joshua leans forward, looking over his shoulder. He almost seems uncomfortable with his role as narc.

"I'm just sucking on it," she says then cuts her eyes to Molly. "I lived on the street for a few weeks, then I heard about this guy who could get me work. So yeah, I started working for him around the time I got here."

Molly leans forward, lowering her voice. "Have you ever seen him with kids?"

Candi frowns. "What do you mean? He's not a pedo if that's what you're asking."

"No," Molly clears her throat. "Does he… *sell out* any kids? Underage kids?"

"I don't know." Candi continues sucking on her fake cigarette. "I don't know who all he works with."

"Okay… Have you ever been made to *work* when you don't want to?" Molly's voice is urgent, pressing.

I'm troubled by how much she's trying to force this issue. I want to argue with her and tell her she has no evidence Gavin, a.k.a. *Brisbee*, would do something like that outside of Guy's control. We can let it go, end the quest…

But she'll never accept that from me.

She needs to eliminate every person associated with what happened to her. I understand her drive, but it doesn't make it any less grueling.

"No," Candi says, and she looks over her shoulder. "Look, I'm sorry I'm not telling you what you want to hear, but Bris treats me right. Now I've got to go."

She stands, and looks over at Josh. "Bye, Josh."

"Wait!" Molly rises, opening her clutch. "Take this. It's my number. I want you to call me or text me if anything like what I described happens. I'll help you."

The girl looks at the card a few moments not taking it. Joshua reaches out and takes the card from Molly then he stands. Candi heads for the door, but Joshua hesitates.

"I'll talk to her." His face is serious, and his eyes move to Molly's. "I'm sorry if that's what happened to you."

She blinks away, her aversion to pity strong.

I reach out and touch his arm. "Thanks."

He tosses a ten on the table and hustles to the door after Candi. I look at Molly. Her dark brows are pulled together, and her arms are crossed.

"Come on," I say, reaching for her. "Let's head on back."

She ignores my hand, and we leave, making our way up the sidewalk quickly to our hotel. She's not talking, and I'm anxious to get back to Jillian and

Mark. Still, I can tell by her eyes, she's thinking.

"What's on your mind?" I nudge her arm with my elbow.

Blinking down to the path in front of us, she pushes a lock of hair behind her ear and doesn't answer.

"You can tell me," I urge, but she turns her head, almost as if she's fighting tears.

"Molly?" My voice is softer. "What are you thinking right now?"

We walk a few more paces in silence, the only noise our heels on the pavement. Until she stops.

"I thought I could expose him for the monster he is. I thought I could do something good here, break up his whole ring..." Her voice cracks, and my heart aches. "Then I find out it was just me. I was the one who was worthless. I was the kid who didn't matter. It was only me... just me."

She stops and turns to face the brick wall, and her shoulders shudder forward. Her arms tighten over her waist, and for a moment, she holds herself tightly as if trying to keep the shattered pieces from flying out into the world.

"Oh, Molly," I touch her shoulder, but she steps forward, away from my comfort.

"I'm sorry." She sniffs, straightening quickly.

She pushes her hair back and shakes the grief away. It's what she always does, and I hate it.

Clearing her throat, she swallows the tears. "So I made a mistake. It doesn't mean I'm wrong."

"Why don't we just do what we originally said?" My voice is gentle. "We can confront him, see if he'll explain himself, maybe even apologize, and put it to bed."

Her lips are a straight line. "I don't want his

explanations."

"I know." I put my arm around her waist. "But sometimes in life, it's the best we can hope for."

It's another of those rare times when she'll let me touch her. They're becoming less and less as time passes. Molly's been pulling away from me since Jilly was born, and now she's far away, somewhere in her mind where she's planning, analyzing, devising.

We're closer to the hotel, and I try one last time. "Killing isn't the answer. It won't bring you peace."

She only steps out of my arm, and enters the hotel ahead of me, going to the stairwell and jogging away, leaving me behind.

I let out a sigh and go to the elevator. On the short ride up, I decide it's time for me to do what I came here to do and heed Roland's advice.

Tonight I'll go to the bar, I'll bring Mark with me, and say what I need to say. Then I'll go home. Molly can stay if she wants. It's time for me to let her go and focus on being a mother... Possibly even a wife?

Sliding my card in the lock, I hear the noise of the shower running, and my mind shifts to what all is included with that title. I think about the comfort of being part of a loving family. It's a dream that tugs at the depths of my soul.

I step out of my shoes just inside the room and move the "Do not disturb" sign to the outside. Turning the latch, a smile curls the side of my mouth, and I quickly pull off my shirt and shimmy out of my jeans. I see his dark form moving behind the sheer white shower curtain, and my lip goes between my teeth. My stomach tightens with anticipation, and I reach out to carefully open the curtain and peek inside.

The sight of his naked body steals my breath. His

arms are raised, and his biceps flex as he slides large hands through his hair, rinsing away the shampoo lather.

Water streams down his powerful shoulders, creating rivulets that highlight the six pack of his abs, the V tracing his obliques, and my inner muscles clench at the sight of his cock, partially aroused and hanging thick and heavy between his thighs.

Without opening his eyes, he turns, giving me another killer view. His ass is tight and square with hand-sized indentions on each side. I don't even realize I'm biting my lip until it hurts.

This man, the father of my baby, could be my future, my life.

I want that.

I'm going after it.

"Hey," I say softly, stepping into the shower. I immediately press my bare breasts against his strong back, circling his narrow waist with my arms and sliding one hand down to stroke him.

His body tenses briefly, and he looks over his shoulder at me. "What are you doing in here?"

Blinking against the drops of water glancing off his skin, I meet his darkening gaze. He turns, placing his hands on my hips, sliding them up to cup my breasts, rolling hard nipples between his fingers.

"I'll give you two guesses." I hold his waist and rise on my toes to kiss him.

He bends down to meet me, and our lips part. The taste of fresh water is in my mouth as our tongues curl together, our bodies slippery and hot under the warm spray. Large hands move down the curve of my back, cover and cup my ass, and I slide my fingers up to his broad shoulders, down to his waist, and around to that tight ass.

I feel his erection rock-hard against my belly, and a low groan ripples through him, vibrating mine. He moves my mouth with his kisses, but I pull away, planting my lips on his chest, moving lower to circle my tongue around his tight nipple before dropping all the way to my knees and lifting him to my lips.

"Lara," he hisses as I slide my tongue around the tip, tracing my nails along his thick shaft.

His hand is on my cheek, and I go lower, tracing my tongue along his sack, feeling his muscles jump at the sensation. Another deep groan, and I slant my eyes up, giving him a naughty grin.

"I think you like that." I do it again, noticing a clear drop of precum.

"You have no idea." His voice is husky.

Moving higher, I pull him into my mouth again, doing my best to take his length as far as I can. I use my hand to fill the gap, pumping and sucking. My hand on his ass feels his muscles flexing tighter with every pass. His brow is furrowed, eyes squinting as he watches me.

Having him in my mouth, feeling his body's response to my touch, tasting his arousal sends burning need coursing through my veins. My pussy is hot and slippery, aching for him to fill me.

I pull him faster, pumping and sucking until the muscle in his jaw flexes, and he opens his mouth with a deep groan.

"Get up." Large hands go under my arms, and he lifts me off my knees in a quick sweep.

He shuts off the water roughly and rips the curtain back, lifting my naked body against his chest. My legs go around his waist, and I grab a fluffy white towel off the rack just before we're out of the bathroom, headed to the bed.

He puts me down fast, turning my body and guiding me forward so I'm on my hands and knees, my ass in the air facing him.

"Mark," I gasp, as he pushes my thighs apart. I'm so ready for him.

With one solid thrust he's inside me. We both groan, and my elbows buckle. My chest drops to the mattress, and I moan loudly as he works me, finishing what I've started with aggressive, demanding thrusts. He holds my hips, pulling me up to meet him, and all I can do is enjoy the ride.

I'm so wet, so hot, when he slides his hand around to find my clit, it only takes a few expert touches to have me breaking, shuddering around him.

"Fuck yes," he hisses, holding steady, and I feel him pulsing, filling me as I clench and spasm around him.

He continues stroking my clit through his orgasm until I grasp his hand, unable to bear the almost-painful bursts of pleasure.

"Oh, God," I whimper, and he guides us farther onto the bed, moving the towel so it's under us as he holds my back against his chest.

One hand is tight around my waist and the other is on my breasts, stroking and caressing one then the other as his lips seal kisses against the top of my shoulder, my neck, the side of my hair.

"Mmm," I sigh, holding his hands, closing my eyes as the residual shimmers of bliss wash over us. "I need to catch you in the shower more often."

A soft tapping at the door interrupts us, and Mark's hand stills on my body. "I ordered room service."

CHAPTER 8

She wasn't looking for a knight, she was looking for a sword.

Mark

Lara sits on the bed across from me wrapped in a white robe. Jillian is on her lap, and an empty pizza box is between us. I might be in heaven.

Roland came and traded Jilly for one of the beers and half the pizza. I finished off the rest, and now I'm sitting in my boxer briefs, holding my empty pint glass, watching as Lara traces her nose along the top of our daughter's head.

She blinks up at me and smiles. "Good?"

"Not bad for hotel pizza."

"Is it as good as the Everything sandwich from your top secret, probably illegal poboy kitchen?"

"Nothing is as good as the Everything sandwich."

She wrinkles her nose and winks. "I can think of something better."

Definitely in heaven.

"I wish we were going to Preservation Hall instead of Montage tonight." Her voice is almost sad.

"Me too." I slide my hand around her ankle. "You never told me how the meeting went?"

With a sigh, she looks down at her twisting fingers. "Candi said she'd never been abused or seen any signs of pedophilia, but Molly's not convinced."

"So were does that leave us?"

She lifts our daughter and turns her so that Jilly's head is at her shoulder. "I still want to see him tonight," she says, gently bouncing the baby. "I'd like to get it over with and go home."

My eyebrows lift slightly at her choice of words. "And Molly?"

"She's going to do what she has to do. I can't be in this anymore." Her voice is soft, but I can hear her frustration.

Or maybe it's exhaustion? I wonder if she'll be able to follow through on letting Molly go. I know how long she's been tied to that girl. Still, if she's made it to this point, I'm not going to let the opportunity pass.

"Where is home?"

Again, her eyes flicker to mine, only this time a question is in them. "Where my family is."

Lifting my hand from her leg, I hold it out to her and wait. She adjusts the baby in her arms and without hesitation places her hand in mine. I give her a gentle pull, and she climbs forward, turning to sit with her back against my side. I wrap my arm around her, our baby secure between us, her little eyes blinking slowly as she drifts to sleep.

I rotate my body so I can hold them closer, Lara's back to my chest. Both arms go around them and kiss first Jillian's head, then Lara's. She turns her face and looks up at me expectantly.

I look down at her, and as much as I don't want to, I remember the night she blew my mind then broke my heart. "I asked you to marry me in Nice, and you said yes." My voice is low, with a slight edge. "Then you left me without a word."

Her chin drops, and she scoots around so her cheek rests against my chest. Jillian dozes against her breast.

"It was the hardest thing I've ever done," she says quietly. "I wanted to be your wife—I still want to be your wife—but I knew what Molly was planning. I couldn't pull you into it."

Residual distrust simmers in my chest. "What's different now?"

Her finger traces a line along our daughter's chubby arm, and she hesitates before answering. "Now that you're here, I can't deny what my soul is telling me."

"Which is?"

"I can't run from you anymore. We have to be together."

Reaching up, I thread my fingers in the back of her hair and gently pull, causing her face to tilt up. Her eyes glisten just before they close, just before I claim her lips, pushing them apart with mine and kissing her deeply.

Our mouths move, tongues curling, and heat simmers low in my pelvis. I want to take her again. I want to slide her robe off and bury myself deep in her clenching heat.

She turns her head, and I relax my fingers, allowing her to press her cheek against mine. "We can get through tonight then start a new life."

Leaning back, I study her eyes, thinking about how much I love her. How much I want to protect her. How much I want her to have a new life.

"I was thinking about it, and I have an idea." Her expression changes, but I keep going. "Molly wants Gavin to go to jail—"

"Molly wants him dead." She moves to the edge of the bed and stands, carrying the baby to the small crib we had delivered this morning.

"I have surveillance equipment. You can wear a wire and see if you can get him to confess."

Baby settled, she turns and crosses her arms over her waist. Her brow is furrowed, and she goes to the closet. "Would it be like a box or something strapped to my torso?"

"No." I go to my suitcase. Digging around, I pull out the wireless receiver. It's as small as the tip of my finger. "We can put this under your collar or in your bra or even behind your ear. I'll be able to hear and record everything he says. Maybe we can kill two birds with one stone."

"Figuratively," she says, coming to where I stand and lifting the square chip from my palm. "It's so tiny."

"They make them small enough now they can be attached to a dragonfly drone."

Her mouth falls open, and she looks up at me wide-eyed. "That's scary. So like an insect could be tracking you, listening to everything you say?"

"Not an actual insect, but yes."

She shakes her head and carries her clothes into the bathroom. I walk over to the crib and watch our daughter sleeping. As a detective, I'm more comforted than alarmed by the availability of such devices. They help me keep this little one safe as well as her mother.

When Lara returns, she's wearing a short skirt and black top, and even without makeup, she's gorgeous, with her dark hair and eyebrows, fair skin, and full pink lips. I can't help a smile.

"Here, let me take her down to Roland's room and get her settled." She reaches in and lifts out the baby. Jillian squirms and makes a noise as she's snuggled into her mother's neck and shoulder. "Get dressed and we can decide how we're going to handle this while I finish my makeup."

She starts to go, but I reach out and catch her by the waist, pulling her to me once more. Sliding my hand to the back of her head, I hold her eyes on mine.

"You don't have to be afraid anymore. I won't let anything happen to you. Or Jillian."

She blinks several times, her blue eyes focused intently on mine. Leaning forward, I capture her soft lips in a kiss once more, just a quick one, but her eyes flutter shut. I let her go and for a moment she seems a little dazed.

"Better get going, the sun's starting to set."

She shakes her head and goes to the door, and I grin, glad to know I have that effect on her. Going to the small dresser, I pull out a pair of jeans and a white tee.

* * *

Lara

"I'm going to ask him how he could let me be hurt, how he could let Molly be hurt." I pace Roland's hotel room with my sleeping daughter in my arms. "I want him to answer for what he's done."

"I've already given you all the answers you need." Roland sits on the edge of the hotel bed with his arms crossed watching me.

"Yes, but you're not him. You can't answer for him."

His lips press into a thin line. "Molly has influenced you in the wrong way. She's got you envisioning justice you're never going to get."

That makes me frown. "So you're saying he wins?"

"Wins?" Roland's eyes flash. "Wins what? This isn't a game, Lara. This is underworld shit, and the answer is yes. *Yes*. In the world of drugs, prostitution, smuggling, gambling, murder, the biggest thug always wins, and he doesn't have to explain himself."

"Maybe not, but if no one ever stands up to him and says 'This is wrong, you're hurting people'... If no one ever makes him acknowledge that simple fact, then he never stops."

"You think you're going to stop him?"

"I don't know." Jillian starts to fuss and squirm on my chest, and I know my agitation is upsetting her.

"Give her to me," he says, lifting her out of my arms.

He puts her on his shoulder, gently rocking until she settles down again.

"You're really good with her," I confess.

"Is Mark going with you? I don't want you doing this alone."

"Yes. I wouldn't do anything stupid now that I have her." I put my hand on Jillian's back and rub it up and down.

"Everything you and Molly have done for the past six years has been stupid, but at least Mark is here now. Maybe he can stop you before it's too late."

My lips tighten, but I don't tell him my plans yet. I'll get this night behind me, then I'll tell him I'm done. "Thanks for watching her."

I lean forward and hug him.

"Let me know when you get back."

Mark is fully dressed in dark jeans, a blue dress shirt, and a black leather jacket when I return to the room. He looks amazing, but I don't have time to think about it. I go to the bathroom and dust powder on my nose, apply some mascara, smooth on some lipstick.

My fingers tremble as I work, and my stomach is tight. All the insecurity and self-doubt are hitting me at once, but I brave through it. We're right at the end, I remind myself.

"Here." Mark stops me at the door, lifting my hand. "I'll attach this inside your sleeve. Try to hold your arm between your bodies to cut down on the background noise."

The sleeves of my sweater hang long over the tops of my hands, and he fastens the tiny device next to the inside of my wrist. I'm wearing a black bodysuit underneath the open-knit sweater and a short black skirt over opaque tights and boots. I look like a club kid. All I need is neon hair.

"How do I do that without being suspicious?" I hold my arm down as I inspect my sleeve for any signs of the bug. It's invisible.

"Get a drink. Hold it in front of you, chest height." He demonstrates with a bottle of water.

It sounds easy enough. I grab my bag, and we're out the door headed to Montage. We walk quickly up the sidewalk holding hands. I'm comforted to have him with me, but my insides are shaky. I can't stop second-guessing myself.

"Where's Molly tonight?" He glances at me, and I assume it's the reason he thinks I'm so antsy.

"I don't know. I texted her a few times, but she hasn't responded." I think back to her moment after our meeting with Candi this afternoon. "I hope she's in her room, but she doesn't tell me much these days."

The crowds grow thicker as we approach the line of bars around Pike and Pine Streets. Mark pulls me to him when we see the sign for our destination.

"You go in alone and see if you can find him. I'll switch on the receiver and hang back out of sight. Don't be afraid. I'll never be too far to save you."

He's big enough to make good on that promise against anyone now. His reason for bulking up warms my insides. *My hero…*

Everything is different from the night so long ago when he tried to save me from the darkness. We were brutally separated that night, and the memory of how it went down makes me hesitant to leave him.

The biggest thug wins…

My eyes are huge, but I step away from him, into the unknown. A shudder passes through my stomach, and I count my steps as I approach the garishly decorated club.

A familiar voice makes me jump. "Lucy!" Looking up, I see Joshua trotting from the alley to me. He's wearing a vintage sharkskin suit, and his hair is now silver.

He stops in front of me, looking around. "You alone tonight?"

"Uh, yeah," I glance at the clump of kids hanging in the alley where he was just standing. "Is Molly with you?"

"Who?" His brow creases.

"I mean… Maggie." I am seriously fucking up the aliases on this job.

His eyes narrow a bit, and I know he's onto us. "Haven't seen her since the Redwood. Is that why you're here? Are you looking for her? I can keep an eye out—"

"No. I actually… I was going to go ahead and talk to Brisbee if he's around."

"Oh, yeah! He's right inside." Joshua's eyes sparkle, and he starts for the door.

My stomach twists, and my feet seem to be rooted to the spot. I can't seem to go forward, insecurity blanketing me in waves. I'm not sure if I can do this. I try making myself go, internally commanding my feet to move, when someone bumps into me from behind, and I stumble forward. I look back to see another skinny kid in jeans and a beanie smoking a cigarette.

"Sorry." He staggers toward the alley, and I'm irritated at his clumsiness. But it worked. It got me moving.

Mark is with me…

He's never too far to save me…

I can do this. I'm not alone. Who knows? I might even get him to say something on the record, and we can send him to jail.

If I'm brave enough to go through with something like that.

One time, a long time ago, Roland told me I was wicked brave. I've never felt brave a day in my life, but having Jilly compels me to do what I know is right. It keeps my feet moving forward, if only to try and rid the world of one more abusive scumbag.

Joshua holds the door, and I go inside. The club is noisy and packed, and a live band is getting ready to play.

"The Hep Cats," Joshua shouts at me, and I frown.

"What?"

"The band. They're called the Hep Cats. They're pretty good."

My eyebrows flicker up, and I nod, trying to seem like I care. The truth is my mind is focused on one thing, and it's twisting my insides into painful knots.

"There he is!" Joshua holds out a hand, and I see Gavin through the crowd.

He's dressed more casually than when he met with Molly, but it only makes him seem taller, more intimidating. I need a drink.

"Can I get a drink first?" I shout to Joshua.

"Sure!" He leads me to the bar, and we face each other. "I'll get you a Capri Sun."

"What's that?"

"Cherry vodka, pomegranate liqueur, limoncello, and sprite."

My nose wrinkles, but he waggles his eyebrows. "You'll love it. It's better than the Dreamcicle shit you were having last time."

"I didn't like that one either."

We stand waiting for the drinks, and Joshua studies me. "I'm not sure what you're up to, but I like you."

Pressing my lips together, I nod. "Thanks. I like your hair."

He grins sheepishly. "I did it for Molly... I mean, oops! Maggie." Our eyes meet, and he starts to laugh. "It's okay. A lot of kids around here change their names. Look at Candi. Her name was Gert. I'd have changed it, too. That sounds like a bodily function."

"Why did you change your hair for Molly?" I ask, trying to stay focused.

He shrugs. "Candi was kind of hard on her."

"She can take it." I lift my drink and sip it. It's not terrible, way less sweet than the neon blue disaster I had before.

"Think she likes me?"

My nose wrinkles, and I search for an answer that won't make Joshua feel bad. "She doesn't really talk to me about stuff like that."

He nods, and his eyes return to the bar. I don't know if he believes me, but I've taken another sip of adult Capri Sun, and I know I have to do this now. Straightening, I lift my drink and step away from the bar.

"I'd better get this over with."

He waves to me. "I'll be here."

He enters a lively discussion with another couple at the bar, and I'm not sure if he knows them or if he's doing with them what he did with Molly and me—making new friends. Just like that.

Either way, the drink has taken the edge off my nerves, and it enables me to hold my hand the way Mark said. I only feel a little squeamish as I cross the crowded space to where Gavin stands at a back wall, his eyes on the band tuning and tweaking their instruments.

I'm within two feet of him when his blue eyes flicker and land on mine. It's like a lightning strike, and the rest of the bar disappears. I'm trapped in his sinister gaze, the once-placid expression transforming into a frown as he recognizes me.

My lips part, and I do my best to control my breathing.

Inhale…

Exhale…

Slowly in and out.

No hyperventilating.

"Lara," he says. "What are you doing here?"

"Gavin." I lift my chin slightly. "Can we go somewhere and talk?"

"What about?"

I swallow my fear, still my hand trembles as I hold the neon orange drink at chest height between our bodies. *Mark is here…*

"Are you afraid?" I manage to sound coy.

"Afraid?" He laughs, pushing off the wall. "Of course not. Follow me. We can talk in my office."

He walks through the crowd, and I do my best to keep up with his fast pace. We go straight up the staircase at the back wall to a room with a large, tinted window overlooking the dance floor and bar below.

"Shut the door behind you," he says, circling a small desk and sitting in the leather chair behind it.

The closed door muffles the noise of the crowd. Do I still need to hold my hand at my chest? I decide not, and put the drink on the edge of the desk, sitting in the wooden chair across from him.

"It's been a long time," he says, his eyes not betraying any emotion. "How have you been?"

He studies me. He's looking for answers, for the reason why I've appeared here out of nowhere. I wonder how much he's even tried to keep up with us since we left with Freddie, since the old place burned to the ground.

"I've been better." My voice is calm, even.

"You look well. I heard you had a baby."

I blink rapidly, my heart hammering in my chest. "Who told you that?"

I was careful, using fake names and staying off the grid when Jillian was born. I didn't want Mark tracking me down, so how did Gavin? A flash of betrayal echoes through me, closing my throat. Only one person could have told him. But has Roland been talking to Gavin behind my back? Why?

"You look like you've seen a ghost," he laughs. "Did I say something wrong?"

"Let's cut the crap, Gavin. If you know about my daughter, I'm sure you know why I'm here."

He leans back, crossing an ankle over his knee. "I only heard about your baby through the grapevine. I actually have no idea why you're here. You'll have to tell me."

If he thinks I believe that…

"Okay." I inhale a steadying breath. "I'm here for answers. I'm here for you to admit what you did and tell me why—"

"Admit what I did?" I'm still breathing rapidly, worked up from the start of my speech, but he leans forward in his chair. "Admit that I took you in, took care of you, gave you a home, food to eat, a chance to live out your dream as a singer?"

"You don't know anything about my dreams."

His eyes are cold, level. "And you know nothing about me."

"I know a little bit. What are you doing here… in Seattle?"

"Running a club. A very successful one, at that. It's so much easier without the constant drain of the theater and the productions and the insurance. God, the insurance." He sits back again, as if he's just a normal businessman talking shop.

I'm not fooled.

"But you're still dipping into the sex trade. I thought Guy was behind it, but it was always you."

His eyes narrow. "Guy was a madman. I had to keep him on a leash."

"Is that why you had the sex club?"

"Is that what you call it?" He chuckles, and my stomach turns. "He had certain tastes, *fetishes* if you will. I did what I could to keep him appeased."

"Fetishes," I say the word as if it's bitter.

"I'm sure you're aware of them. Virgins?"

"Is that why you gave him Molly? Why you gave him me?" My voice rises on the last word, and I'm losing control of my emotions.

Gavin's expression is closed. "I did everything in my power to keep you away from him. You made that deal yourself."

"I did it to protect Molly."

"Molly... Molly," he mocks me. "Get out of here, Lara. I've had enough of your sentimental notions. Go home and leave me alone."

He stands as if he's through with this conversation, but I'm on my feet just as fast. "I'm not finished yet."

"Yes. You are." In three steps he's right in front of me, bearing down with his intimidating gaze. "Don't cross swords with me, girl. You have more to lose in this than I do."

I take a staggering step back, but my leg bumps into the chair. "I-I don't know what you mean... I don't have anything to lose."

His lips part with an evil grin, blue eyes glittering. "You have everything to lose. You don't want what I know getting out. You don't want the truth going public."

"You're wrong. I want the truth now."

"What truth? About the body in the salon?"

"What bod—"

"The body I helped cover up. The one that was never completely destroyed?"

"No." My vision clouds, and I fumble for the door.

I rip at my sleeve, scratching at the hem, trying to get the bug off of me, trying to keep Mark from hearing these words...

"*You* arranged your experience with Guy against my warnings and attempts to help you." My hands slip along the wall, searching for the door to run, but he's behind me, on top of me, pushing me down with his accusations. "I told you to stay away from him, but you ignored me. You lured him into your dressing room, then you brutally murdered him."

"No!" I scream, my hands cupped over my ears.

"Yes, little Dark Angel. I have it all recorded. Every room in that theater was under surveillance, yours included, and Landry has the thumb drive. Come at me, and you will lose everything. Your daughter, your freedom, your life."

I shudder violently, as if frigid cold water is being poured down my back. My fingers finally locate the doorknob, and I turn it, slamming the door wide open and racing down the stairs.

All the words he said are screaming in my mind. Cameras, surveillance, the secret I thought was hidden, burned up in the fire. Landry, the corrupt New Orleans cop... He dug it up, and now he's just waiting to send my world crashing down around my head.

I'm out the door, running for the hotel, when Mark steps out of the alley, blocking my path.

"Oh!" I pull up short, holding up my arms as if to defend myself.

"Easy," he says.

I'm breathing fast, and we're far enough away from the bar that the noise is subtler, muted.

"Mark..." My voice trembles and breaks.

He watches me, blue eyes distant, withdrawn. He looks at me like I'm someone new, someone he doesn't know. He's a cop, a hero. Long ago he told me he wanted to be one of the good guys. Now he knows

I'm just as bad as all the bad guys we've left littered across the continent. My sins are out, and I'm no different than the rest of the fallen angels in the hell we left behind.

"We need to get to the hotel." He takes a step to the side and puts his hands in his pockets.

All the gestures of love, the embraces, the warmth, are gone. Now he addresses me as if I'm a person of interest, a suspect to question. I wonder if he'll read me my rights.

He only tilts his head to the side. "We have to talk."

CHAPTER 9

The darkest place I've ever seen was inside me, and nothing scared me more.

Mark

Every room in the theater was under surveillance...

We're walking fast to the hotel, and my insides are humming. I'm searching my memory for everything I can remember about my time working with Gavin, from my very first job to the night I was dragged out nearly dead, tied up, and thrown into a wooden crate.

Wooden crates I saw loaded onto a barge heading out of Algiers that cold fall morning. How many of those crates held bodies?

My very first job was cleaning up a crime scene. Gavin stood over me and told me I was in his world now, and Landry stood there with that smarmy look on his face, grinning in agreement.

My stomach tightens with disgust. Nothing is worse than a corrupt cop.

He had the crooked pharmacist; he had a money laundering business uptown... None of those help me, because I never kept records of any of it.

Years ago, when I first became a cop and started searching for Lara, I wanted to shut him down, bust him for all the rotten things he'd made me do, for what he'd done to her. But the theater was burned, and I thought everything was gone.

He just blew the lid off that theory. Surveillance

cameras. Fucking Landry. If he has one crime on video, he has them all—whatever happened in that room is on camera. All the abuse, Molly's rape, Lara's rape, my beating... My fists clench with rage, and one thing is blindingly clear. I've got to get back to New Orleans.

Lara keeps pace beside me, her arms tight across her waist. Her dark hair fans around her shoulders, and she seems shell-shocked, spiraling. I want to put my arms around her. I want to tell her to breathe, stay calm, there's no fucking way in hell I'll let that asshole take anything from her. Only, I'm not sure she's ready to hear me.

She looks like a wounded animal who's cornered, as if she's afraid I'm going to hurt her, too.

Like I would ever do anything like that.

I need to get her somewhere she feels safe, where she can breathe and tell me exactly what happened, exactly how she killed him.

She killed him...

Swallowing the knot in my throat, I scrub my forehead with my fingers. I'm having a hard time putting an image to those words in my mind. From the first day I met Lara, she's always been committed to following the rules. Molly might be bent on revenge, but Lara is not a killer.

Only... if what Gavin said is true, it seems she is.

And once again, she's kept a pretty fucking serious piece of information from me.

My jaw is clenched so tight, I might break a tooth, and looking up, I'm thankful we're finally at the hotel. I need answers.

I step forward to hold the door, and she glances up at me as she passes. All these facts are still a storm in my mind, and when she sees the anger in my eyes, she quickly pulls away. *Wait until we're in the room…*

The elevator hums as we ride higher. I watch the numbers; she stares at the shiny tiles lining the floor. The chime sounds, and we start down the hallway until she pulls up short.

"I want to get Jillian." Her voice is soft, but I reach out to catch her arm.

"Just wait. We have to talk first."

Another wide-eyed look of fear. It twists my guts, but I need to know what she's thinking. I need to assess if she's about to run again or if she's going to let me help her. She has to let me help her, for Jillian's sake.

For our sake.

Guiding her down the hall, I pull out the card and usher her inside. The heavy door slams shut, and she stops in the center of the room. Her arms are wrapped around her waist, but her back is to me. She's still shaking, and I slip off my leather jacket, dropping it on the back of the chair.

I go to the mini fridge and take out a small bottle of Jack Daniels. It's not my favorite, but I need a drink.

"Would you like something?" I ask, and she shakes her head, not meeting my eyes.

I toss back the shot and clear my throat as it burns on the way down. Again, I scrub my fingers against my forehead. I walk around so I'm in front of her, so I can see her expression as we speak.

"Tell me what happened."

Her brow furrows, and she keeps her eyes fixed on the floor. "Why?"

"Why?" My voice is more forceful than I intend, but our track record on disclosure isn't the best. "Because I need to know how bad this is."

At that her eyes meet mine, defiant. "I killed a man. Gavin has it on video. How much worse can it get?"

We stand for a moment facing each other. Her defenses are up but so are mine. I fall back on my interrogation training. I take a deep breath, step away, and bring the tension down.

Softening my voice, I start again. "He said you lured Guy into your dressing room and killed him... I'm going to assume this was after he—"

"You were gone." Her voice cracks, and when I look into her eyes this time, I see she's at the breaking point. "It was only me, alone with Molly. I was still in pain... I still hurt. I physically *hurt*." She takes a shaky inhale, and her eyes glisten with unshed tears. "He burst into the room after a show, and he tried... He tried..."

Her bottom lip trembles, and her eyes squeeze shut as if she's in agony. I'm across the space, pulling her body to mine before she can say another word.

"Come here." My hands are on her back, holding her close. "Just breathe," I whisper, and she melts into me, quivering.

I hold her tighter, pouring my strength into her broken heart. "It's going to be okay," I say softly, putting my hand on the back of her hair and stroking it down.

Lowering my chin, I kiss her head, and I feel it slowly moving back and forth.

"No," she whispers. "It's not going to be okay. He's going to hold this over me, hold me prisoner with it..."

Her voice breaks off, and I tighten my arms around her waist. "I will never let that happen." Sliding my hands up and down her body, I hold her until her shaking starts to subside. Until she's able to speak without crying.

"Talk to me," I urge. "The more you tell me, the more I can help you."

She steps out of my arms and goes to the bathroom, runs water in the sink, and I open another tiny bottle. I should call room service and get them to send up a fifth, but I don't.

Finally she returns holding a damp washcloth to her cheeks. "I'm sorry. I never thought…"

She doesn't finish, but I'm pretty sure I know what her words would be. If she had known Gavin would say the things he did tonight, she would never have agreed to wear a wire. It's cynical, but I can't deny it based on our history—she would never have told me about Guy.

"Who else knows about this?"

"Roland. He was there when it happened."

"In your dressing room?" I rise to my feet, encouraged by this additional information. "He can verify what you're saying—that Guy was attacking you. It was self defense."

Her head bows, and the guilt returns. "He wasn't attacking me when it happened."

"What do you mean? Why else—"

"He came into the room like I said, but Roland came in behind him and knocked him out with a stage pin."

"Are you sure that didn't kill him?"

She nods, stepping to the mini fridge and taking out a mini bottle of wine. I wait as she unscrews the cap and pours a glass.

"Roland only knocked him out. He was trying to get me to safety. Roland was gathering my clothes when Guy started to wake up…"

"And then he attacked you?"

Her lips press together, and her eyes are downcast. "I didn't give him a chance."

She doesn't need to say another word. Standing, I go to where she is and pull her into my arms again. I don't blame her for what she did. I remember Guy, but even more, I remember the overwhelming pressure of being in that place. I was caught up in it, but she was trapped.

I guide us to the bed and sit against the headboard. She curls up beside me, her head on my chest, and I cradle her in my arms. I think about the sharp conflict between my duty as an officer of the law and the fact that the love of my life has committed murder, a crime so heinous, it has no statute of limitations.

In my mind, there's no debate over what I should do. I was present when she was being abused, being held captive by a madman. I was nearly killed trying to stop what happened to her, and if that puts me in direct conflict with my oath as an officer, then fuck it. I'll walk away from that oath.

But I won't have to make that decision.

"You acted in self defense," I say with finality. "If anyone knows that, it's me, and I'm going to prove it. I will never let you be punished for what you've done."

"Mark," she whispers, wrapping a slim arm around my waist. "I was so afraid I'd lost you."

Her lips press against my neck, and her breath hiccups. I reach for her chin and lift her lips to mine, kissing her gently. I taste the salt of her tears; I feel the damp on her cheek, and everything in me is focused on comforting her.

For the first time since we left the club, the

tension in my chest eases. I tighten my hold on this woman who *will* be my wife. This woman I will *never* let go to prison for ridding the world of one of the most hideous monsters I've ever encountered.

I kiss her head, wanting to hold her until the fear subsides. At the same time, we don't have a moment to lose. Gavin has shown his hand, and we have to move fast before he starts destroying evidence we can use against him. If Gavin recorded everything, that means he has Lara's reason for killing Guy somewhere on video as well.

I intend to find it.

"Lara?" My voice is gentle. "I love you."

Her body relaxes more, and I hug her closer. I can't remember if I've said those words out loud since our reunion. I've shown her so many ways, with my body, with my plans. I've asked her to marry me…

"I love you," she whispers, and my planning momentarily stalls. I'm fucking king of the world.

I hug her closer, kissing her head, relishing this moment, and my mind is flying, hours down the road.

"We have to go to New Orleans, my love." I kiss her head again. "Now. We don't have time to lose."

She nods against my chest, seeming to understand the urgency. I hold her a bit longer until she sits up and pushes her hair away from her face. She touches the tears away, and with all the warmth burning in my chest, I watch as she summons that incredible strength she's always had.

I saw it the first time she climbed the ladder after falling. I saw it again on that train to Canada, and now, after being hit with a low blow, I see it rise again.

"I'll tell Roland. We can be ready to leave as soon as you are."

121

***

Lara

Molly stands at the dresser, looking at my reflection in the mirror.

She's defiant, but she doesn't know what I'm up against. She wasn't there when I killed Guy, and I've never seen a reason to tell her about it. I'm not looking to give her another excuse to justify her vigilantism.

"We're going back to New Orleans. Mark booked us tickets to leave in two hours."

"I'm not going back there." Her eyes are flinty, and I know we've reached the fork in the road, the place where we go our separate ways.

"I thought you might say that."

"So?" She shakes her silver mane off her shoulders. "Why are you here?"

"I wanted to know your plans. What will you do?"

She goes to the closet and carefully takes her jacket off the hanger. "For starters, I'll find a place to live." She places the garment in the base of her suitcase then continues to her toiletries, collecting them in order of use, morning first.

"Did you have something in mind? What about a job?"

"Joshua offered to let me crash at his place until I find something." Her expression is neutral as she arranges the breakable items between socks and underwear.

"He has a crush on you."

"A crush." She says the words like they smell bad. "I'm nineteen years old, Lara."

"I didn't say you had a crush on him." I step back,

allowing her access to the drawers where her shirts are arranged by color. "I only thought you should know he might have more of an ulterior motive than sheer generosity."

"I don't think Joshua has an ulterior bone in his body." She places the shirts in her bag ordered by color.

Thinking of his silver hair tonight, I nod. "He's a sweet kid."

"He's not a kid. He's twenty-one."

"No shit." Crossing my arms, I step out of the way again. She's moving fast, gathering her things, but I can't tell if she's angry. "In that case, you should be even more aware he has feelings for you."

"He's not going to hurt me."

"If I thought that, I wouldn't be so calm about it."

Blue eyes cut up to mine before she continues stuffing her few belongings into her small suitcase. I can't help remembering the day we left the theater so long ago. We had half as much as we do now. Still, we travel light.

"You don't have to leave tonight, you know. We've paid through tomorrow morning."

"It's okay. It's easier to catch up with everyone at night." The last of her belongings are in the case, and she zips it up. "They hang around the same places."

We're out the door, walking slowly down the hall. Mark has our bags in the lobby, waiting for a Lyft to the airport. Roland meets us with sleeping Jillian on his arm.

"Goodbye for now, shortcake," he says, stepping forward to kiss her cheek. "Make good choices. Don't do drugs."

"You, too." She holds her face up like she always does. Her eyes glide over my sleeping infant then up to me. "We can take the elevator together."

"Of course." We follow Roland, and my stomach feels like a lead weight is dragging it down to my feet.

For almost seven years, we've been inseparable. We left New Orleans together, and as she's gone through all of these changes, as she's confronted and slain her demons, I've been with her, taking care of her, making sure she's safe. Even as she's pulled away from me, we've still only been steps apart.

Now a strange fear clutches at my chest.

"I'm not abandoning you." I need to have those words on the record. "I have to take care of… a matter back in the city. Roland has to get back to work. Mark—"

"Mark is going wherever you go. He's in love with you."

We're in the elevator, and Roland pretends to be occupied with Jilly, but I know he's listening to every word we say.

"I love him," I say softly.

She nods. "Then it's going to work out. You'll get married. You already have a baby. You'll get your happily ever after."

If only it were that simple.

The doors open, and we emerge from the elevator. Mark is at the front desk, and when he sees us all together, when he sees Molly's suitcase, he turns to the attendant again.

"Looks like we're all checking out tonight." The man nods and types on his computer screen.

Molly keeps walking, and I follow her to the revolving door.

"Wait," I say, reaching out to catch her arm. She stops, and looks up at me. "I'll call you. I'm only going to New Orleans. It's not the end of the world."

"I never said it was." She almost laughs, and I feel silly.

It's strange to feel like I'm the only one who remembers when she used to wake up in the night crying, fearful and clinging to me in our tiny theater room. I remember being barely awake, exhausted and making up stories about her dancer mother or our escape plan to Paris, her little dog.

"I'll check on Pierre for you."

Her head tilts to the side. "I told Evie she could keep him. She fell in love with him when we were there last."

Oh.

"Well, take care of yourself." I release her arm and pat it, unsure if I get a hug.

Her shoulders drop, and her lips quirk into a half smile. Stepping forward, she puts her arms around my shoulders. I wrap my arms around her waist, doing my best to fight the heat in my eyes.

"Keep in touch," I manage through the thickness in my throat.

She turns, catching the handle of her rolling suitcase, and takes off. I only stand and watch her go, disappearing swiftly into the damp night, returning to the streets where I found her.

"Don't worry, darling, she'll be fine." Roland is beside me, and I take Jillian out of his arms. She kicks her little legs, but her eyes are closed as I hug her against my chest, running my nose along her head.

"I hope so." I allow my baby to soothe the pain in my chest.

"She will." He places a hand on my back. "Girls like her always land on their feet."

Warmth swirls behind us, and I glance up to see Mark is with us. "It's time to catch a plane. It'll be tomorrow when we get to New Orleans, and we have a lot of catching up to do."

One last glance up the sidewalk, and I step into the car waiting to take us to the airport.

CHAPTER 10

The best view comes after the hardest climb.

Mark

"I never should have worked for him as long as I did." My eyes follow the swaying of the topless dancers in the private booths behind the bar, but my mind is years away, remembering my role in the sins of this city.

Terrence sits beside me at the bar, a pint of Guinness in front of him. "You can't blame yourself for trying to earn a living."

"I could have gone to the Bahamas with you."

He slaps my arm. "And leave behind the love of your life?"

My eyes drop to my beer. "I was always pretty obvious back then."

"He took advantage of your character. You showed your hand when you grabbed that rope. It put you on the radar just as sure as a nice rack would've in that place."

I look up at the girls swaying side to side. They wear less clothes at the jazz club now — pasties and thongs instead of skimpy bras and tiny shorts. None of them are as gorgeous as Lara.

"How did you get mixed up in that racket anyway?" He fumbles with an unlit cigarette.

"They let me smoke at work," he says with a laugh. "No, it was good pay. I knew where to draw the line. When to walk away."

"You didn't have to work there. You could've charged more for rent."

"Then how would I have met you?" He gives me a wink. "I've never been too worried about money. You get on that hamster wheel and you never get off."

"So what motivates you?"

He shrugs. "Beauty, freedom."

"And?"

"Pretty girls showing their tits."

That makes me laugh. "I have to figure out a way to use what I know to bring them down. Will you help me, T?"

"Why you so worried about those guys now? They're gone."

Tension is in my chest, and I can't tell my friend the whole truth. "Gavin's holding something over Lara's head."

"Always the romantic." He laughs, taking a long sip of dark beer. "I'll do what I can, but I stayed away from those guys. I worked for Darby, and when he said we were done, I went fishing."

"You also married Bea."

"Can you blame me?"

"No." We both sit in silence a little while. Then I prop my elbow on the bar. "I need to find Landry. He's not at the NOPD. Any idea where he might have gone?"

"He never left the city, but I don't know where he is now."

"Could you find out?"

He shrugs, lips poking out. "I still see Eddie every now and then. He might know something."

"Text me if you do. I'm at Roland's place for now."

He slides off the stool, and I follow suit, ready to get back to Lara and the baby. We still need to figure out where we're going to stay, and I'm sure Roland has to get to the club.

Terrence stops at the corner and lights up. "Landry's not going to tell you anything. He's not that stupid."

"Maybe not, but maybe I can convince him it's in his best interest to cooperate."

Specifically, it's in his best interest to give me that fucking thumb drive.

"What exactly are you looking for?"

Shoving my hands in my pockets I study my friend. I've known Terrence as long as anybody in this city, and he's always been a stand-up guy.

"They had cameras in every room. I need to get my hands on those recordings."

His expression changes halfway through my explanation, as if he understands immediately what the introduction of surveillance means. He was the one who told me about the private dances, after all.

"I got you. I'll see what I can find out."

We shake hands, and I head north on Orleans Street. Roland's place is just a few blocks away, but I want to make a slight detour first.

* * *

Lara

Mark texted he's on his way back from meeting with Terrence, and I'm in Jillian's closet-room. I'm not interested in staying here any longer than it takes to pack her things and leave.

"I'll talk to Bill and see if we can do another

129

concert this—" Roland stops in the doorway, but I don't look up. "What are you doing?"

Jillian is in her crib kicking her little feet while she coos at her animal mobile. I'm emptying her drawers into my suitcase.

"We're leaving."

"Why?" He's with me in two steps trying to catch my hands. I only push his away.

"I wouldn't stay here another day if you paid me."

"What the hell? Why are you acting this way?"

He's still trying to stop me, so I pivot to face him. "How long have you been spying on me? Telling everything I do to Gavin?"

Anger burns under my skin, and I know it's blazing from my eyes. I've been holding onto this confrontation since I faced Gavin in Seattle.

Roland takes a step back. "I haven't spoken to Gavin in…" He shakes his head, his eyes roaming as if searching for an answer. "Five years? Since he left here."

"I'm not listening to lies anymore. From anyone."

I'm back to the bureau, pulling open the last drawer. He puts his palm on it and slams it shut. Jillian emits a squeal just before she hiccups and starts to cry. He leaves me and goes to lift her out of the crib, but I follow.

"Put her down."

"I will not put her down." Brown eyes flash at me. "You're going to tell me what the hell this is about. What are you accusing me of doing?"

Jilly cries more, and I imagine it's the first time she's heard Roland raise his voice. Still, I'm not backing down.

"When we were in Seattle, when I met with Gavin. How did he know I had a baby? Only one person knew about her birth." My eyes flashed, and I poke my finger in his chest. "You."

"Did he say I told him?"

"No—"

"Then what the fuck, Lara? Are you kidding me?" Jilly's cries grow louder, stronger, and he turns her so her little face is against his chest. He hugs her close and goes to the door, ducking as he leaves the room.

I stay behind a few moments, attempting to calm my emotions so I can calm my little girl. When I walk out, he's swaying side to side, smoothing her back with his hand.

"Shh, princess. It's okay." His voice is soft, and he kisses her little head.

She's still fretting, but she's not screaming anymore.

"We went to a small, private hospital. I used an alias." My voice has an edge, but I'm holding it steady. "No one knew she was born except Molly and you."

"Then what did you do?" His voice matches mine, edgy but calm.

"What do you mean? We came back here and stayed with you. It all comes back to you."

Jilly's bottom lip quivers, and two tears hang in perfect little spheres on her bottom lashes. I reach for her, but he turns away, hugging her closer.

"What else did you do when you came here?" he asks.

My brow furrows. "What do you mean?"

"Did you enter a convent?" Sarcasm.

"No, we—"

"You lived your life. You visited with Evie, you went out, you sang with me in the club... How do you think Mark found you?" His eyes flash, and he turns to me again.

Jilly scrubs her face against his shoulder and he inhales a few times, calming his voice. "Everybody saw you. Everybody knew you'd had a baby. Anyone could have told anyone, and it got back to him. How dare you accuse me?"

My throat is tight, and my heart is still thundering, but I can't argue with him. The shock and fear of Gavin knowing everything about me is still so fresh, I'm not ready to let him off the hook so fast.

Still, he has a point. We didn't go into hiding. We were out and about in the Quarter—where any number of Gavin's old acquaintances might have seen us.

"Can I have her now?"

"No." My jaw drops, but he continues. "All I've ever done is help and protect you, and since Jilly came, it's been the same with her. You know where my loyalty lies."

"Give her to me."

The muscle in his jaw flexes, but he hands her over. I hug her close to me, and she puts her head on my shoulder. Two fingers are in her mouth, and she grips my hair in her little fist. Roland watches us, his expression stricken.

"Do you really think I'd do that?" His voice cracks, all anger gone. "I love you, Lara. I love Jilly. Soon you'll be leaving, and I won't see you... possibly ever again. Tell me you don't believe I would hurt you."

Swallowing the thickness in my throat, I hug my baby tighter before fixing my eyes on the floor. "So much has happened, I don't know who to trust—"

"You know me." He steps closer, so close Jilly's back is against his chest. "You've known me all your life. I have always been there for you, through everything." My own eyes heat, and I blink up to see the heartbreak in his. "Haven't I?"

We stand here, and all the memories flash across my mind.

Being a teenager and being in love with him.

Him teaching me to kiss, encouraging me to sing.

His fury when I fell; his fury when I told him my bargain with Gavin.

Him slipping Rohypnol into the Sazerac to save me.

Him nursing me back to my feet after I was hurt.

Hiding me in his home and covering up my crime.

Finding Freddie to carry us away from this nightmare like a handsome prince in some fairytale.

Treating Jillian like she's his own daughter…

A tear spills onto my cheek, and I shake my head. "I'm sorry, Roland. I don't know what to say."

His arms are around me at once, around both of us. He places his hand on Jilly's back and turns me so we're not squishing her. She doesn't fuss. She's so used to the two of us showering her with love and affection.

"You've been through so much, my love." My head is against his chin, and he gives me one more squeeze before releasing me.

"I feel like I don't know who to trust, I don't know when it's all going to end."

"Mark is determined to end this, and if anyone can do it… Well, *you* can. I saw you do it with my own eyes. Gavin had better watch his step."

He grins, but I don't want to think about what I did. "I don't even remember that night."

"I do, and trust me. You are fierce. Wicked brave."

Jilly's head lifts and she looks at him, at me. Her blue eyes are so big, and I sniff before laughing. "She's never seen us fight."

"Give me my girl." He holds out his hands, and she immediately leans into him.

I let her go, and he bounces her against his chest. "Mommy was a bit out of sorts, darling. You have to be patient with her. She hasn't had it as easy as you."

I roll my eyes, dropping onto the couch. "You spoil her so bad."

"Back to what I was saying before all this recent unpleasantness." He does a little wave as if to sweep it all away. "I'm going to talk to Bill tonight. As long as you're here, I want to do another concert. The crowd loved it last time."

"I don't know. I don't really feel like singing—"

"You do and you will. It's the only time I get to play my old songs." He carries Jilly to the kitchen. "We can do a mix of standards and Roland Desjardin originals. Do you know 'Big Spender'? 'The Man I Love'?"

Taking a deep breath, I exhale loudly. "Yes."

Movement at the front door causes my eyes to flicker up. They key turns in the lock, and when it opens Mark is here. All my paranoia and anxiety melts away when our eyes meet.

He smiles, toeing off his boots. "How are my girls?"

I'm about to answer when my stomach growls, and I notice the large white bag in his hand emitting the most amazing aroma. "What did you bring us?"

"They've gone legit." He holds up the bag with a teasing frown. "I only hope it's still as good."

"Petit Monjou is your secret poboy kitchen? They're the best!"

Dropping onto the couch beside me, he leans forward to kiss my lips before pulling a bundle wrapped in white paper from the bag.

"The line was out the door."

"It's always like that. Roland took us there when we first got back. I wish I'd known…"

He unrolls the foot-long sandwich, and I have to stop speaking. My mouth is literally watering. "No more Everything poboy. Now they call it the Three-fer."

"I don't care what they call it. Give me some."

He laughs, passing half to me, and I take an enormous bite, my eyes rolling with delight as the tangy rémoulade fills my mouth along with perfectly fried seafood.

Mark lets out a little groan as well. "Still the best," he manages around his bite.

I'm grinning as we devour our dinner in record time. The day we sat on the river chatting and getting to know each other is on my mind. We were so young, falling in love on the brink of disaster.

Leaning my head on my hand, I trace my finger over his shoulder, my belly happily full. "How did it go with Terrence?"

He nods. "He's going to see if Eddie knows anything." I can't help a shudder at that name. His eyebrows lower. "Yeah, I don't like that guy either."

"Good. You're here." Roland enters the living room with Jilly and a bottle. "I have to go, but it's time for her dinner. She'll need a bath, and then this little princess is ready for bed."

"I actually remember how to take care of my child." Impatience is in my tone.

"Yeah, but it helps me," Mark jumps in, but I elbow his side.

"Don't encourage him. He thinks he knows everything about babies."

"I think he might," Mark whispers close to my ear.

Roland only gives me a superior look. "Unpack her things. You're not going anywhere."

At that Mark pulls back, brows furrowed.

I grip his forearm. "We had a fight. I was going to tell you—"

"Fight? What about?" His muscles relax.

"Lara was overly tired." Roland hands me Jilly's bottle, and I cradle her in my arms. "Now, I have to get to work. Practice those songs."

Mark hops off the couch and holds out the white bag. "Hey, I got one for you."

Roland stops at the door and glances at the offering. "It's not often I say this…" He takes the bag. "I was wrong about you. You're very good for Lara, even without money or connections."

Mark exhales a laugh. "Thanks?"

Roland pats him on the arm and takes off. Mark locks the door behind him before turning to face me. I've got Jilly cradled in my arm, and her eyes are blinking slowly as she drinks her bottle.

"I never really know what to make of him," Mark says, coming to sit beside me on the couch.

"He means well." I lift my chin for another kiss.

Warm lips cover mine, and our tongues meet briefly. It's just enough to send a tingle through my lower stomach. When he pulls back, our eyes lock, and my chest tightens. *When this is over…*

"Hey, can I give her the bottle?" He sits, and I look down.

Jilly's just a little stowaway in the midst of all this turmoil. She's so innocent, so trusting.

"Yes—of course!" I gently pull the bottle out of her mouth.

She immediately fusses, but I hand her to her daddy. Her head is so small cradled in the crook of his arm. I help him move her higher, then we position the bottle in her mouth again. She eagerly takes it, and her big blue eyes move around his face as she eats.

"She's so beautiful," he says, and the love expanding in my chest is so strong. It's bigger than all my fears.

Resting my head on his shoulder, I touch her little arm. "She looks like you."

"I think she looks like you." He turns his smiling face and captures my lips again.

Just like that.

It's so casual, so proprietary.

I love it.

"I love you," I say softly, and he does it again.

"I love you."

We're quiet as our baby finishes her bottle. Once she's done, I show him how to place her on his shoulder and burp her.

"Roland always says I do it wrong. I say I warm her up, and he just finishes her off."

"I have no idea—"

He's interrupted by a loud, sailor-burp out of our dainty little girl, and we both burst into laughter.

"I think you're the king. She's never burped that fast!"

He shrugs. "Beginner's luck."

"Come on." I unfold my legs and stand. "You can

help me bathe her." His eyes are worried when they meet mine, but I smile. "It's not hard. Come on."

Roland and I have always bathed her in the kitchen sink. It's fun and old school, and she can't slip away so easily. I put a towel on the bottom and run a mini bath of warm water. Jilly is braced over my forearm, and she bends her knees quickly, bouncing up and down and splashing water all over both of us.

"I think she likes this," he says, holding up a hand and laughing.

"She always makes the biggest mess."

She laughs and coos, and I grip her slippery little body as I direct her daddy.

"She doesn't get very dirty. Just try to clean all her crevices."

"I feel like I'm invading her privacy."

"She's a baby, Mark."

"Still." He dabs the washcloth at her little butt barely making contact.

"Nevermind, she'll be okay for tonight. Grab that towel."

Jilly squeals and slaps the water. I lift her out and place her in the fluffy white towel her dad wraps around her little body. We carry her to our bedroom and dry her, put on her diaper. I smooth lavender lotion on her shoulders and legs then I zip her up in a long-sleeved onesie. Her legs kick and she waves her fists watching us.

"Ready to sleep little girl?" I say, picking her up and situating her on my shoulder.

We walk into the living room, and Mark sits on the couch. "Want to sit?"

"She goes to sleep quicker this way." I hold her in my arms, swaying side to side.

He watches us smiling. "You should sing to her."

My nose wrinkles, and I don't know why I feel shy. "It's been so long. I don't know…"

"Roland wants you to practice. What did he say?"

"He said a couple of different things."

"Pick one." His voice is warm, and his blue eyes hold mine.

The lift of a song moves through me, and I close my eyes thinking of my favorite Gershwin tune. Closing my eyes, I slow my swaying as I hum the bridge of that old standard. It's a wish about meeting the man I love… someday, maybe on a Tuesday…

Building a home…

Never roam…

The melody slips from my lips as easily as pulling on a silk dress. *"And so all else above, I'm waiting for the man I love…"*

When my eyes flutter open, Mark is watching me like he used to so long ago from the catwalk far above the stage floor. Butterflies take flight in my stomach, and I want to laugh and cry and sing and dance all at once. The cutest little snore comes from my shoulder, and I look down to see Jilly fast asleep on my arm.

My heart warms with all the love in this room. "I'll put her in her crib," I whisper. "Meet me in the bedroom?"

His low voice sets my body humming in all the right places. "I thought you'd never ask."

CHAPTER 11

"At the end of the day, we can endure much more than we think we can." –Frida Kahlo

Mark

Lara is on my lap riding, bucking her hips, and sending me to fucking heaven.

My cock is buried deep inside her, and I clutch her ass, lifting her and doing my best to hold out until she finishes.

The lines in her torso deepen as she moves. Her long, dark waves curl at the tips of her nipples, and I lean forward, capturing a tight peak between my lips and giving it a pull, a little bite.

"Oh!" she moans, and spasms break out around my dick.

"Fuck me," I hiss, right on the edge of coming hard. "Come on, baby."

Her hips move faster, and she leans forward, gripping the headboard behind me. Her beautiful breasts sway right at my lips, and I cover them with kisses.

She's moaning, making those sexy little noises, and I slide my hand around to find her clit. The moment I touch it, her back arches, and she lets out the most beautiful cry. She comes hard and fast, and I let go, pulsing deep inside, riding that wave with her. God, it feels so good.

She falls forward onto my chest, and my arms go around her, holding her close. My eyes close, and we hold each other to the end, humming with afterglow, our bodies slick with sweat and perfectly spent. It's the best workout ever.

Her body moves, and a happy sigh escapes on her exhale. It makes me smile, and as much as I hate it, I pull out and rotate us so she's lying beside me in the bed. I want to see her face.

"You are the most beautiful woman I've ever known," I say, smoothing dark hair off her cheek. "I'm taking you tomorrow to pick out a ring."

Her hand is at her mouth, and she blinks those ocean blue eyes up at me. "Husband," she says softly, reaching out to touch my face.

Damn, I never thought a word could fill my heart with so much joy. I capture her hand and pull it to my mouth, kissing her palm.

"Love, cherish, protect." She blinks rapidly, and a beautiful smile spreads across her lips.

"In sickness and health, good times and bad."

"After this, it's nothing but good times." She slides forward, pressing her cheek to my chest. I wrap my arms around her.

The light fades to black, but the sounds of the street keep going. Several hours pass, and I doze, waking when Roland arrives back at the house. My mind can't stop running through the things Terrence said, Gavin said, my promise to Lara. I want all of this behind us before we take that next step.

Lara turns in her sleep, her breasts slowly rising and falling with her sleep. My beautiful wife...

The task ahead of me feels impossible, but it's not the first time I've run into secrets, buried evidence, criminals who think they hold all the cards. If I can't get that thumb drive from Landry, I can at least get my hands on the video evidence of why Lara did what she did — something I need to do no matter what.

Thumb drives can be lost. They can be bought, sold, copied…

Tomorrow I'll return to the theater and dig through the wreckage. The structure is still in place. Gavin owns the land and the building, and it's never been torn down. I can't help wondering why — if there's something still there, hidden in the rooms. Now that we've had our confrontation, I feel a greater sense of urgency. He'll be expecting us to dig, and I won't let him cover any more of his tracks. We only need one card to fall for the whole house to collapse.

I'm sure I'll never sleep. My throat is tight, and I want to get started now. When I open my eyes again, light streams through the sheer curtains. I hear voices in the other room, and Lara's not in the bed. She's up with our daughter, feeding her a bottle on the couch. Jillian threads her chubby fingers in her mother's hair, and I lean down to kiss my fiancée's lips.

"Still up for ring shopping?" I ask.

"Hmm, I am if you are." She reaches up and pets my arm. "You didn't sleep much last night."

"I'm sorry if I kept you awake." I walk around to sit beside her. "I couldn't stop thinking about what we need to do. I want to go there today — this morning — and see if anything's left."

Her eyes are round as she watches me. "I'll go with you."

"What about…" I look down at Jilly, who studies me with bright eyes. Reaching down, I slip my finger into her strong little grip. "She doesn't need to be there."

"I'm sure Evie or Roland will be glad to keep an eye on her for us. She'll probably sleep the whole time we're gone anyway."

A door opens, and the man in question emerges from his bedroom wearing loose sweatpants and a tee. "What will she sleep through?"

"Mark wants to go to the old theater and see if we can find evidence."

"That sounds dangerous... and possibly illegal?" Roland doesn't even stop on his way to the kitchen.

"So will you watch Jilly while we're gone?" she calls from the couch.

I shake my head. "He's right. You stay here. If I get caught, I can at least show my badge."

"No." Her blue eyes flash, and she grips my arm tightly. "Let me go with you."

"Lara—"

"I want to go. I want to see it." She pauses for breath. "I haven't been able to do it before, but now that you're here... Take me with you, Mark. I have to close that door."

My lips tighten, and I let out a frustrated breath. "I don't like putting you in harm's way."

"I'll be with you." She smiles, and she's so earnest, I cave.

"Get dressed. We need to go now before too many people are walking around."

The early morning light barely penetrates the looming walls of the burned out building. Soot and ash cover the floors, and the red velvet curtains are black and torn. Lara's hand is tight on my arm as we step over rotten boards and fallen red bricks.

"I thought I'd be glad it's gone." Her body is close to my side, behind me as we pick our way through the empty hall. "I never expected to be sad."

Looking up, I see the balcony rails broken-out like missing teeth. The windows are dark holes, and the seats in the house are torn metal husks.

"It's eerie," I agree. "I remember it being lit up, every seat sold out, and all of you glittering on that stage."

We take the short stairway up to the stage floor. Lara looks up, and I follow her gaze to the catwalk so far above our heads.

"It's still there," she says.

Black steel rods are broken and dangling, but the thin strip of wood and the assortment of canned lights and pulleys hang from the ceiling.

"The place where it all began," I say, remembering Terrence's words about showing my character. "Although, I'd already spotted you way before that night."

"The first time you saved my life." She lifts my hand and spreads her palm over mine. "Not the last."

"We need to go down, below the stage."

She takes a deep breath and nods. Our hands unite, and I guide her through the broken steel doors. Large dents and stripped paint make me think a battering ram must've been used to break through these in the fire. We go down the short flight of metal stairs to the trap room below the wooden stage. Doors are broken off and burned, leaving holes like Swiss cheese in the stage floor above.

"Did they ever say what caused it?" She's still whispering. "We were in France when it happened, and I didn't want to know anything then."

"Faulty wiring," I say, shining the flashlight on the door to the hidden suite of rooms. "But the fire department couldn't rule out arson."

The closer we get, I see a crack in the door. Behind it is pitch black. Lara's hand tightens on my bicep, and she pulls back. Stopping, I turn and see her eyes are huge. Her chest is rising and falling rapidly.

"Can you do this?" I ask, taking both her hands.

"I think so." She isn't whispering anymore, but her voice is very small. "It's strange how the memories make it feel so scary."

"No one's here but you and me. I won't let anything happen to you."

She nods, and I push the door open. Adrenaline spikes in my veins, and while I meant every word I said to her, I'm also feeling the cold breath of memories sneaking up on us. The last time I was in this place, I found Lara on her knees. A silk mask was in her hand, and she was confused. She'd been drugged, and she thought I was Guy.

Then his thugs found me. They seemed to appear out of nowhere, and I fought...

"I've always wanted to find the other entrance. The one they dragged me out. I want to know where it leads."

"I was only here once. I came in the way we entered."

Sweeping my flashlight along the floor, the carpets and the wallpaper don't seem burned. I can see the sprinkler system went off — water stains are on the walls and warped paper is scattered around — but it appears the fire never made it this deep into the structure. I lead us past the room where Lara had been, and instead I go to the very first room I visited in this place.

Pushing the door open, I see the bed against the wall. When my light hits the sheets, Lara pulls my arm back suddenly.

"Oh, God!" she hisses.

The pillow and top portion of the mattress are stained black. They appear to have been drenched in whatever it was… I know what it was.

"Blood," I say, going toward it.

Lara's hand slips off my arm, and she stays at the door.

I shine my light all over the mattress, the sheets, then up the wall to the ceiling overhead. When Gavin brought me here the first time, I noticed the little domes for surveillance. I didn't think he'd keep recordings of the horrors occurring here.

My light lands on a small round disc that looks like a smoke detector. In the center is a tiny black dome. Panasonic is stamped on the outside.

"That's one." I shine my light all around it.

I need to find the receiver, the computer that monitored this device. Turning to the door, I see Lara is in the hall clutching the doorjamb. She's peeking through the door, but she seems shaken.

"Are you okay?" Holding out my hand, I wait for her to put hers in mine.

"That's where Roland put him after…" Her eyes are wide, haunted as she looks at the bloodstained bed. "So much blood. I never knew."

No longer waiting for her to put her hand in mine, I step forward and pull her body to my chest.

"You did what you had to do." She's shivering, and I hug her tighter.

"I don't even remember doing it."

"Let's go. I need to try and find the computer these cameras fed into. If they're down here, it's possible the hard drives weren't damaged."

Her mouth drops open, and she seems to understand immediately what I'm thinking. "Would Gavin have been that careless?"

"Probably not, but only one way to know."

We're back in the hallway, and I open every door,

sweeping my flashlight around the walls and furniture for any sign of a computer.

"His office was off the lobby. Could it have been there?"

"I hope not. The first floor had the most damage." We double back, and I go into the open sitting room where I once observed trays of food and champagne glasses.

An open doorway is beside the fireplace, and I see from the hinges a swinging door was formerly here. We charge through it and find ourselves at the base of another concrete stairway leading straight up. Light shines through the opening, and it appears to lead out to the street. Lara and I exchange a glance.

"Hang on." I leave her standing at the exit and run back to the room where Roland hid Guy, where I now realize the authorities recovered his body.

Once again, I scan my flashlight all around the walls and ceiling. I don't see any holes in the roof. No fixtures have fallen. My brow furrows, and I recall the cause of death. It would have been impossible for cause of death to be what was described in that report. Not a single beam or heavy object is anywhere to be found.

"Mark?" Lara calls into the room, but I have my phone out.

Quickly, I take several photographs of the bed, the ceiling above it — all the details of the crime scene. I might not be able to reveal how it went down, but I can at least throw the report into question.

"I'm here." Returning my phone to my pocket, I carefully step through the main room to the exit beside the fireplace. "It seems strange a door leading out wouldn't have a lock."

"That's because we can't get out this way." Lara points to the door at the top of the stairs. It's covered in black iron burglar bars. "It's locked."

I trot up the stairs and pull on the black bars. They don't budge, and I see the silver lock below the doorknob. The door leads to the other side of the parking lot behind the theater. A large brown dumpster shields this entrance from the street, and to the left is a red brick wall covered in English ivy.

Turning, I walk down slowly. I don't need my flashlight since the exterior door has been ripped off. Sunlight streams through the bars.

Lara stands waiting for me at the base, and I take her hand. "No signs of an office or computers down here. If they were all housed upstairs, they're likely all destroyed."

Our feet scuff through the dirt and debris coating the floor, and the sense of ghosts lurking in the shadows is diminished as we make our way out.

"Aren't computers usually backed up?" Lara seems stronger as well as we emerge from below the stage.

"If he knew this was going to happen, I'm sure he copied everything he needed to cover his ass."

We're standing at the top of the narrow hallway leading to the private dressing rooms where she lived for so long. Lara looks into the passage, and I stand beside her, waiting for her decision.

"Do you need to go down there?" Blue eyes travel around my face.

"I can make one quick sweep to be sure there isn't a room I never noticed before."

Her chin drops, and she looks at her fingers. "I'll wait for you outside, in the square."

Turning my arm, I inspect my watch. "I'll be with

you in ten minutes. Got your phone on?" She nods, and I touch her cheek. "Watch your step."

* * *

Lara

The square fills with tourists holding café au lait and beignets. The street artists, tarot card readers, and musicians are still setting up, and I dodge them on my way to the nearest iron bench to sit and put my head in my hands.

Being back there, seeing it all broken, burned, and covered in ash... Looking down the passage to the dressing room where I lived, being in that room, all the emotions crashed down on me, and as much as I hated that place, as tormented as I'd been by fear all the years I was there, it hurt. It feels like a piece of my history isn't just gone, it's been violently destroyed.

Memories of my mother were there.

Molly grew up there.

I met Mark there.

"Are you okay?" Mark sits beside me on the bench, pulling me to him.

I'm not sure I'll ever get enough of his love, his strong arms protecting me.

"I didn't expect to react that way." I rest my chin on his chest and look up at the cathedral spires stretching tall, slate gray in the misty blue sky.

His hand is on my back, smoothing the anxiety, helping me let go of the past.

"My uncle was the reason I moved here..."

Pulling away, I meet his eyes. "Your uncle who died?"

"Rick." His lips press together a moment. "I was

here less than five days when I found him shot to death."

"Oh, Mark!" I cup his cheek. "I'm so sorry… You didn't tell me—"

"I didn't really know the guy. I didn't even like him much. Still, I was pretty upset to find him dead like that."

Frowning, I study his handsome face, trying to understand. "You were so young. You'd probably never seen a dead body before."

"I'd seen a dead body. But even when something in your life is ugly or you don't care about it, if it's part of your story, losing it hurts."

My chin drops, and I think about what he's saying. I think about this part of him I never knew.

"Did you ever find out who did it?"

"No. I probably never will, but he was the catalyst." I frown, but he smiles. "Without him, I'd never have met you."

Leaning forward, I wrap my arms around him. I do my best to give back to him the strength he's always given to me.

"I love you," I say, kissing his cheek.

His large hand cups my jaw. His thumb caresses my cheek, and he kisses the bridge of my nose. My heart expands, and I lift my chin to find his lips. Our mouths open briefly, and our tongues lightly touch. It always sends a shimmer of happiness laced with desire through my stomach.

"Let's go look at rings." He reaches out, and I put my hand in his.

Joyeaux Bijoux is just across the square, and the storefront, the display case, all of it provokes a wave of nostalgia. "The last time I was here…"

"You were pawning your mother's pen for

shoes."

Blue eyes meet mine, and I don't know what to say. "It was like a different life."

A different time.

A different girl.

"Let's see if Gerard remembers us."

The little bell rings when we enter the store, and I hang back, looking in the assorted cases. I never shopped in this store. It was only a means to an end for me.

"Good morning! *Bonjour*! May I help you find something today? A beautiful diamond for a beautiful lady, perhaps?"

Mark gives me a wink. "I think that sounds perfect. We're looking for an engagement ring. Something unique and beautiful, like my angel."

Shaking my head, I wrinkle my nose. *Too far...*

"Ah, an angel, indeed! Does the miss, the *mademoiselle*, prefer gold, rose gold, or platinum?"

Gerard looks at me expectantly, and I hesitate, waiting. Does he really not recognize me?

"I... don't have a preference," I say, waiting for him to realize.

"I'd like something I've never seen before." Mark is playing it up. "Something that symbolizes our love — strong. One of a kind."

"Do you share a particular symbol? Are you open to suggestions?"

"What do you suggest?"

Reaching under the case, Gerard produces a narrow tray with several different rings arranged on it. My eye goes immediately to an unusual band. It's shaped like a tree limb, curved with the stone caught in two of the tendrils like the moon moving through the branches at night. The stone is cloudy.

"What is this?" I can't resist touching it.

"Ah, no." Gerard frowns, shaking his head. "That is a moonstone. It is a nice piece, artistic, but not for an engagement ring."

"Moonstone?" Mark leans closer, studying the rose gold setting. "It's dull."

"The luminescence comes from within." He moves it side to side under the light, and I see the translucent blue sheen glowing from deep inside. "It's an unusual stone, but not valuable like a diamond."

Mark straightens, frowning. "I'm getting you a diamond."

Returning to the cases, I study the engagement rings. Yellow, white, pink... Some are square surrounded by clusters of smaller gems, or princess cut, or ovals, or heart shapes. They're all so brilliant, glittering and perfect—nothing like us.

"Freddie gave me diamonds," I say quietly. "They didn't mean anything to me."

"It means something to me." Mark's voice is equally quiet. "I want to give you the best."

"But those rings aren't us." Going back to the curved branches with the moon. "We fell in love outside the theater, away from the lights and the façade. We fell in love in the night, under the stars."

I slide the ring onto my third finger. It fits perfectly, and I can't take my eyes off it. It's like it was made for my hand, and when I tilt it side to side, the light emanates from deep inside, from the heart of the stone.

Mark exhales beside me. "We'll start with the moonstone."

Gerard's shoulder's droop, and a smile curls my lips. "If you insist. Right this way." He holds out a hand toward the register. "We can finish over here."

"Hang on," Mark says, coming back to where I stand. "Give me the ring."

My smile dims, and I slip it off, handing it to him.

"Now, give me your hand."

My smile is back—I hold out my left hand, and he lifts the unusual ring. "It's not a diamond—yet. But I love the way it makes you smile."

"I never wanted you to give me diamonds."

Those precious stones were part of my escape plan. They were a fantasy I made up to help Molly and me survive. I've already had them, and they left me empty and unhappy.

"Will you be my wife?" he asks, holding the delicate piece at my third finger.

"Yes. Yes, please." Rising on my toes, I slide my fingers into the band.

My hand continues around his neck. Our mouths meet, lips part, and our tongues curl together. Another sizzle of blissed-out sensuality moves through my stomach, and I know this is exactly right. I feel entirely different.

I'm liberated, free.

Holding out my hand, I admire the strength of our symbol, the promise of everlasting love. No matter what comes our way, we're strong enough to face it together and keep growing like the tree, like these branches, our light shining from within.

CHAPTER 12

"Stars can't shine without darkness."

Mark

Walking back to Roland's, my jaw is tight. Tension is in my arms, but Lara is practically floating at my side. She keeps holding out her hand, tilting it side to side.

"I'm still getting you a diamond."

"You're a snob, Mark Fitzhugh."

I'm about to defend myself when my phone buzzes in my pocket.

"You deserve a diamond." Reading the face, I see Terrence has texted me.

Eddie is nervous. Come now if you can.

We're only a block north of Terrence's house on Bourbon, and I stop walking. "I need to go back. Terrence said Eddie will talk."

Her hand tightens on my arm. "I'm coming with you."

Acid burns in my chest. "I don't want you there. I don't like you around these guys."

Again, blue eyes flash. "You're meeting with these men, searching for evidence because of me. I have a right to know what they know... what they say."

"Lara..."

"Mark, all of this is about me and what happened to me and Molly."

"Not all of it. Some of it has to do with the things

155

I did when I was working for Gavin, and trust me, they were not good things."

Her brows clutch together. "You think I'll think less of you?"

"I think these guys know leverage when they see it." I put my hands on the tops of her shoulders and look deeply into her eyes. "I don't want you to get hurt."

She puts her hands on my forearms. "I need to come with you. Please don't keep me out. I know Eddie. I know Terrence. They're not going to hurt me."

We stand a few moments facing off, but I ultimately give in. Without a word, I take her hand and lead her up the walk towards the old house where I lived those few months, long ago.

Terrence meets me at the door, and when he sees Lara, his eyebrows shoot up. "It's been a long time. You've only gotten more beautiful."

Lara smiles and shoves a piece of dark hair behind her ear. I step in front of her, eager to get this over with. "Where is he?"

My former landlord takes the stairs to the loft room. "I really like what you did up here. Bea and I've been living here. Not sure why I didn't think of it before."

"Bea?" Lara scans the large, empty space.

"Oh, she's not here. She doesn't know about this."

We follow him through the open loft to the area laid out as a living room. The asshat I recognize from those days working backstage is waiting. His eyes land on Lara, and he leers at her body. He's just as slimy as he ever was, and my fists tighten. If he says a word to her... I'm one smart remark away from punching him in the face.

"You two are finally together." He digs out a cigarette and lights it with dirty fingers. His brown hair is greasy and shoved behind his ears.

"Terrence said you know where I can find Landry?"

"No." He flicks the lighter, and my eyes go from him to my friend as I wait for him to finish.

Terrence jumps in. "Sorry, I didn't mean to mislead you. He has information."

"I'm not getting pulled into this," Eddie says. "I'm only doing it because… I feel bad about what happened."

Lara's posture relaxes slightly. "I don't remember you being there." Her voice is soft. "You couldn't have known what would happen."

Eddie sits forward, becoming more animated. "That's what I said! It was only supposed to slip. It wasn't supposed to break. It was only supposed to ruin your act… Which I guess it did."

A knot tightens in my throat, and my vision darkens. *Is this fucker saying what I think he's saying?*

"What are you talking about?" My tone is low, edgy.

"The pulley. You didn't know… about that?"

I'm on him before he can even finish speaking. I jerk him off the couch by the neck and throw him across the room. He lands with an *Oof!* and I close the gap fast, giving him a swift kick to the stomach.

"Mark!" Terrence chases me, but he can't stop me. I drop to my knee, gripping the front of Eddie's shirt, hauling him up and slamming him against the floor again.

"Stop! Mark, stop!" Terrence has me around the chest, but my fist is flying.

I slam it into Eddie's nose, and the satisfying crunch of bone echoes up my arm.

"No!" Eddie howls, but I land another punch to his mouth before Terrence throws the entire weight of his body against me, knocking me off the bastard.

"You could have killed her!" My voice is savage, and Terrence struggles to hold me back. "If I hadn't been there —"

"Stop, Mark. He's got information about Landry!" Terrence wrestles me to the other side of the couch, but I'm breathing hard, my eyes burning with rage, adrenaline racing through my body.

Lara sits slowly in a chair, her expression stunned. "You caused the accident? The first night I was on the swing?"

Eddie rolls onto his stomach, still on the floor. "I'm sorry," he moans. Brown-red stains smear his nose and mouth, and he shakes his head as if trying to wake up. "It was for Vanessa." Strings of spit and blood dribble from his open mouth onto his arm as he speaks. "She wanted to take your place."

I lunge against Terrence, but he holds me, bracing his foot against the chair. "You'd better say what you know about Landry now."

The fucker on the floor shakes his head again. "I caught him transferring computer files, bragging about a secret Internet he had. I didn't understand, but he said everything was there. They put everything on it."

Lara's eyes meet mine. "What does it mean? A secret Internet?"

She's confused, but I'm not.

My voice is like sandpaper, and I'm barely holding it together. All I can see is Lara's body plummeting to the floor, the horrible purple bruise around her waist from where the belt almost cut her in half... I'm not even counting my shredded palms from grabbing the rope to catch her. I'm ready to kill this guy, but I force myself to find control. What he's saying is important.

"Was it on a server or in the cloud?" I snarl.

"Neither." Eddie shakes his head again. "He said it was somewhere else. A secret internet."

He keeps repeating the same phrase, and I know it's because he doesn't know what he's talking about. Terrence looks at me, and I shrug, pretending like I don't know.

Only I do know. I know very well what he's talking about.

"Come on, Lara." I go to her and pull her up and into my arms. "We better go before I kill this guy."

Terrence follows us down the stairs to the front door. "I'm sorry, man, I didn't know he was behind that accident."

"It's okay." I clap his shoulder. "Thanks for digging him up."

"I hope he told you something you can use. I thought it might be more than that."

Nodding, I put my hand on Lara's waist and guide her out to the sidewalk. "I think I can figure out what he means. Thanks, T."

Terrence nods and disappears into the apartment again. Lara looks up at me, a mixture of relief and disappointment on her face.

"Eddie did it," she says softly. "All this time we thought it was a mechanical failure."

"I never thought it was a mechanical failure." I pull her to me as we walk, holding my arm around her torso. "It's why I hated letting you be up there without me. I checked that fucking thing twice the night it broke. I knew someone had tampered with it."

A shiver moves across her shoulders, and I hug her closer. We continue a ways in silence until Roland's house is in view. Before we climb the steps, she turns to me, studying my face.

"Do you know what he means by a secret Internet?" Her brow is furrowed, and I nod.

"Have you ever heard of the dark web?"

Her lips part, and I can see the wheels turning behind her eyes. "Molly's mentioned the dark web before. It *is* like a secret Internet!"

"I've only used it to…" My lips press together, and I glance down. "Well, to track Molly. It's how she finds her targets. They use it to make transactions no one can trace."

"Transactions… Like for prostitution? Drugs?"

"Exactly, and they pay with digital money like Bitcoin. It's anonymous and very dangerous."

"I don't understand." Her hand is on my arm, and I cover it with mine.

"You don't really need to understand it. Just know it exists, and it sounds like that's where Gavin is storing the videos."

"If it's anonymous, how will you find it?"

I look up at the house we're standing beside. "I'm not an expert in this stuff. I've only dabbled in it, downloaded a few Tor browsers and poked around, followed Molly. Her user ID was DollBaby."

Lara winces, but she's doing her best to keep up. "And a Tor browser is…?"

"A web browser. It's how you access the deep web and the dark web."

Just then the front door opens, and we both jump as if we've been caught doing something illegal. Lara's hand clasps mine hard, but she relaxes when

Evie steps out carrying our little girl.

"I thought I heard your voice!" She scampers over to Lara and hugs her.

Jillian reaches for her mother, and Lara pulls her into her arms. "When did you get here?"

"Just a few minutes ago. Roland said you're going to sing with him tonight."

Lara's eyes fly to mine. "I don't know if we have time anymore—"

"Sure we do," I interrupt. Jilly sits up straight in her mothers arms, and I put my hand on her back. "You've been practicing. I love to hear you sing."

"But what about…?" Worried blue eyes meet mine, and I give her what I hope is a reassuring smile.

"We've got time for tonight."

"I can't wait!" Evie bounces on her toes. "I'll bring Jilly and stay until she gets restless, then we can come back here and put her to bed. Don't worry about a thing."

"Oh. I wasn't… I mean, I didn't mean…"

"What's this?" Evie takes her hand off Jilly's back, admiring the new ring.

Now Lara's smiling, seeming shy. "Isn't it beautiful? It's my engagement ring."

"Engagement!" Her friend shrieks, and the baby fusses.

I reach for my daughter. "Let me have her so you can talk."

My little girl's face is against my neck, and I step inside, leaving the two of them on the front porch discussing everything from how I proposed to me insisting on a diamond and failing. For now.

Roland is inside, sitting at the upright piano, tapping out notes and then scribbling on a sheet of paper in front of him. "Find anything useful?"

"Not much at the theater, but Terrence connected us with Eddie."

"That idiot stagehand who followed Vanessa around like a puppy?" Roland shivers. "God, Vanessa was the worst. Remember how she tried to talk all the songs instead of singing them?"

I remember fighting off her naked body on the catwalk those few nights Lara was recovering. "He tampered with the pulley system—he broke the mechanism the night Lara fell."

Roland's fists slam on the piano keys, and he's on his feet, eyes flashing. "Where is that bastard?"

I hold up my hand, turning it so he can see the slight swelling. "I left him at Terrence's place with a broken nose and possibly a few missing teeth."

His jaw is clenched, and any doubts I ever had about this guy are gone. "He'll have more than that if I see him."

"He would've had more than that if Terrence hadn't been there." Moving Jilly to my other arm, I start for the kitchen to wash the blood off my hand. "He had some intel, though. It seems Landry was loading files onto the dark web."

Roland has followed me, and when I turn on the water, he takes the baby. "I'm not familiar with that."

The water stings the cuts on my knuckles, and I hiss. "I'm no expert myself, but I know someone who is."

He waits, and I rinse the soap off my hands, turning over my idea in my mind. It has to work, and I have to go alone. I don't like having Lara around these people, but I especially don't like having Jillian where I can't keep my eye on her, away from people I trust to protect her.

"Are you going to tell me or keep me in suspense?"

"Oh, sorry," I glance up to meet Roland's impatient glare. "Molly. She's an expert. I have to go back to Seattle, only I don't want to take—"

"You are going to take me." Stepping back, I see Lara has joined us in the kitchen.

"Lara." My shoulders drop, and I grab the towel, stepping over to her. "I don't want Jillian there. It's too dangerous."

"So Jillian stays with me," Roland says. "It's how we'd planned it the first time."

"You're going to Seattle again?" Evie's voice is a playful whine, but Lara's eyes are fixed on mine. She's not backing down.

"Looks like we both are," I say.

"Go ahead and book our tickets," she says. "We can leave in the morning."

You reach for me, and I disappear.
My heart is what you long to share…

Lara's voice unfolds like rich caramel through the darkened club. Roland's hands on the piano keys are the perfect accompaniment, smooth and flowing, point and counterpoint, and the rapt crowd listens, hanging on every word, every note.

She's dressed in a floor-length, dark green silk dress. It has spaghetti straps, and almost looks like a negligée. Her long hair falls in shiny waves down her back, and one side is pinned up with a butterfly barrette that sparkles in the light. I'd only been a bit miffed when she told me it was a gift from Freddie.

Roland said I was being an idiot, so I let it go.

———
163

Now I sit at one of the small wooden tables, mesmerized by her performance as always. Evie and Armand are at the table with me, and Jillian has gone from bouncing on my arm to being cradled in Evie's as she takes her bottle. She's perfectly relaxed and seems to be falling asleep to the gorgeous strains of her mother's voice.

"She's so good," Evie whispers. "I think she's better than when we were in the show together."

"I can't tell." My eyes are fixed on my beautiful fiancée. "I've always been in love with her voice."

"Her voice, and other things." I glance at Evie, and she grins. "She said you're looking for Landry?"

Sitting forward, I give her my full attention. Those words are the only thing able to distract me from Lara.

"Do you know where he is?"

"Not me." She shakes her head and tilts it toward her date. "But Armand and I ran into him about a month ago... We were in the park walking Jilly. He made some crack about Armand and I having a baby, and I told him she was Lara's."

Another puzzle piece clicks into place, I think, remembering how alarmed Lara had been that Gavin knew she had a baby. How panicked she was trying to figure out if he was keeping tabs on her or if one of our friends was a spy. I make a mental note to tell her after the show. Her friend Evie doesn't always use the best judgment.

"What happened then?"

"He's a boorish bastard." Armand's elegant voice cuts into our conversation. "I have no interest in his obvious attempts at friendship. It was clear he was digging for information."

"I know." Evie's chin drops, and her expression

is guilty. "Armand fussed at me for telling him who Jillian is."

"It's probably best to keep information like that off the record for now," I say, hoping to reinforce Armand's instincts and shut her up.

Armand's brown eyes cut to mine. "You're a police officer now?"

"Detective."

His expression tightens in a way that makes me suspicious. Still, he continues. "If you're looking for him, I know where he lives — or where he lived as of a few months ago."

I swallow the anticipation in my throat. "Please. That would be very helpful."

"He was on the west bank, in a cottage in Algiers near the docks. It's a nice place — formerly a duplex he's converted into a single home."

"You think he's there now?"

"I don't know his hours, but it's where he was for the longest time. He's always been into shady dealings around the shipyards."

Leaning back in my chair, I study Lara on the stage singing and looking like a goddess. I don't want to leave during her show, but we fly out first thing in the morning. I hate to risk her being angry with me, but we haven't a moment to lose.

"Evie." I lean over the table. "I've got to follow up on this. Would you let Lara know what I'm doing?"

Her eyes flit from me to Armand and back. "You're going now? But what about the show?"

"We're leaving in the morning. I need to do this now — if you don't mind helping me."

"Of course I don't!" Her eyes are wide, and she hugs Jillian close. "I love keeping the baby. It's going to break my heart when you move away. Roland's, too!"

She's been dropping hints about us staying in New Orleans all afternoon, but it's difficult to think further down the road than the enormous problem staring us in the face… A problem she knows nothing about as far as I can tell.

Lara finishes her number and announces a short break. Her eyes were on me as I talked to Evie, and I know her radar is on high alert. She's watching for anything I might do.

The audience claps, and she does a little head bow before holding her hand out to Roland. He stands and applauds her, and she makes her way to where we sit, blue eyes lasered on mine.

"Darling!" Evie intercepts her before she makes it to me. "Your voice just gets better and better. I tell you, you're one of the greats in the making. It'll be Ella, Billie, Peggy, and Lara!"

"Evie." She hugs her friend before taking Jillian out of her arms. Our baby nestles against her mother's neck, and while she's chatting, she never lets me out of her sight. "You're so sweet. I'm nowhere near the same league as those great ladies."

"Oh, but you are! Phillip is so sorry he couldn't be here tonight. He's on this insane deadline, and —"

My throat is tight as I watch them. I know she's going to pin me down, and I am not letting her go with me to meet Landry. That's where I draw the line.

"Tell him I completely understand. Now let me chat with my man before I have to get back up there."

She grins, and gives Armand a little wave, but the minute her back is turned to them, it's all seriousness.

"What's going on?" She steps close to my chest, looking down and pretending to show me something with the baby.

I slide my hand over Jilly's back, speaking low in Lara's ear. "Armand just told me Landry's address."

Wide eyes blink up to mine. "You're going there?"

"I'm walking out the door as soon as you go back onstage."

She grabs my arm. "You can't go alone."

"I'm going alone."

Roland trots up beside us. "I didn't know we scheduled a break there."

Lara's lips press together, and she glances down. "I… needed to get a sip of water."

"Well, come on. We've got to stay on schedule or the natives get restless."

He starts to go, but I catch his arm. "Would you mind if I borrow your car?"

Shock flickers in his eyes, and he glances between the two of us. "You're not staying?"

"I need to run an errand before we leave tomorrow." I'm doing my best to infuse my voice with calm — nothing to worry about here.

"Sure. Fill the tank." He winks, and I do a little nod at the joke.

Lara scans the area around us, and her hand remains on my arm. Jillian sucks her little finger as she watches me. "You can't go. You'll raise suspicion. He'll call Gavin, and our advantage will be gone —"

"Stop." I put my hands on her shoulders. "I'll only ask him some questions. I won't give him any indication we're tracking him or how much we know —"

"I won't be able to sing." Her whisper breaks. She's breathing fast, and I recognize this panic. "What if something happens to you? What if he —"

"Hey…" I trace my thumbs along the tops of her cheeks. I look into her eyes and give her a gentle smile. "Don't you trust me by now?"

"No," she shakes her head, blinking rapidly. "You have a temper. You'll fight. If something happens to you—"

"Nothing is going to happen to me." I'm tense, but I won't let her see it. "I'm a big bad detective now. He can't hurt me. It'll get back to my superiors."

"These guys know how to get rid of bodies."

Roland plays notes on the piano. It's her cue to head back to the stage, and Evie steps up to take Jillian out of her arms. Lara kisses the baby quickly before handing her over and holding both my hands.

"I'm going with you."

"You're going up there to finish your set."

"Mark!" Her eyes flash, but her expression is so scared.

"Listen to me." My jaw is tight, and as much as I love her—because I love her—my tone is sharp. "I gave in to you earlier because the situation directly involved you. What happened with Landry is about me, not you, and you're not coming with me. You're going to sing with Roland, finish your set, and I'll be at the house before you get back tonight."

She gazes into my eyes. She's always trusted me since that night on the catwalk, and I'm asking a lot of her now.

Still, she nods, swallowing her fear. "I'll see you in a few hours."

"I'm sorry to miss the rest of your show." Leaning down, I kiss her cheek, careful not to smudge her makeup. "I love your voice."

"I love you."

Before I go, I kiss my baby girl, telling Evie I'll

meet her back at the house. Fear isn't my strongest emotion right now. Anticipation, adrenaline, expectation... These are the feelings surging in my veins.

I'm ready to face him. I want to look him in the eye and let him know I'm better than he is. I'm not in Gavin's pocket anymore, because I got away from the lies, the corruption. I'm more than a police officer now; I'm a detective. I'm one of the good guys — No, I'm *the* good guy who's going to bring his crooked ass to justice...

Yeah, it's possible I'm feeling a bit cocky.

I'm ready to look in this asshole's face and make him eat the words he said to me years ago. Then I'll get that fucking thumb drive.

CHAPTER 13

A flower simply blooms.

Lara

Fear is a fist in my chest.

Closing my eyes, I sing the jazz standard while Roland accompanies me on the piano, and the vibrations of the song, the melody in my heart, my lungs, my mind, take me away from this place.

They always do.

Opening my eyes, I go straight into one of Roland's songs. His eyes are fixed on the keys as he plays, and he listens, following my lead, his head tilted to the side.

I suppose this is his dream as well. When we were in the old theater, he talked about writing songs for me to sing. He convinced Gavin to let him compose an entirely new show with me as the lead…

Only it never happened.

Until now.

That old place burned to the ground and those players are all gone, but his songs remain. We're here in front of a live audience, and they're enraptured. I'm his mouthpiece, and the lyrics are beautiful, the bridge, the refrain, the verses leading into the chorus.

For so long, I only thought about my lost dream, the chance that never appeared. Or the chance that appeared only to be so quickly taken away. Now I look at him and wonder what dreams he left behind along the way.

You're in my arms and it feels so right.
But it's simply an illusion.

We harmonize on the *an* as always, holding it out for a bit longer, a dotted quarter note. He brings the night to a close with the final measures, a sweeping denouement of harmonious chords.

The audience cheers, our tip jar overflows, and it's after two. Fear slams into me again, and I'm ready to go, to get to the house. Mark said he would be there...

Evie and Armand took Jillian home a while ago. Mark left for his errand in Algiers before that. It's taken all my strength to focus on the songs and trust him. He knows what he's doing. He's been a police detective for so long, I'm sure he has encountered danger before, confronted criminals. I've seen him beat the shit out of guys—Eddie, for starters, this afternoon.

He's strong and he's trained and he's ready.

Still...

Sitting on the piano bench with my back to Roland as he makes his final notes on the score and collects our money, I think about the broken pulley and Eddie confessing he did it all for Vanessa.

"Vanessa," I say to myself, and Roland glances over his shoulder.

"Wanted to take your place," he says as if completing my thought. "Can you imagine her speaking the words? Not even singing them?" He does a little shiver then seems to notice my worried expression. "What's wrong? Why do you bring her up?"

"I was thinking about her getting Eddie to break that pulley. I could have died." It was so long ago, but

I remember that terror. "Mark saved my life, but I honestly thought that belt had cut me in half."

"It's a wonder you didn't have internal injuries."

"I didn't have any friends in that place." Gazing around the near-empty bar, I think about this type of work and how competitive it can be.

"You had me, Evie, Molly… Rosa went back and forth in her loyalties." He tilts his head side to side. "Bea wasn't so bad, and Tanya could be a friend when she wasn't wasted."

"And Mark," I say softly.

My chest aches with longing.

His lips press into a grin. "That, my dear, was your very own special gift. Finding him in a place like that… There's no accounting for it."

"I got lucky."

"You've been lucky more than once." He stands, sliding the papers together and zipping them into the leather portfolio where he stores them. "You have a pure heart, and you're generous. It earns you good karma."

Wrinkling my nose, I stand and follow him out of the bar. "I don't think I believe in that."

"Whether you believe it or not, it's the truth."

The cool night is not as damp, and the clouds have drifted away. The moon is a fingernail, and I slip my hand into the crook of Roland's arm as we walk to his house.

"As long as it holds out just a little bit longer," I say, wishing on those stars blinking to life high above the city. *Let him be home…*

"You don't need luck anymore."

"Don't we always need luck?"

"Not this time. This time justice will balance out the darkness and the crimes those men did here.

You're not acting on your own. You're simply the tool bringing order back into the universe.

Our heels click on the pavement, and I fight the urge to run ahead. I think about the night he saved me from my crime. So much has changed, but so much feels the same.

Finally, we're at his house, and he holds the short black gate for me. I dash through it, crossing the tiny lawn quickly.

"Slow down before you trip," he chuckles.

Pausing at the front porch, I place my hand on my chest, calming my breathing. "Sorry, I feel like old ghosts are chasing me tonight."

Our eyes meet in the darkness, and his teeth glow as his smiles. "We've beaten those ghosts before."

"It seems like they have a way of coming back. Like being trapped in a horror movie."

He shakes his head. "You need to pack."

I run up the steps. Mark said he would be here when I got home.

Reaching for the doorknob, my breath stills…

* * *

Mark

The waning moon casts long shadows around the house on Alix Street. A white picket fence lines the yard, and a short crepe myrtle tree stretches in front of one window. It looks too normal, too nice for the thug I'm trying to find.

I park Roland's car around the corner, partially hidden near a small grocery store and step out into the damp night air. It's almost eleven, so the store is closed. The smell of the river hangs in the air, tangy mud and fish mixed with exhaust from the barges.

Slipping the key in my pocket, I walk the half-block to the house. The exterior is cypress painted a deep orange color. The trim is dark green, and it looks trendy, designer. It's unexpected a crooked cop like Landry would have an artistic sensibility. You just never know with these guys.

Large round crates hold small, white flowers on each side of the steps leading to the porch. I take the short flight of concrete stairs and stop at the front door.

On the drive here, I decided to change my approach from full-on attack to something more contrite. If I want answers, if I ever want to get that thumb drive or get close enough to destroy it, I have to play it cool, act casual.

This is going to be hard.

Two short knocks, and I hear his gravelly bark on the other side. "Who's there?"

Adrenaline spikes in my veins, but I rein it in. "Reese Landry? It's Mark Fitzhugh." A shadow passes over the window, and I step back so the streetlight can hit my face. "Remember me?"

More rustling, and the slow crank of a deadbolt sounds before the door opens a crack. "Mark Fitzhugh?" He's standing in the dark opening. "What the fuck are you doing here?"

Control.

Calm.

"Looking for work, actually. I thought I might get on with you again."

It's so quiet, I can hear the hiss of traffic crossing the river behind me.

"How did you find me?"

I'm still in the light, allowing him to see my face

and empty hands. I glance down at my boots and do my best to appear non-threatening.

"It's the damndest thing." I try to laugh. "I ran into that piano player, Roland Degrassi? Dennou?"

"Desjardin."

"Shit, that's it. I suck at names."

The crack in the door narrows, and his voice drops an octave. "What about him?"

Fuck. "He said you might be living in the same place as before... And here you are."

"You didn't know where I lived."

"Clearly I did." I grin, opening my arms. "I'm full of surprises."

"I don't like surprises."

A moment passes, and I keep my eyes averted, doing my best to hide the impatience simmering just below the surface, my primal desire to grab him by the throat and force him to talk, confess his crimes, and give me what I want.

"You're smart." I nod. "But since I'm here, can we talk? I'm looking for work and with the theater burned—"

"The Hudsons are gone."

"I'm willing to work for you." A truck passes slowly on the narrow road behind me, and I glance to my right.

I don't know anything about this neighborhood. It could be a harmless resident returning home from a trip to the store or a night out... Or it could be one of Landry's associates making sure he doesn't need help.

Suddenly I feel very alone and exposed.

Returning my attention, I'm encouraged his door is still open a crack. "Would you mind if I step inside? I'd rather talk in private."

"I don't do business with people who aren't referred to me."

My teeth press together, but I hold on. "Seriously?" I force out a chuckle. "We worked together for months."

"Yeah, and you're supposed to be dead. How do I know you're not on some revenge mission?"

He's not stupid, which makes this even more dangerous.

Leveling my gaze, I infuse my voice with confidence as I lie through my teeth. "Because I'm not."

Several seconds pass. The screech of cicadas slices through the air around me. Frogs cry from the nearby delta. My breath stills while I wait to see what's about to happen.

The door opens slowly, and he doesn't attempt to conceal the .45 clutched in his fist. "I'll give you five minutes to say something I want to hear. Then you're out. Try anything, and…" He tilts the gun, making sure I see it.

I see it.

All of my police training tells me this is a bad idea. I'm alone, and I'm not wearing Kevlar. No one knows I'm here—well, one person knows I'm here, and I promised her I'd be back in three hours…

My boots thud on the wooden porch as I step through the doorway into a nicely furnished living area. A brown, distressed leather couch is in the center of the room, and a leather chair with large brass studs and tweed-covered cushions is beside a round table holding a blue and white Asian-style lamp. It casts a soft yellow glow, and pictures in frames are arranged at its base.

"Nice place," I say, stepping to the center of a

Persian rug. "Should I sit?"

"Don't get comfortable."

A scotch sits on the end table near a chair. Landry is wearing jeans and a short-sleeved button-up shirt. He looks like he's been out playing cards or possibly on a job?

"So I was in the Quarter hanging out at one of the bars, and I thought about all the shit we used to do. We made good money."

"I've retired from strippers."

"Still, there's other business in the city. Maybe you know someone who needs a guy?"

"I don't recommend people I haven't vetted."

Landry hasn't changed. His dark hair is slicked away from his pockmarked face. He's still short and stocky with suspicious black eyes, and he picks up the scotch with short, meaty fingers.

Losing the veneer of cool, I lower my brow. Sometimes these guys only respond to their own kind, and I'm ready to step into that role.

"How do I get *vetted*?" Glancing around his house, I start suggesting. "When Gavin was here, I oversaw cargo deliveries to container ships. I know my way around the docks."

He goes to the small table and tops off his drink. "What have you been doing for the past six years? When you were supposed to be dead."

When you thought you'd killed me is more like it.

"Alaska, Canada. It's good country up there, wild and remote. Perfect for entrepreneurs."

Black eyes lock onto mine. "I heard you're a cop."

Now the way he's acting makes sense.

This asshole knows everything.

Still, I'm not losing after coming this far.

Sustaining my act, I shift my approach in an attempt to make us allies, to put myself on his level.

It turns my stomach.

"You know as well as I do, being a cop is an asset around here." Pointing to his glass, I nod. "Mind if I have one of those?"

"Help yourself." He steps to the side and smiles. It feels more threatening than his glower.

Taking the crystal stopper out of the decanter, I pour two fingers of what I thought was scotch. The scent tells me it's bourbon.

"Cheers." I clink my glass against his and take a sip. My lips curl, and I hiss at the burn all the way down.

"You were pretty young when you left here," he says. "You're still young."

"Is that a bad thing?"

"You tell me." He takes a sip from his glass. "Young people get wild ideas, think they're invincible. Do you think you're invincible, Mark Fitzhugh?"

"I remember being told once heroes don't last long around here."

"Did you internalize that message?"

Stepping over to the table, I pick up one of the picture frames. A black and white photograph of a skinny woman with a 1940s hairstyle wearing a cotton dress.

"My first job I cleaned up one of the rooms below the theater." I return the picture to the table. "I've always wondered if it was a man or a woman..."

"You wonder too much. You remind me of Rick."

My breath disappears. It's like I've been sucker punched, and I'm glad my back is turned so he can't see the expression on my face.

"You knew my uncle?" Lifting the tumbler, I take another sip. I need another sip.

"Rick was curious. Started asking questions." He walks around to the side so he can see my face. "Only Rick wasn't an idiot. He didn't come at me when he had something to lose."

I don't know if my expression is under control. Anger burns just below my skin. "What does that mean?"

His glittering smile turns sinister. "Rick fell in love with Tanya's mother. She blamed Gavin for her daughter being a junky when we all knew her daughter learned that shit at her mother's knee. Still, that crazy bitch had something to lose."

"So it was a woman."

"Now here you are, coming at me. You have a kid, too..."

My stomach tightens. *Is this bastard threatening Jillian?* The anger simmering under my skin blazes into an inferno in my chest, fueled by the bourbon I've drunk.

The thumb drive is forgotten.

Tricking this guy into trusting me is forgotten.

Everything fades in the face of protecting my baby girl.

With precise, even movements, I unbutton my coat. "Sounds like I'm wasting your time. Let me give you my card in case you change your mind..."

His eyes land on the holster at my chest and several things happen at once.

The clink of crystal glances off the end table before crashing to the floor.

Boots thump on hardwoods.

His pistol flies up, and I feint to the left just as the staccato *pop!* of gunfire echoes in the room.

Pain blasts through my temple, and I'm thrown back as warm liquid gushes down my face

"Fuck!" I shout, whipping up my pistol and pulling the trigger before he can shoot again.

Another sharp *pop!* echoes in the room, and Landry flies back, hitting the opposite wall with a slam. My head is spinning. My ears ring, and I'm disoriented. This is bad—I can't tell where I'm going, but I can't stay here.

Wiping the blood from my eyes, I stagger to the door. I've got to get out. If Landry's not dead, if he's simply wounded, he could be up and on me fast.

Pulling the door open, I stumble onto the front porch and down the steps, gripping the rail. My boots crunch on gravel, and I weave through the darkness, across the short asphalt road to the corner. Roland's car is ahead, hidden around the corner from the store.

"Jesus," I gasp, using the force of will to keep my heavy feet moving. I have to make it to that car before I pass out.

Reaching in my pocket, I grab the key and jerk it out.

One more step, and my knees hit the grass.

It's damp and muddy, cold water seeping through the material to my skin.

Holding out my hand, I catch the fender, pushing away so I don't hit it as I go down.

"Lara," I whisper.

I won't be home when she gets there.

CHAPTER 14

I am not a survivor. I am a warrior.

Lara

Armand is on the couch, and I hear noises in the kitchen.

Running through Roland's small house, I spin on my heel in the dining area. I slam my bedroom door open, but it's dark and silent.

"Are you okay?" Evie's light brows are pulled together as she steps into the room.

"Where is he?" My insides break. "He's not here."

"Who?"

"Mark!" I push past her to Jilly's room, but she catches me before I open the door.

"The baby's sleeping, Lara. Mark hasn't been here. Was he supposed to be?"

"Oh God… Oh God, Oh God." I'm in my bedroom ripping the silk dress over my head and jerking on a pair of jeans.

Slamming drawers open and closed, I pull on a long-sleeved tee and a pair of thick socks.

"What's going on?" Roland is at the door.

"We have to go — Armand!" I run out to the living room. "Armand, I need your help, please!"

His dark brow quirks. "What is it?"

"Mark said he would be here before I got home. Something's happened. He's in trouble or he'd be here."

Armand stands slowly. He's wearing a dark, tailored suit, and it makes him look even taller, slimmer.

"He went to Landry's." He opens his blazer and takes out a small handgun. "We can take my car."

"You carry a gun?"

"Darling, I'm not as nice as you think I am."

"I never thought you were nice." My voice is just above a whisper. I didn't mean to say it out loud, and I press my lips together quickly.

He gives me a wry smile, and my stomach is tight. I realize how little I know about Evie's boyfriend — other than he loves her. I guess that counts for something?

I don't have time to sort out my feelings right now.

Roland's voice is sharp. "Just hold the fuck up a minute. What the hell is happening here?"

I'm already at the door. "There's no time — Roland, come on! Mark wanted to confront Landry, but I didn't want him to go. I wanted him to wait..." My voice breaks, and tears heat my eyes. "He's so stubborn. Oh, God, I knew something was going to happen."

"That's why he borrowed my car?" Roland dashes to the tall cabinet in his living room and opens a small drawer. He takes out a black case shaped like a gun, and his eyes level on Armand's. "Let's hope it's not too late."

My knees go weak, but I get it together. We've got to get to Algiers.

"What's happening?" Evie's voice is panicky. "Armand, I don't like this..."

"Evie," I rush over and grip her arm. "We have to go. Please stay here with Jilly."

"We should call the police. Mark is a policeman. They'll help him, and you won't be in danger—"

"We don't have time, Evie. Please. Mark could be hurt."

"I don't want any of you being hurt!"

Armand steps to her, putting his hand on her waist and leaning into her ear. I watch as her panicked blue eyes blink down, and she nods slowly.

He kisses her cheek and turns to us. "Let's go," he says, leading the way.

"I still don't like it!" Evie calls as the three of us rush out the door.

Armand's black Audi is parked on the street, and once we're in, he whips it around heading north in the direction of the interstate.

"I'll go to the door," he tells Roland, never taking his eyes from the road. "You go around to the back and see if you can get inside through a window or an unlocked door—"

"What do I do?" I'm on edge in the back, gripping the tops of both front seats.

"You'll stay in this fucking car," Roland snaps.

"I will not!"

Armand interrupts. "Can you drive?"

My chin drops, and I shake my head. "No."

"Shit," he hisses.

Roland cuts his eyes to me. "I knew there was something I should've taught you to do."

"I never needed to know." My voice is panicky. "It's not like I had a car…"

We're crossing the river, and streetlights flicker fast across Armand's face. His dark hair is short, and he's clean-shaven. The muscle in his jaw move back and forth as he thinks.

"Do you know anything about driving? It would be helpful in case we need to leave fast."

"Roland can do it. I can go around back and check for open windows or doors."

"*That* is not going to happen," Roland says under his breath.

I'm furious, ready to shout at both of them. I don't know why this car won't go any faster. I'm sure I'll scream when the blinker goes on, and Armand exits the interstate.

"We'll figure it out when we see what we're dealing with." The ominous tone in his voice draws more heat to my eyes.

Oh, God, not again…

Not Mark…

This side of the river is dark and feels very remote. The houses are small and grouped in little clusters with open spaces of flat grassland between them. The levee rises high on the opposite side of the road like a wall.

Armand cuts his speed and switches the headlights to dim. My throat is so tight, I can barely breathe. The two-lane street is narrow, and we're approaching a tall wooden structure painted white. A metal sign hangs on the corner.

"Is that my car?" Roland leans forward, and I strain my eyes in the darkness.

Only one streetlight is up ahead on the corner, and Roland's black Fiat is on the shoulder in an alley. It's partially hidden, and Armand guides his car to a stop behind it.

"Be careful," he says, but I'm out the back door before he finishes speaking.

"Lara!" Roland's door opens and slams shut.

I'm running to the small car, cupping my hands on the windows and looking inside. It looks normal... Nothing is disturbed or broken.

"He's not here," I cry, my voice breaking.

Looking wildly around, I don't know where Landry's house is, but it has to be near if Mark left the car hidden here.

Roland stands beside me, his jaw tight. "I don't have my keys."

Armand walks to where we're standing. "Landry's house is just up the road there, behind the blue house on the corner."

My eyes fly to where the lone street lamp illuminates a two-story blue residence, and I'm about to run to it when Roland's strong grip closes over my arm, jerking me back.

"Stop!" he growls. "You do not run off like that here. These guys are dangerous. This one in particular is a killer."

Armand looks up the short distance. "I'll go—"

A low groan cuts him off, and I grab my mouth, squeezing my lips together to silence my scream. Roland releases me, hustling to the other side of the car.

"Mark?" Roland drops to a squat, and I'm right behind him, falling to my knees and reaching for my fiancé.

"Oh, God!" I whisper, tears dropping onto my cheeks. "Mark!"

He's lying on his side, one hand outstretched to the car. His skin is ghastly white, and the left half of his face is smeared with blood.

Roland feels all around in the grass beside him. "Thank fuck, here's the key. Get him into the car." He's on his feet unlocking the Fiat.

Carefully reaching out, I touch his face. "Mark?"

"Have to get away," he groans.

His skin is so cold, but his eyes blink open slowly. I'm simultaneously relieved and panicked.

"Lara?" He grabs my shoulder. "Go... We have to go."

"Help me, Armand." Roland has the back door open, and he's grasping one of Mark's arms.

Armand takes the other. "Can you stand?"

Mark groans again, but he manages to get one of his legs under him. They struggle helping him to his feet, but as soon as he's up, he collapses hard against the side of the car.

"It's okay," I say, not sure of anything. "You're going to be okay."

"Just a few steps to the left," Roland says.

Armand helps, but he keeps looking over his shoulder in the direction of Landry's house. "We need to get out of here."

I rush forward and hold Mark's waist, steadying him with my shoulder against his chest, my hip at his thigh.

"You can do it," I urge. "Come on."

His muscles flex as he holds the door, easing himself into the backseat. I'm right behind him, jumping inside as Roland slams the door shut.

"It's okay," I whisper, wrapping my arm around his shoulder, cradling his head against my neck. My eyes are so hot, and my insides are vibrating with fear, worry, and cautious relief. "Roland, do you have a tissue or a napkin?"

He leans forward and digs in the glove box, pulling out a small white towel. "What happened?"

Mark alternates between resting his head against my neck and trying to hold it up. "He shot me... I-I lost consciousness."

Again, his head falls against my neck, and my heart plunges. "Mark?" I place my hand against his cheek. "Let me see your head."

He moves again, and I rotate my body to see his injury better. "I don't think you're bleeding anymore. He's not bleeding," I call up to Roland. Still, I hold the towel against his head. "He's warmer."

"What happened, Mark?" Roland speaks louder, and Mark stirs against my arm.

"Stop," he says, reaching out to grasp the back of the front seat. "Roland, stop! We have to go back."

"We are not going back there." Roland doesn't even break his speed. We're on the highway headed for the interstate and the Mississippi River Bridge.

Mark's entire body goes rigid against mine, and he pulls himself forward. "Go back. We have to make sure he's dead."

"What the fuck?" Roland cries. "You killed him?"

"I don't know." Mark's head rests on his fist against the top of the passenger seat. "We have to go back and be sure."

Again, no break in speed or direction. "It's not going to happen."

Scooting forward, I place my hand on his shoulder. "Can't we just call 911 and make an anonymous report?"

"No," he grinds out. "We have to go back there. He threatened Jillian!"

At once, the car's speed drops, and Roland flicks on the blinker. He eases into the turn lane, and grabs his phone off the passenger's seat, tossing it to me.

"Call Armand and tell him we have to go back. Ask him to come with us. Mark is in no shape to do anything."

I barely have time to register the panic flaring in my chest at Mark's words. We race toward the house behind the levee, and my fingers tremble as I press the buttons for the call log and find Armand's number.

When Mark realizes we've turned and we're heading back, he once more collapses against the backseat.

* * *

Mark

My fucking head aches like a motherfucker, and the world won't stop spinning.

For a brief moment, I allow myself to take comfort in the softness of Lara's neck, the sweet scent of her little flower perfume, the warmth of her skin against mine.

Then Landry's threat rears its ugly head, and adrenaline fires in my veins like electricity, cutting through the dizziness.

"I can help," I say, trying again to pull myself forward.

Lara's soft hand caresses my cheek. "Shh," she whispers, kissing my lips. "Let me check your head."

Blinking up, I see worry in her blue eyes. "You said he shot you, but it looks like the bullet just broke the skin." Her dark hair falls over her shoulders, and her slim brows are pulled together.

Reaching out, I put my hands on her waist, sliding my thumbs along the soft skin of her stomach, just under her shirt. I'm so glad to see her, but my insides are tight. We have to make sure that fucker is dead.

"He barely missed me then. I dropped when I saw him raise the gun." Her eyes meet mine, and I try to smile. "Use your phone to see if my eyes are dilated."

"How…" She reaches down, fumbling with the phone until the light blazes.

"Shine it in my eyes." Holding steady, it hurts like hell when the white light sears into my eyes. "Fuck," I hiss.

"I'm sorry!" Her voice is so worried, but I hold her, tracing my thumbs along the line of her jeans.

"Are they dilated?"

"No." She quickly lowers the phone, killing the light. "Your pupils narrowed immediately."

"That's good." Releasing her waist, I push against the seat, doing my best to steady myself. "I can help, Roland. I'm just so fucking dizzy."

"You need to stay in the car with Lara."

We pull up at the store, and I look out in the direction of the house. The front door is still open, and the soft yellow light from inside is cancelled out by the harshness of the streetlight on the corner.

Roland gets out of the car, and Armand joins him. Summoning all my willpower, I grasp the door handle and open it, using the side for balance.

"We can't just walk up to the front door," Roland is saying.

"I'm going with you." I'm able to stand without holding the door, but the ground still tilts.

Armand grasps my shoulder. "It's a foolish thing to go up there in your condition. You'll only put us all in danger."

Lifting my chin, I meet his dark eyes. My jaw is set, but I know he's right. If I can't focus my gaze on the horizon, what the fuck makes me think I can focus on a moving target?

Roland joins him. "Lara needs you. Jilly needs you. We'll go back there and try to get a visual through the window."

"Don't get yourself killed," I relent, leaning against the side of the small black car as they take off into the darkness.

Lara's head rises out of the vehicle beside me. "I saw a water bottle in Armand's car," she says softly. "Stay here while I get it."

Her feet crunch in the fine gravel, and she opens the door of Armand's car. My eyes strain in the direction of Landry's quiet house. I lost sight of the guys when they went around the corner. Staying back here is killing me. If something happens to them, and it's my fault…

"I hope this doesn't hurt." Lara is at my side again, pouring water onto that white towel from before. "Drink the rest."

"I'm sorry," I say, taking the water bottle as she gently wipes the blood from my cheek. "When I came over here I thought I could get him to trust me, maybe even confess, go on record to verify any of the shit we did. I thought I could get inside, find the thumb drive… None of that happened."

"He threatened Jilly," she says softly, not smiling. She pauses briefly, catching my gaze before returning to her progress cleaning my face.

"I never expected—"

"I hope you killed him." This time her blue eyes stay on mine, and ferocity is in them.

My lips tighten, and I look away from her gaze. Taking a long drink of water, I try to see anything happening at the house. "I want to be the one to do it. I want to go back there and finish this myself…"

As I'm speaking, two figures emerge from the bushes and run up the front porch steps.

"Get in the car and lock the doors." I take off in the direction of the house, shaking away the remnants of the vertigo.

I'm not as sure-footed as usual, but I jog the half-block and cross the narrow road. My boots scuff in the gravel as I cross the street, thudding up the stairs, but when I reach the door, both Armand and Roland are inside, standing side-by-side and blocking my view of where Landry fell.

Heat rises in my neck, and conflict cyclones in my chest.

I'm a cop, and even though I have the head injury to prove I acted in self-defense, even though I know this guy is responsible for many crimes, I don't relish taking a life.

But when this motherfucker threatened my baby, "Is he dead?" I step forward, and Roland steps to the side.

My eyes go to the spot they were inspecting and see...

It's empty.

"He's gone." Armand pivots to face me, his jaw clenched. "Either he staggered out on his own, which means he could turn up dead in the swamp tomorrow, or someone came and got him, which means we need to get back to Evie. *Now*."

"Fuck," I hiss, looking at the bloody stain on the floor. "Did you see any kind of a trail... anything out back that shows where he went?"

"Nothing." Roland's expression is grim.

"We have to go," Armand says, breaking the spell. "We have to decide what to do about the baby, your trip to Seattle..."

I step back, shoving my hand in the front of my hair, wincing as my fingers hit the wound on my scalp. "We can't leave like this. What about Jillian?"

"You're not taking her to Seattle," Roland snaps. "Not if you plan to go after Gavin. He'll retaliate."

My eyes clash with his, and I can't hide how I feel. "And what happens if this guy is alive and decides to come after you and Jilly while I'm gone?"

"Taking her with you makes you vulnerable." Roland steps back and starts for the door. "Before we do anything, let's get back to my place."

The three of us head for the door, quickly going down the steps. I have to pause a moment at the bottom for the world to catch up to me.

"If anything happens to her..." I can't even complete the sentence. I've only known my daughter a short while, but she's an irreplaceable part of my life.

"Nothing is going to happen to Jillian, I promise you that." Roland's eyes flash to Armand, and the tall fellow nods.

"Evie loves her. I've become fond of her as well..."

"So you'll help us?"

Armand shrugs. "I doubt I'll have a choice."

We're back at the store, and I'm pleased to see Lara unlock the door and step out when we get close enough for her to recognize us.

Her voice is soft, hopeful. "Is he dead?"

I go to her, pulling her against my chest and holding her so close. Just the feel of her body against mine renews my strength.

"He's gone," I say against her ear. "It's clear I shot him, but we couldn't find any sign of where he went or where he might be."

She pulls away, and I relax my hold on her. "What do we do now?" Her eyes move back and forth, and her anxiety reflects my own.

"We need to get back to the house." Roland opens the door to his car, taking the front while we take the back.

Once we're inside, I pull Lara against my chest again. The events of the evening, my injury and Landry's words all churn in my mind and in my stomach.

"If he's still alive, he's going to come after me," I say softly. She lifts her chin to study my face.

"Roland has a plan—something with Armand he wants to discuss when we get to the house." Through the windshield, I study the black Audi leading us across the bridge and into the city. "I'm willing to listen, but I won't leave if I'm not sure Jillian is safe. We won't do anything until we're sure she's protected."

Lara relaxes in my arms, but my body is tense. I'm not used to putting my trust in others, especially people I don't know well. What I need to do is get back into Landry's house and search for that thumb drive... Destroy Gavin's power, but getting back to Jillian overrides that plan. She's my priority tonight.

We have to stick to our first idea. We have to locate those old recordings—the ones that prove Lara acted in self-defense. The ones that show all the crimes committed under Gavin's watch.

Going to Seattle, getting Molly to help us is a long shot, and I have no guarantees the path I've laid out in my mind will work or if we'll even be able to find what we need once we're on the dark web. So far, nothing has gone the way I've planned.

Everything has backfired and ended up in violence or gunfire.

Fuck. This situation has to turn around.

We've got to get ahead of these guys for once.

CHAPTER 15

Don't be afraid. Just believe.

Lara

Jilly is in my arms. Her little back is straight, and her bright eyes follow the men in the room just like mine do.

"We're not going anywhere until I'm satisfied she's safe." Mark's arms are crossed, and his jaw is set.

His face is clean and a butterfly bandage holds the sides of the cut above his left brow closed. I'm relieved his dizziness seems to have passed.

Roland leans against the back of the couch, an unlit cigarette between his fingers. "The house alarm has motion sensors, broken glass sensors. No one is getting in here tonight. Or any other night it's activated... which will be every night until I'm convinced this threat is over."

"He wouldn't be stupid enough to try and get to you here." The anger in Mark's voice makes my heart beat faster. "He'll wait until you go out, jump you in a fucking alley on your way to work or while you're walking home."

Jilly jerks around to face me, and I kiss her little head.

Armand's smooth voice injects a much-needed level of calm. "Which is why my personal security will escort both of them everywhere."

Mark's eyes narrow at him. "Remind me what you do again. Why you need personal security."

"It's best if we don't dig too deeply into the whys of my situation. Just trust that I won't let anything happen to Jillian."

"Sorry." Mark shakes his head. "That's not good enough. You're going to have to give me something."

Armand's lips curl in that knowing smile. "I can assure you all my personal business dealings are legitimate. Unfortunately, my family—my father, uncle, brother—they're still involved with less transparent enterprises. Which means I'm always careful. I don't take chances with my valuables."

Evie returns to the room quickly, and Armand's eyes meet hers just before he sits in the leather chair beside the couch. "Nothing will happen to your daughter while you're away," he finishes.

"You know I'll never let anyone hurt her." Roland's eyes are on my little girl.

I hug Jilly closer against my chest, and Mark's gaze meets mine. His is stormy with concern, but I'm inclined to trust our friends, especially after the way they helped us tonight.

"Armand's men are so nice," Evie says, sitting beside me on the couch. "They're always close, but you never feel crowded or in danger."

"Would it be better if she stays with Evie?" My eyes move quickly from Roland to Evie to Armand. "If that's not a problem, I mean."

Armand watches as Evie rubs Jilly's little back. "She's welcome to stay with us if it makes you feel more secure."

"Oh, I'd love that!" Evie's face brightens with her smile, and she reaches for the baby, taking her out of my arms.

"Would you like to stay with Aunt Evie? Yes? Yes?"

Jillian smiles and pats her cheek, making one of her sweet baby noises. My heart is so twisted, I don't know what to do.

Mark paces the room, shoving his hands in his hair and exhaling a soft growl. "If we didn't need those files, I'd say fuck it. But not having that thumb drive, not knowing if Landry is dead or alive … It's our only chance of ensuring Lara's safety."

I go to him and put my arms around his waist, placing my cheek against his firm chest. His heart beats steadily, calming my fears.

"It's a terrible place to be… but I trust Evie and Roland." Blinking up, I smile at Armand. "And Armand."

He smiles at me from where he sits in the chair. I've never known him well. Phillip has always been the more social of Evie's boyfriends. Their situation is so unorthodox, but I do know I can trust her.

Roland tosses the unlit cigarette on the top of his piano. "I don't want her out of my house. I'd step in front of a bullet for her."

"I'd rather it didn't come to that," Mark says, still holding me close. "I'm not happy leaving… but we have to do it for Lara. We can't wait for Gavin to learn what we're doing and destroy everything. It could already be too late."

Stepping back, I catch his eye. "Should we call Molly now? Ask her to start searching tonight?"

He puts his hands on my shoulders. "I already did. I didn't want to share too much information in case anyone is listening. I basically asked her to search for things from the past." He passes a hand over his mouth. "I don't know if that's enough or if we'll be starting from the beginning when we get there."

Armand uncrosses his legs and stands. "If you feel well enough tonight, we're taking off. It's almost four."

"I'm so sorry. It doesn't feel so late…" Jilly has fallen asleep on Evie's shoulder, and my friend's eyes are drooping as well, her head resting on a pillow.

"Adrenaline," Roland says. "You could spend the night here if you'd like."

"I'd like to sleep in a bed—if only for a few hours."

I take the baby from Evie, who wakes at once. "Did I fall asleep?" She looks around, and I smile.

We all say our goodnights, and Roland activates the house alarm once they're gone. Jilly is asleep on my chest, but I don't want to put her in her room.

"Can we move her crib to our bedroom?"

Mark smiles, and goes to her little room. Roland stands in front of me, smoothing his hand down my arm.

"You know I'll protect her with my life, right?"

Nodding, I step forward to give him a half-hug. It's the best I can do while holding my sleeping baby.

"I hate leaving this way."

"Just do what you need to make sure you're safe. I'll also never let you be taken to prison for getting rid of—"

"I won't let that happen." Mark passes behind us, Jillian's portable crib in his hand. "Let's try to get a few hours of sleep."

* * *

Mark

Lara's head is on my bare chest. I'm propped up against the pillows listening to the soft shush of my daughter's breathing from her small crib at the side of our bed.

My forehead has stopped bleeding, but it still throbs with every heartbeat. The streetlight illuminates the window, and the house alarm is activated.

Still I can't sleep.

I thread my fingers through Lara's silky hair, thinking about everything that happened tonight. Landry, the bastard. I hope he's dead. Armand, the mystery. He's turning into an interesting ally. Roland and Evie, the faithful ones.

The beautiful woman in my arms…

I think about how sexy she was tonight in that green silk dress. Her voice has always hit me like a storm surge — knocking me out, destroying me, claiming me, since the first night I saw her.

My mind drifts to that first night so long ago. We were so young, and she appeared at the top of that ladder wrapped in her dressing gown. She was shy. Then she took off the robe, and *damn*…

Her incredible body was on full display, and I pretty much had blue balls for a week.

Her lashes move against my chest. "Are you awake?" I ask softly.

"Can't sleep," she says, and I slide to the side, down so our faces are a breath apart.

"Are you afraid?"

She shakes her head, her eyes blinking to my lips. "I'm never afraid with you here. And Jilly's there… safe." A little sigh. "I just can't sleep."

201

I trace my finger along the line of her hair, sliding a dark lock away from her face. Her cheek is silvery in the moonlight. I remember falling in love with her under the stars.

"Remember the night we ran around the city?"

Her cheeks rise with her smile. "I remember you slipped and fell."

Warmth floods my chest for the first time in ages. "I remember you laughed."

"I fell in love with you that night."

Reaching out, I slide my hand under the thin cotton tank she's wearing, placing my palm against the warmth of her bare skin. "I'd been in love with you for weeks."

"In lust, you mean."

My hand travels higher to cup her soft breast. "Sure, lust came first. I won't try to deny it. You have the most beautiful body."

I drag her to me, pushing her shirt up so I can pull a tight nipple between my lips. I'm rewarded with a soft gasp. Kissing a line to the other side, I capture that soft peak, pulling her nipple between my teeth. She lets out a moan, and I reach up to place my fingers at her lips.

"Shh," I speak against her warm skin. "Don't wake the baby."

My fingers leave her lips and move down, sliding between her thighs. She's already wet, and heat surges below my waist.

"I fell in love the more I got to know you." I say, sliding my tongue around her nipple as my fingers circle her core. Both tighten at my touch.

"Mark," she whispers.

"I loved your loyalty, your bravery."

I give her breast another suck, and she threads her fingers in my hair. "Does your head still hurt?"

"Not a bit." My erection strains in my boxer briefs.

Moving down, I catch the sides of her panties, dragging them down her long legs, past her slim ankles. Her hips lift, and I watch her fingers tighten against the mattress in anticipation.

Placing my palms flat on her skin, I open her thighs, letting my eyes travel the length of her body to her core. She's beautiful, mouthwatering, and ready. Her lower stomach trembles, and I lean closer, running my nose along her inner thigh.

"Mark..." Her voice breaks on a little cry. "Please."

I can't help smiling at her eagerness. I'm about to lose it for wanting her, and I'm gratified to see her so on edge, so ready. Leaning down, I trace my tongue along that line where her thigh meets her hip. Her whole body jumps, and she lets out another whimper.

"What do you want?" I say, moving slightly higher to kiss her stomach.

"Please kiss me... there." Her hips move, and I kiss her stomach lower.

"There?"

"Ohh... You know where."

A grin splits my cheeks, and I drag my tongue slowly along the line of her beautiful pussy. Her voice rises in a soft cry as I do it.

"Yes," she whispers, and I lean in closer, giving her clit a suck.

Her body jumps. I dip my tongue lower, and her hips rotate in time with my mouth. I'm kissing her, tasting her, tracing my tongue all over her most sensitive parts, focusing my efforts on that taut little bud.

When her hips start to jump, shudders breaking out in her thighs, I give her two more passes. Then I make my way higher. My erection aches for her. Her fingernails scratch along my hips, ripping at my briefs, dragging them down my hips.

"Now," she whispers, "I want you in me now."

Rising higher, I capture her mouth with mine, pulling her lips with mine, curling my tongue against hers. Her legs part, and I feel her hips pressing to meet me. Reaching down between us, I drag my cock up and down her slippery folds.

She breaks away with a moan. "Oh, please... you're killing me..."

I won't make her beg.

With a solid thrust, I'm buried to the hilt in her tight, wet depths.

"Fuck yeah," I gasp, my eyes squeezing shut at the onslaught of pleasure.

Her clenching heat massages and pulls my cock. It's the greatest feeling I've ever known. My hips begin to move, pumping and rocking, deeper and harder. She bucks her hips, meeting me thrust for thrust.

"Lara," I groan, biting the soft skin of her shoulder.

"Oh!" She moans, spasms breaking out all around my dick. "Mark... Oh!"

She's coming hard, and I feel the shimmers moving like waves through her body. She pulls me under with her, and I close my eyes as the surges of ecstasy race up my thighs, centering in my pelvis, as I come, pulsing and filling her, following her through the stars to that blissful place of oneness.

I wrap my arms around her and hold on as we drift through the clouds. Memories of putting a ring on her finger, dreams of our future life together…

It's so good.

She sighs and holds my shoulders tight. Her legs are around my waist, and my cheek rests on her breast. She's my angel, and I'm in heaven.

"I love you." Her voice is so soft and happy.

With every heartbeat, I'm whole. "You're mine," I say, lifting my head to kiss her lips. "You're always mine. I'll protect you now and forever."

"It's all I ever wanted."

I wrap her in my arms and hold her.

Dangerous times are ahead of us, but right here, in this moment, I'm confident we'll slay the demons. Holding her right now, I can see the future.

Happiness is just within reach.

CHAPTER 16

I survived because the fire inside me burned brighter than the fire around me.

Lara

Molly meets us at the charter lot.

After agreeing Jillian should stay at Roland's, with Evie and a man from Armand's private security taking over when he has to go out, Armand insisted we take his private jet.

Mark surprised me by accepting quickly.

One of the perks is it can be ready to go in as little as twenty minutes—or however long the pilot needs to file the flight plans. So after an endless night, we slept most of the day, and flew out of the city at three.

Traveling back in time, we arrive in Seattle after six, quickly leaving the plane with our small carry-on bags.

Molly's lips are tight. She won't meet my eyes, and while I have no idea what it could be, I can tell something has happened. She's wearing a short-sleeved black sweater and black pants. Her silver hair is swept over one shoulder.

"You've lost weight," I say, giving her a brief hug she doesn't return.

"I don't have time to eat much." She takes the handle of my rolling case and walks ahead of me, leading us quickly to the waiting Lyft.

We can't talk about anything important with a stranger driving the car, and I spend most the time chewing my lip in frustration. So much needs to happen in such a short period of time, and the pressure of what's hanging over us, what's to come, makes it difficult to think of anything neutral.

"What's this?" Molly lifts my hand to study the engagement ring on my finger.

"It's an engagement ring." I manage to smile. "Mark and I are getting married."

She nods, dropping my hand. "It's different. Pretty."

Her face turns to the window, and I lift my hand, studying my ring. The branches and tiny twigs that compose the band shine with newness. I haven't had time to think much about the fact we're getting married. We haven't even set a date.

"It's a moonstone." I tilt it to the side, allowing light to filter through the iridescent gem. The lavender-blue heart glows deep in the center like an opal.

"Not a diamond."

I can't tell by her tone if Molly really cares, but I try to answer honestly.

"Diamonds seemed too perfect, too…" I still can't seem to find the right words for why the brilliant, traditional stones don't fit what Mark and I share.

He continues to disagree, insisting he will buy me a diamond once all of this is behind us.

Molly doesn't pursue it. Instead she looks back, tilting her head to the side. "Where is… it? The precious cargo."

My eyes go to Mark, who is silent in the front seat. His eyes never leave the road, but the muscle in his jaw moves. I can tell he's thinking, planning.

"Somewhere safe."

A little nod, and Molly returns to looking at the

scenery. We pass under a bridge where a large sand sculpture of a troll reaches toward the road. It's cartoonish, but it puts lead in my stomach. It reminds me of the evil closing in around us, reaching for us at every turn.

"It must be nice always knowing exactly what to do," she says. "Always making the right decision."

I don't understand the edge in her voice.

I study her stony expression before trying to answer. "I wouldn't say always."

"But you give orders like you're never wrong."

I'm so confused. My face wrinkles with my frown. "Give orders? Never wrong? What are you—"

"We're here," she says, leaning forward as the car slows to a stop and opening the door before I've finished speaking.

Mark takes our suitcases out of the trunk, and we hustle up the steps to Joshua's apartment. It's a big, warehouse loft only partially converted to a living space. A wall of windows gives us a nice view of the city. A double bed is situated beneath it, and a desk with a large Mac is against the other wall.

A small sofa and vintage chairs are arranged in the center, and a small kitchenette is in the corner. A door I assume leads to a bathroom is beside it, and in the corner, partially hidden behind a screen sits an air mattress with blankets spread over it. I can't help wondering how Josh can afford a place like this in the city.

"Is that for us?" I ask, nodding toward the air mattress.

"It's the best we could do on short notice."

"It's great. Thanks. Is Joshua here?"

"He's out," Molly says, going to the small living area and dropping her phone on the table.

"Hopefully we won't be here long." Mark leaves our carry-on bags against the wall behind the door. "Did you understand my message? I didn't want to say too much in case anyone was keeping tabs on us, but I worried it was confusing. I wasn't sure you'd understand—"

"I found something." Molly walks ahead of us, going straight to the desk holding the oversized monitor. "Something very... educational."

She moves the mouse, and the dark screen flickers to life. In the center is a black rectangle with an arrow centered at the bottom. It's a video, and she doesn't hesitate to hit play.

The feed is like something from a gas station camera or a drive-through monitor. It's black and white and tinged with a faint, greenish hue. Two figures are moving quickly around a small room, and it takes me a minute to recognize... I'm one of them.

"Pack, fast!" The one in the closet is pulling down clothes, speaking swiftly.

It's Roland.

My heart beats harder as the realization washes over me. I don't have time to stop this before the figure of me on the screen makes a startled cry, and snatches a large block of wood off the small bed.

The breath leaves my body so fast.

I can't stop it.

I can't stop what's coming...

I watch as the image of me slams the club against the body on the floor over and over.

Black chunks fly up around my arms.

One lands on my cheek, sliding down and leaving a dark smear.

The noise is so loud, repeating and constant.

Wham! Wham! Wham!

The thing on the floor doesn't move.

It makes a low noise and the image of me beats it faster, harder.

I'm like a wild animal, my dark hair flying.

Vomit burns hot at the base of my throat.

I'm going to be sick.

"Stop this!" Mark lunges forward, taking the mouse out of Molly's hand.

Still, it takes several seconds before he's able to shut it off.

My eyes are fixed on the flickering video of me beating Guy until finally Roland is able to catch my hands and stop me.

His palms smear what I know is blood in wide swaths up my forearms until the club stops over my head. His eyes are round and full of horror.

I collapse to my knees where I'm standing in the center of Joshua's apartment. Leaning down, I put my forehead on my fists. All the feelings of that night when Guy burst into my dressing room, his eyes blazing with abusive lust assault me at once.

I'm back in that place again, unable to catch my breath and shaking all over. It's fight or flight, and I'm cornered.

Flight isn't an option. I have to fight, and I'm frenzied enough to beat a man to death with my bare hands.

I thought I forgot how this feels.

I'll never forget.

* * *

Mark

"What the fuck, Molly?" Anger burns in my

chest.

At the same time, the savagery captured on video has me shaken. I've never seen anything like what flashed before us in harsh black and white. Lara's actions were so brutal, so crazed, they could only have been driven by deep trauma.

Trauma I never want her to relive.

Molly's arms are crossed and her brow set as she stares at the image on the screen. The picture is of Lara with her arms raised. Roland is behind her holding them steady, holding a club the size of a baseball bat above her head. The top half of it is dark, covered with gore like her forearms, her cheek.

Even in poor-quality video, the scene is nightmarish.

"You lied to me," Molly turns her back to the computer. "You let me believe he died in the fire."

"No…" Lara's voice is muffled. Her head moves side to side, and the sound is more of a moan.

"Give up this quest." The girl's voice is sarcastic, mocking. "Killing won't bring you peace. It won't take the hurt away. Yet there you are, seizing your peace with a baseball bat."

Now that I've stopped the fucking playback, I drop to my knees and gather Lara in my arms.

"It's okay," I whisper, kissing her temple, smoothing back her hair.

She's not crying. Her body trembles and her breathing is shallow, and I know she's close to the edge. As long as I've known her, it's her one weakness, her body's involuntary defense against the onslaught of memory.

"Listen to me," I speak softly in her ear, wrapping her in my arms. "It's over. It was over years ago. I've got you. I'll keep you safe now. Always. I promise."

Another shudder moves through her, and I hug her tighter to my chest. My hand covers the back of her head, and I hold her forehead steady against my neck, skin against skin.

"I was so afraid," she says barely above a whisper. "He was going to hurt me again. He was going to hurt Molly. It was never going to stop—"

"I know." Rubbing my hands up and down her back, I soothe away the past. "I know why you did it. You had no choice."

"You were gone... I'd lost you." She takes a shuddering breath. "Roland said to live with it. He said Guy would grow tired of me and move on to someone new."

Her voice is faint, as if she's still there, caught in that dark place and struggling to break free.

"You couldn't do that. You could never let that happen again."

Her chin dips, and her hands tighten on my arms. She puts her feet under her, and I help her stand, help her find her footing. For a moment, she holds my arms, her head still bowed, but I can see she's rallying. Another breath, another shake of her head.

"I didn't have a choice," she says, her voice growing stronger. She steps back from me, and there she is. She's with us again, determined to survive. It's another reason I love her, another reason I'll never let her fight alone.

Turning to Molly, Lara meets her head-on. "What happened in that room wasn't about revenge. It wasn't cold or calculated."

"You're right." Molly's expression is angry. "It was spontaneous and fierce. It was vengeance. It was what I do."

Lara shakes her head no, wrapping her arms

around her waist. My lips tighten, and while I know she's had her own share of trauma, I don't like how Molly drives her.

"If I hadn't stopped Guy, he would've gone on abusing me… and you… and the next girl… or boy. Just like he abused Roland before us."

Silence falls on the room, and we're momentarily derailed. Molly's hyper-controlled exterior falters and her lips part. Lara dropped a bomb neither of us saw coming.

"Roland?" Molly's response is hushed.

"It's not my place to tell his story. He's as much a victim of this as you and I. It's why he took care of us…"

"Then I'm doing this for him, too." Molly's voice grows louder, stronger. "If Gavin would sacrifice him, you, the ones he claimed to care about… He's a bastard. A worthless bastard who deserves to die."

"He never cared about me. It's like I told you then. We were always very secondary to him."

Molly paces the room, silver hair fanning over her shoulders. Her arms remain crossed, and her slim brow is furrowed. "I'm so close to taking him down. So close…"

"Can we get back to the recordings?" Jillian is on my mind, and I don't want to be away from her longer than necessary. "Is this the only one you found? Are there more?"

She stops moving. "It was my first hit after three days of searching." Moving to the computer, she drops into the black desk chair. "It's not as easy to find things as it sounds. I used all sorts of search terms. It's possible he's deleting the files."

Ice filters down my spine. It's what I feared the most—losing evidence to show Lara acted in self-

214

defense. "Can he delete them once they're on the web? I thought nothing ever died on the Internet."

"He can delete them. If he knows how to hide them, he knows how to get rid of them."

My muscles tense, and I look from her to the computer. "Show me what you've done. We have to find the evidence before it's too late."

"The video of my rape?" Her blue eyes are cold, her distance a wall.

"Molly..." Lara's voice is a whispered plea.

"I don't know what happened to you," she says, looking at Lara. "I wasn't there, and again, no one bothered to tell me the truth—"

"Does it help that they're all close in time?" Lara cuts her off. "Molly's was first, then Mark... then me."

"I tried to save Lara... unsuccessfully."

"It wasn't a fair fight." Lara puts her hand on my forearm. "He tried to get me away from Guy. Two men attacked him... They nearly killed him."

Molly's hands are on the keyboard typing quickly. "I found the one of Lara killing Guy using the terms *dark angel*, *lights*, and *pussycat*. Time and date stamps are helpful, but sometimes they muddy the waters. A lot of files are uploaded every day."

She's working in an unusual web browser, and it looks like she's simply scrolling through lists of filenames on a white screen.

"It's a database?" I ask, watching the list filter up the screen.

"If you didn't know what you were looking for, you'd think it was just another pirate site. Porn videos or bootleg movies, ebooks, songs..."

A soft chirp sounds, and her eyes flicker to the

smart phone lying facedown on the desk. She stands, leaving the screen open.

"I have to go. You're welcome to search. I'll help you again later."

"Later?" Lara steps between her and the door. "Where are you going?"

"It's nothing for you to worry about." Molly's eyes divert, and she tries to step around Lara.

"I always worry about you. I've worried about you since you were a girl."

"Don't." Blue eyes flash, and I see the two of them hitting that wall. I remember a time when it didn't exist, a day in Jackson Square when Molly was still a happy kid holding Lara's hand.

"Will you tell us what you've been doing here?"

"No."

She snatches up her phone and goes to the door. "Search for what you need. If I can help you, I will. Otherwise, stay out of my way."

Lara's eyes meet mine, but it's just like before. It's like it's always been. We can't stop Molly from doing what she's driven to do, fighting her demons, and now that we have Jillian, we're even less able to chase after her.

"We have to find the videos," I say. "It's why we're here."

I won't let Gavin threaten Lara. I won't let him hold this over her head forever. The videos are our only hope, and the thought of losing them forever, drives me harder than whatever mess Molly is mixed up in.

The metal door slams shut, and I drop into the chair typing in phrases.

Dark angel, lights, pussycat…

I've got to find them.

CHAPTER 17

Sometimes following your heart means losing your head.

Lara

"Dark angel is what he called me," I say, pacing the room behind Mark. "It might locate more videos of me."

His fingers fly over the keys then scrolling, scrolling, scrolling…

I stand behind him helpless with only the one computer, and I can't stop worrying about what new dangerous thing Molly is doing. Her words from the last time we were here, from today echo in my mind—she wants Gavin dead—and now that she knows I killed Guy, it's like she has my permission.

The video shook me to the core. It was like a little earthquake, bringing all the horror, the pain, the anger to the surface…

It overwhelmed me, but it also forced me to see the truth. For the first time, I see the wicked strength Roland has always told me I possessed.

I've texted Molly several times. No reply.

She can't do this alone. Gavin isn't like the other men she's faced from her past. He knows we're coming, and he has no intention of being a victim. He will fight her. He'll gladly kill her. Even back in those days, she was worthless to him.

Chewing my lip, I open the messenger app and send a quick text to Joshua. It's possible he'll help me... I'll make him help me.

"Are you hungry?" I switch over to the maps program.

I remember the layout from our last visit to the city. Everything is clustered in the same four-block area.

"What?" Mark looks up, but he's distracted by his search.

"I'm going to get us food. It's late, and we never had lunch."

Nodding, he returns to the screen. "Thanks."

I'm out the door, headed up the sidewalk in the direction of the Brewhouse. Joshua hasn't texted back, but the last time I was here, he stayed mostly in and around this area. I hope wherever he is, he can meet me for a few minutes.

Clouds are rolling in, and the temperature has dropped since we arrived. A light breeze is blowing, and I wish I'd grabbed a sweater before I left. I'm too far to go back now, so I duck my head and walk quickly up the block.

Inside, the crowd is light. The rich aroma of brewing coffee greets me, and the shop is heated. I go to the counter and order an Americano and two Reuben sandwiches to go.

They hand me my coffee pretty quick, and I carry it across the black tiled floor to a tall wooden table in front of the glass windows lining the front wall. I'll wait for our food and hopefully Joshua will appear.

My phone is in my hand, and I watch it for any reply as I sip my drink. The warm liquid helps me relax, but it's not enough to cancel out the tension of this day, of this trip, of my fucking life so far. God, will I ever get a break?

A crisp ring from the bell above the door causes me to look up, and I immediately smile. "Joshua!" Hopping off the stool, I give him a hug.

"You're here!" He smiles in that friendly way of his and hugs me back. "Sorry about the air mattress, we—"

His nose wrinkles, but I wave his apology away.

"I'm sorry to invade your privacy. We would've stayed at a hotel, but we hope to find what we're looking for and go home as soon as possible."

His hair is still silver, short on the sides and long and floppy on top, and he's dressed in a gray suit with a white shirt underneath. He looks really handsome and professional.

"Were you at work?" I can't imagine what kind of job he has. I can't imagine Joshua working. "You're so formal and businesslike."

He grins. "Yeah, I'm at the men's store around the corner. It was time for my break, so I've got a few minutes."

"Are you getting coffee?"

"Sure." I wait as he goes to the counter and orders the daily brew. They pass him a white cup with a dark brown sleeve, and he joins me at the high table. "So what's going on?"

"Molly met us at the airport—"

"You mean Maggie Mae?" He gives me a wink.

"I'm sorry about that. We didn't know who to trust, and we were alone."

"It's okay. Molly told me the story." His eyes blink to the ring on my hand. "I really like her, you know?"

Sitting back, I put my hands in my lap. "I noticed she's still living with you. Are you two… together?"

"I don't think Molly does 'together.'" His gray

eyes meet mine, and his smile is less sunny. "But we have moments."

Something shifts in my chest. "I'm glad. I didn't know if she would ever be able to do that. If she would ever recover."

"Whatever happened to her was pretty bad, wasn't it?"

I only nod. "It's something she'll have to tell you when she's ready."

"I know. She's told me a little. Not much, but I'm fine with waiting."

My lips press into a smile, and I really like this friendly guy who picked us out on a crowded street one Friday night. I hope he's able to break through to her, to touch her heart.

I touch his hand again. "You're pretty brave, you know that?"

A chuckle breaks from his lips, and his smile shows off his straight white teeth. "Yeah, but I'm stupid when it comes to pretty girls."

The guy at the counter calls my name, and I hold up a finger before hopping off my stool to grab the waiting bag. It smells delicious—no Everything Poboy, but not bad.

"What's going on, Josh? She was only with us in the apartment for a few minutes before her phone pinged and she left in a hurry. We need her help, but it seems something's more important…"

His eyes flicker away, and he leans up, taking a sip of his coffee. I can tell he's trying to evade my questioning, but I'm not about to let him. Reaching out, I grasp his forearm.

"Please tell me what she's doing." Our eyes meet, and he studies my face a moment before standing as well.

"She'll be mad at me if I tell you anything." He sets the cup on the table, his eyes fixed on the lid.

"I'm not going to try and stop her. I just need to know, and we actually do need her help."

He doesn't answer right away. He seems to be thinking, weighing the options.

"Let's walk while we talk."

Outside, it's growing darker and the breeze is stronger. I hold the bag to my chest and sip my hot drink, doing my best to stave off the chill.

Joshua's hands are in the pockets of his gray slacks. "She's been going out with Candi for the last two weeks."

My chest plunges. "Candi… the hooker? Doing what?"

"Watching out for her. Making sure she isn't hurt." He lifts his chin. "I told her I didn't like it. She told me she's being careful."

It's the best he can hope for. I know from personal experience.

"Does Candi know Molly is there?"

"Yeah, I think she likes having Molly there, even though she acts like she doesn't."

I remember Candi, the young girl we met at the Redwood. She acted like a ditzy blonde, an act I've seen Molly use to lure her victims, make them believe they're safe. But when pushed in a corner, Candi turned stabby… another trick I've seen Molly use.

"Gavin has a new kid, a girl named Brittanie." The muscle in his jaw moves, and I can tell this is where things are getting bad. "She's only thirteen, but she looks older. She needs to go home, but she won't."

"Where is her home?"

"I don't know. Foster care, probably. She's like a lot of the kids around here, a runaway. Maybe her parents are into drugs. Maybe she's a lesbian, and they kicked her out. Either way, she's on the street."

We keep walking, and I see the men's clothing store up ahead. "Do you have to go back to work?"

"Yeah, but I can tell you things are getting close. I'm worried."

A knot tightens my throat, and I try to swallow it away. "Why are you worried?"

"They've been going out more. Molly gave Brit her phone number, and every time it goes off, she leaves. She won't tell me where they go, but I think I know."

"Will you tell me?"

His lips press together, and he ducks his head before leaning in close to my ear. "It's a private club. It floats—meets at different places, tattoo parlors, hotels. I don't know all the spots. It's dangerous. The men pay money to have... *experiences*."

A block of ice is in my stomach. It's the same setup as in New Orleans, the underground club where men paid to have sex with strippers or to have a ménage or to have sex with a teenage girl...

I know what Molly wants to do. She wants to kill them all, and I'm terrified she'll fail horribly.

"Do you know when they meet?"

He shakes his head. "All I know is last week, she bought a gun."

Reaching out, I take his arm. "Mark's here. He's a cop, a detective. He can help us. Please call me the next time you hear anything, even if it's just a hunch. If you think she's going with them, let me know. Please, Josh."

He pokes out his lips. "Okay. I gotta get back, but maybe we can all go out when I get home."

"I'd like that."

I wait a moment as he heads up the block toward the store. My stomach is once again twisted with fear. I knew she was mixed up in something, but I didn't know it had gotten so critical.

A gun, Candi, a teenage girl…

I need to get back to the apartment.

* * *

Mark

"Fuck!" I push the wireless keyboard forward on the desk. "Where the fuck is Molly?"

Nobody's in the apartment, and I push the chair back, shoving my hands in my hair. I hit the cut on my head and swear again at the pain.

We came all this way, we don't have fucking time, and Molly just takes off. What the hell is she doing? I grab my phone and text her again, but there's no response. Behind me, the deadbolt turns, and for a split second, I think it might be her.

Lara pushes through the door, a brown bag in one hand and a go-cup of coffee in the other.

Her eyebrows go up. "Did you find anything?"

The hope in her eyes pisses me off even more. "Where's Molly?" I growl.

Her expression falls. "I don't know, but I talked to Joshua."

"Yeah? What did he say?"

"Come to the table." She holds out her hand, and I follow her into the small kitchen area.

She takes two large paper-wrapped bundles from the bag. I can only assume they're sandwiches.

"What'd you get?" My stomach pinches, and I realize it's been a while since I've eaten... hours. Glancing at the clock, I realize it's way past dinner time for us.

"Reubens." She places one in front of me, and I tear into it, lifting the marble rye out of the wax paper.

White juice drips from the side as I take a large bite, and the tang of sauerkraut mixed with corned beef and Thousand Island dressing fills my mouth.

"This might be the best thing I've eaten all year."

She grins and kisses my head. "Not true. You had a Three-fer last week."

Nodding, I take another large bite. "I wasn't starving then."

She sits across from me at the small table and opens her sandwich. It's the same size, but she takes a less ravenous wild-animal-sized bite. She even touches away the juice with a napkin.

"How's it going?" She studies me with worried eyes.

"Tedious." I grab a napkin, wiping my hands, my mouth. "I need Molly. It's the whole reason we're here. We came all this way, and she just disappeared."

I don't want to take my frustrations out on Lara, but they're right at the surface.

Lara shakes her head. "She's off playing guardian angel... or angel of vengeance... or justice. I don't know."

"What does that mean?" I'm finished with my food, but Lara has only taken two bites.

"Joshua said she's been going out with these girls... Prostitutes. I know she has Gavin in her sights, but she can't face him on her own."

Her voice wavers, and I go to her, lifting her into my arms, against my chest. This is all so fucking hard.

My hands slide up and down her back. "You okay? That shit this afternoon was brutal."

Her head nods fast, and she holds my arms, pushing out of them. "Yes. Yes, I'm fine. Once again, you've saved me from a meltdown."

An edge is in her voice. It makes me frown, and I catch her jaw. "What the hell does that mean?"

Angry blue eyes blink to mine. "It means for once I'd like to be able to face a problem without the threat of flying off the cliff. I don't have to be rescued all the time."

My chin drops, and I try to think of a nice way to say this.

Fuck it.

"Well, that's too damn bad." My eyes lock on hers. "I'm going to keep pulling you back from that cliff as long as you need me to do it. Every time." Reaching down, I grab her finger, lifting it by the engagement ring. "That's the whole point of this right here."

Shaking her head, she gazes at the not-diamond on her finger. "We haven't set a date." Her voice is soft.

A tiny smile plays at the corner of her mouth, and I know she heard me. Maybe she finally internalized the message. She hasn't shown any signs of running since that ring.

"I'm ready. We can go down to the courthouse now, be back by the time Molly drags ass in here."

That gets me a little laugh. "Roland would kill us."

"I know." Pulling Lara to me again, I kiss the top of her head. "You probably want a big wedding and all the trimmings…"

"I never really imagined my wedding."

I don't know if that's a good thing or a bad thing, but I do know we're stuck here waiting until Molly decides to return. It gives me an idea… something to release the tension. The lights of the city spread out below us. It's a beautiful view.

"As soon as this is over." Catching her cheeks with my hands, I kiss her lips. "As soon as we can get it planned, it's happening."

Her hands move to my waist, fumbling with the edge of my shirt until they find my bare skin. "I'll be your wife."

The words heat my blood, and I kiss her deeper, tasting her spicy mouth. I find the edge of her shirt and lift it over her head. She's standing in her jeans and a black lace bra, her nipples peaked and pointing right at me. I'm instantly hard.

Leaning down, I kiss the top of her shoulder, lowering her bra strap. "I thought we might try for a little brother or sister for Jillian."

Cool fingers unfasten my jeans, pushing them down my hips. "I'm on the pill." It's a light quip, a touch of seduction, and it makes me smile.

"I know it's too soon." Moving my mouth higher, I pull the skin of her neck between my teeth. "Just know I'm ready when you are."

She shivers and lets out a little moan that registers straight to my cock.

"When this is over." She has my shirt open, and the touch of her mouth against my skin is electric. She sucks and pulls at my nipple, and fuck me, that's sensitive. "We can think about so many things."

Leading her to the silly air mattress, I remove the last of her clothes. Dropping to my knees, I pausing to kiss her flat stomach, looking at it a moment, thinking.

"I don't want to miss anything. Ever again."

Her fingers thread in my hair, and regret fills her eyes. "You won't."

She leans down, and our mouths collide. I want to kiss the pain away, the fear. The anxiety she doesn't want to have, but she can't deny. With all the crime and danger surrounding us, nothing has ever been able to stop our love.

Our bodies slide together. Her thighs part and her hips rise to meet me. I sink into her warm depths with a groan.

"It's always been this way," she sighs, her fingers cutting into my arms. "No matter what happens, I always want you."

Stretching down, I capture her lips, pulling them with mine. "Will you still want me without all the danger?"

"Hmm," she grins, picking up on my tease. "It'll be so boring."

"I'll find a way to be your hero." I rock my hips, giving her a hard thrust, glistening on the edge of orgasm.

She moans, eyes fluttering shut. "Always."

CHAPTER 18

Challenging me will be your last mistake.

Mark

The bang of the metal door rouses us. I'm lying on my back, dozing in the afterglow, but Lara jerks the blankets over her breasts and stands.

"Sorry, didn't mean to disturb you." Molly goes to the sink and runs water. Her tone doesn't sound sorry.

Lara steps into her jeans and pulls my tank over her head before storming around the screen. I push off the mattress, grabbing my pants.

"Where were you?" Lara's voice is sharp. "You disappeared for hours, and you know we came all this way for help."

Molly's is equally sharp. "I'm sorry. My life wasn't on hold waiting for you to show up. I had a prior commitment."

"Where? What did you do?"

"I don't have to answer that."

Stepping into the room, I try to ease the tension. "I wish you'd at least answer my texts. I get it. You have shit going on, but this is urgent, Mol."

She takes a breath and holds out her hand. "Show me what you've found."

"Nothing." We go to the computer, and I show her what I've done. "I searched the terms you said, but they only brought up that one video."

Dropping into the chair her thin brows pull together. "You also have to use what you know about the time, the place, the people." Her fingers fly over the keys, and I watch her type in *sex club, underground, backstage, floating, exclusive, teens.*

The screen fills with lists, and she scrolls quicker than me.

"You're more familiar with this environment."

Her eyes scan. Her lips are pressed into a straight line. "The population here isn't that big. It's a lot of the same shit repeated over and over. You learn to recognize it."

The tension in my neck is back. "You said you've been searching for three days? So you think he's deleted it?"

"It's possible. I still might be able to find traces."

Lara paces the room behind us. Her arms are crossed over her waist, and anger radiates off her. "Do people have usernames in this dark web? Couldn't that be a clue?"

"No." Molly's voice is flat. "It's about anonymity. Nobody uses traceable IDs here. It's one of the first rules of a tor browser—no cookies, no storing passwords."

My fists clench. "Dammit, Molly. He can't have deleted everything."

Her hand stills, and she hesitates over a listing. Faster than I can keep up, she clicks it. A window opens, and she scans the contents before closing it again just as fast. I only caught the first sentence, *Third meeting, same day, same time, Black Pony...*

Her cheeks are flushed, but she closes window and continues scrolling as if nothing happened.

"What was that?" My eyes go from the screen to her face and back. "You found something?"

She shakes her head. "It was a false alarm. I thought it was something. I was wrong."

Years as a policeman have made me pretty good at spotting a guilty face. "Was it something else? Something related?"

Blue eyes flash at me. "You're looking for videos to exonerate Lara? Or at least give her an alibi for what she did?"

"Yes."

"That wasn't a video." Her face is back on the screen, and her fingers move faster than ever, leaving whatever that was far behind us on the path.

The next search term makes her stop. "What's this?"

I grab a chair from the table and pull it beside her so I can sit. The link opens a window to another video screen.

"This looks like a hit." Her voice is high, and my chest squeezes.

"Play it."

She taps the triangle below the black frame, and images start moving. Again, it's black and white, very poor quality. We watch as a figure, a man, enters a room carrying a long pole. He leaves for a moment then returns with a bucket.

"Wait…" I lean forward, studying the screen, running my eyes past the man to the setting around him.

It's a bedroom with dark walls and ornate light fixtures. A couch is against one wall, and trash is on the floor. A table is smashed, a lamp overturned.

The figure returns and puts his hands on his hips, staring at the room for so long, I'm worried the video is corrupted and has stopped playing. Then he takes the pole, which I realize now is a mop, and dunks it in the bucket.

"It's me," I say softly. "It's my first job... for Gavin. I had to clean blood from a room and burn the sheets."

Watching myself from all those years ago in that place, I understand the feelings Lara wrestled with earlier. It's haunting, but more than that, it's alarming to think everything was recorded and is somewhere on video. It's similar to someone reading your old diary, discovering the worst things you've ever done from long ago.

The events are dragged from the hidden depths of memory to the front of my mind, no longer buried under rationalizations.

"He kept the ones that incriminate us. None of the videos showing his involvement, the crimes that happened there, are still around."

The truth is a lead weight in my stomach.

Molly watches me cleaning the bloody room in silence until I start to strip the bed.

Lara speaks from behind me. "Do you know whose blood it is?"

Glancing up at her, I nod. "I do now. I didn't then."

She waits, but I shake my head. I don't even know Tanya's mother's name. "Someone Landry knew."

Snapping out of her trance, Molly touches my hand. "It's possible something is still out there. If he hid things, it's possible he forgot where."

I pull back. "Are you being optimistic?"

The tension in her brow returns as quickly as it left. "I'm only saying what I've seen. People hide things then they forget where they hid them. It happens a lot, especially with old guys."

"Right." I meet her cocky glare with my own. "It's how DollBaby was able to find Esterhaus."

Her eyes widen, and she's out of the chair. "I've got to go out."

"I'm going with you." Lara is right behind her, grabbing her sweater off the chair.

Molly doesn't even pause. "No, you're not."

"It's after midnight."

"Which to you feels like 2 a.m." Molly pulls a black jacket over her shoulders, and snatches a small duffel off the floor. "I have to meet Joshua."

"I want to see Joshua." Lara hasn't stopped moving, and I know she won't back down. Not after what she learned today.

"Hang on." I'm on my feet again. "Can we run another search first?"

"I don't have time." Molly's voice is a low exhale, and she's gone.

Lara is still pulling on her boots, but she stops to tap out a text. "She thinks she's going to race out that door, but Joshua will tell me where he is."

Digging in my case, I take out a long-sleeved shirt. "I'm coming with you."

"No, you're not."

I almost laugh. "Between you and Molly, I don't know who's more stubborn."

"If she's doing what I think, you'll only attract attention." Her boots are on, and she's at the door, but I stride across the room and lift her off her feet.

"Mark!" She yelps, trying to struggle. "Put me down!"

My grip on her is solid, and I deposit her roughly on the bed. "I'm a cop. I know how to blend in."

"Don't you need to do more searching?"

"I can't do it without Molly, and if she's doing what you think she's doing, you need me with you."

We're out on the street and a gust of wind hits us right in the face. Lara gasps, and I stop at a small souvenir shop and grab a black hoodie.

"Put this on." She shoves her arms in the sleeves and I zip it up. "You should put the hood on. Or put your hair in a ponytail. Gavin will recognize you."

"What about you?"

"I'm a lot bigger than I was the last time he saw me."

Her phone buzzes, and she lifts it. "Josh says he's at the Pony."

She starts out, but I catch her arm. "Pony?" My mind races back to the link Molly followed; the one she said was nothing. "Did he say a color?"

"No." Her fingers move quickly as she texts him back. "I'm asking for the address now."

"Molly said Gavin is doing the same thing here he did in New Orleans…" I think about the work I did for him, the rooms I guarded.

I try to remember the search terms she used. She said them so quickly, but I remember *sex club*, *exclusive*, and *teens*. She was searching for their next meeting.

"Here's the address." She sends it to me, and I pull it up on my map. A quick study, and I'm almost jogging up the sidewalk.

She's right beside me. "What's happening?"

"It isn't what we came here for, but maybe we can end this tonight. If we're lucky."

"How? What do you know? Did Molly find something?"

"Is Joshua a part of whatever she's doing?"

"I don't think so. He knows what she's doing, but I don't think he's involved."

We're a block from the bar, and the red neon sign in the shape of a horse's torso juts out over the sidewalk ahead of us. I glance at Lara, and her head is uncovered, her long hair moving in the wind. Her lips are full and pink, and she's the most eye-catching thing I've ever seen.

"I don't think I'm exaggerating when I say everyone is going to stop and look at you when we walk in there."

"It's a gay bar, Mark. If anyone turns heads, it'll be you."

"Doesn't mean everyone in there is gay. We're meeting Joshua here. Isn't he into Molly?"

"He could be bisexual."

"Bisexuals will notice you." Turning her around, I gather her long hair in my hands and put it down the back of the fleece jacket then I lift the hood over her head. "Tie that close around your face."

"This will attract even more attention," she grumbles. "I look like an idiot."

"Stay close behind me. Keep your face down."

We approach the small bar that looks like a piece of modern art. The façade is a curved strip of black metal with studs around the top, and a cheeky, hand-written sign warns prudes to stay away.

The message on the website flashes in my memory. *Black pony…*

This is it.

I'm ready to charge inside, when Joshua steps out and intercepts us. "Come with me."

He walks away from the club at a brisk pace, but Lara and I both hesitate.

"Hang on," Lara calls after him, "Josh… wait."

"The message said it was—"

Joshua pivots on his heel and rushes to us, grabbing my arm hard and pulling us close. "Stop talking." He raises his voice. "Great to see you!"

He glances around us. Two men in dresses and blond wigs smile broadly and skip past us into the bar.

He smiles and nods before leaning in to speak. "Anyone hears you, they make one call, and it's gone."

I've only been around this guy a few times, but he's usually smiling, pretty casual and laid-back. This change has me on edge.

He takes off again, and we follow behind him, keeping our heads down. After a few blocks, he turns into a coffee shop and slides into a wooden booth beside the door.

"What's going on, Josh?" Lara pulls the hood off her head.

"Candi texted. She's out tonight." His hands are clasped on the table in front of him, knuckles white. "This group is dangerous. Ultra freaks and criminals."

My jaw clenches, and I'm glad I put on my shoulder holster before we left the apartment. "How do you know where they are?"

"I don't. I only know the Pony is where they go to pay and get the real address. They have a guy there waiting. It could be anybody, and if they think the cops know—"

"Makes sense," I say nodding. "But what do we do now?"

"Wait for Candi to text me again."

A waitress appears at the end of the bar, and we all order coffees. She leaves, and I lean back against the wooden booth. This is way more action than I anticipated coming to this town.

"We need a plan," Lara says. "The three of us can't storm into a… a place like that and expect to get away with it."

"She's right." I lean forward. "When I worked for Gavin, only the people who knew about the club showed up at the door, and even then, they were only let in with special cards."

Joshua's brow quirks. "What kind of cards?"

"Business cards but different every time, impossible to forge."

Three coffees are set in front of us, and the server disappears in the growing crowd. Lara shifts in her seat, the tension rippling off her in waves.

"What are we going to do?" she asks softly. "We can't just sit and wait while who knows what's happening."

Joshua picks at the paper sleeve surrounding his cup of coffee. None of us drink the hot beverages.

"Once we know where they are, we can figure it out." Joshua's eyes flicker up from his cup to mine. "It's impossible when we don't know what type of venue we're dealing with, if there are windows or doors—"

"If it's like the old club, there won't be any windows." My voice is grave and my eyes focus on the cup in my hand. "And only one door."

"Two," Lara softly adds. "One for the girls."

"And it's bolted once everyone is inside."

Joshua leans back in his seat and lets out a groan. "Molly…"

"I need to walk," I say, standing. "Is there any chance you have an idea where the place might be?"

"None." Josh shakes his head. "It could be anywhere."

"Take us to any potential spots, anywhere that has back rooms or hidden passages. Do you know any places like that?"

His lips poke out and he nods. "A few."

"Let's start with that. At least we'll be moving around, and who knows. We might get lucky."

"The only luck I want is finding Molly." His voice is low as he stands. "And it not being too late to save her."

CHAPTER 19

Revenge is beneath me, but accidents happen.

Lara

The wind slams into my face, stealing my breath, and my heart thuds in my chest. Nothing is going the way we planned... as usual.

Taking out my phone, I shoot a quick text to Evie, *How are you? How's my little angel?*

Her reply comes pretty fast, considering it's after midnight where she is. *Sleeping like a baby. House alarm set. Pete outside guarding.*

Thanks so much, I type. *Hope to be back soon.*

Any luck with the search?

The guys stop in front of me, and I almost bounce off Mark's back.

"Let's go in here," Joshua says, holding the door for a funky art-deco bar that has murals drawn all over the exterior.

"It doesn't have any hidden rooms I know of," he continues, "but a lot of the local kids hang out here. They might know where Candi or Brittanie are tonight."

My stomach sinks. "You think Brittanie is a part of what's happening?"

"I don't know why else Molly would have wanted to go." His jaw tightens.

We step into the neon-lit bar. It's crowded, and a DJ behind a raised table at the opposite end of the dance floor plays house music loudly.

"I need a beer," he says in my ear. "You want anything?"

I shake my head no, and Mark goes to the bar. Evie is waiting on my reply to her text, and I'm trying to decide how to tell her everything with my thumbs. Ultimately, I settle on, *Still working. Hope to have more soon.*

Good luck, she replies.

Take care of my baby for me. As I type the words, my chest hurts. I miss my little girl so much.

Don't worry.

I wish that were possible.

"Who are you texting?" Joshua is across from me looking as anxious as I feel.

"A friend. She's watching our little girl."

He nods in the direction of the bar. "He's a good guy. How long have you been together?"

My mind races through the ups and downs of Mark and me, from the day he saved me at the theater to him taking me down the alley for food, to our night on the town, to his attempt to fight off Guy's men, to our surprise meeting on the train in Canada, to the glorious weeks we spent in Nice when I was pregnant, to him finding me again at Roland's...

"Almost eight years... sort of."

"Sort of?"

"It's so complicated."

Mark returns carrying two beers. He hands one to Josh. "Figured you could use this."

Joshua takes it and clinks their glasses. "Thanks. Cheers."

They take long sips, and the house music seems to grow louder around us. We're in the middle of a sea of bodies swaying, nodding, or full-on dancing. Lights strobe and flicker in excited patterns, and I'm not feeling any of it.

My lungs are too tight to breathe, and all I can think of is Molly in a deadly situation. Not to mention, we haven't done what we came here to do, if it's even possible anymore.

Mark said Gavin only saved the videos that incriminate us. Is it just for insurance in the event we come after him, or is he building a case against us, trying to trap us? We can't take that chance.

"Want a sip?" Mark holds his beer toward me, and I smile before taking a long gulp.

His warm hand finds my waist, fingers tracing the skin just above my waistband. It gives me comfort in the way only Mark is able to do, and just when I think I'll go crazy from waiting, Joshua nudges me and lifts his phone.

He studies the face, my heart beating faster, then he types a quick reply.

"What's happening?" I ask.

"Candi's on her way here. She said one of the girls who works with Brittanie at the piercing salon is with her. She might know where they went."

"They'd be that lax with security?" Mark's deep voice is near my cheek.

"I doubt it." Josh takes another sip of beer. "But Brittanie would. She's pretty immature, talks a lot."

I cringe at the implication. Of course Molly is all over this situation. It's her own nightmare replaying in front of her.

Mark's hand tightens around my waist. "If this piercing chick knows anything, I'd say Gavin is slipping."

I glance up at him. "Or he's getting cocky."

"That'd be great for us. Cocky means careless, and we need them to be careless."

"Here they are." Joshua leaves us standing by the bar to go and meet rainbow-haired Candi and another girl, who's far less colorful.

Piercing girl has a short asymmetrical haircut dyed jet black, and she's wearing the usual skinny black dress under a long-sleeved flannel shirt, torn black leggings, and combat boots. Her face has an assortment of jewelry, from her lip to her nose, and all along her eyebrow. Joshua seems out of place still dressed in his work clothes.

The three of them talk, but they don't come to where we're standing. Candi glances in my direction, but she acts like she doesn't know me. The other girl never looks our way.

A new song starts, and the group breaks up. Piercing girl heads out to the dance floor, arms over her head. Candi goes to the door and leaves. Joshua returns to where we're standing.

"They didn't have a definite location." Mark lets out a groan, but Josh is undeterred. "But Rhiannon has acted in the club before. She said there's a tattoo parlor closer to the park with a back room like a speakeasy."

"Makes sense," Mark says, and I look up at him wondering why. "If there's a raid, they can run into the park and escape, or hide."

"She suggested we head that direction. I've got the address here. I'll text it to you."

We're back on the street walking fast past taverns and bistros, past sushi restaurants, and brew pubs. It's crowded as always, even though a light drizzle has begun. I pull the hoodie over my head and snuggle close to Mark's side.

"A tattoo shop with a back room?" Mark looks to Joshua, who's at my other side.

"Not sure they're one and the same. They could just share the building." He shakes his head, watching his feet cover ground. "But I don't know. All of this is new to me."

We're getting closer, and we still don't have a plan for how to get inside. The security on these places is so tight. Mark knows you have to have the right credentials. I've only been inside once, and I'd been roofied.

My mind races for anything that could work when I spot a costume shop ahead.

"I have an idea." I grip Mark's arm. "You're not going to like it, but it's the only thing that will work at this late hour."

He frowns, but I jog ahead into the elaborately decorated shop. Feather boas, mannequin heads with Pulp Fiction-style wigs in black, blue, hot pink, and rainbow are in the window. I start grabbing supplies.

Ten minutes later, we're back on the street heading up the last block before we get to the tattoo speakeasy.

"You're right, I don't like this." Mark's teeth are clenched as he speaks.

"If you have a better idea, I'm all ears. Otherwise, this is the only way."

Joshua only shakes his head. His jaw has been on the ground since he learned I was a burlesque dancer in New Orleans. Now he just follows my lead.

Stopping at the alley around the corner, I take off the hoodie. "Give me your blazer."

Josh takes off the grey sharkskin and hands it over. I give him the hoodie, which he pulls over his white dress shirt. He looks more like the Emo kid I'm used to seeing in it.

"Wow," he says, as I remove the rest of my clothes, leaving me dressed in a black bustier and thigh-high fishnets.

Sky-high black stilettoes complete the look, and I pull the hot pink Pulp Fiction wig over the skullcap stocking on my head. My lips are a deep, sparkling pink, and I've painted huge black wings around my eyes.

"I don't like this at all." Mark's eyes are burning.

"I know what I'm doing." It's a lie. It's one of the biggest lies I've ever told, but I do have a kernel of an idea. "I know how this place works. I'll act like I'm supposed to be there, I won't eat or drink a thing, then when they're all doing what they do, I'll see if I can find a door to let you in."

"Lara…" Mark's warm hands grip the tops of my shoulders. His blue eyes sear into mine, but he knows I'm right.

We don't have another choice.

This has to work.

Waves of déjà vu hit me as I walk around the room unrecognized by anyone. It's two rooms connected by an open wall. In the main one are several hard couches with thin cushions, making it easy to have sex. The décor is the usual black, red, velvet and curtains. Small tables hold finger foods and champagne. It's very warm, and the scent of sweat and come is in the air.

When I walked down the narrow hallway on the main floor above, the doorman was confused. I didn't have an invitation. I was at the wrong door for the girls, but I acted like I knew what I was doing. I flirted a bit, which didn't work, and when I threatened to call Brisbee, he caved and let me inside.

I'm confused by what's happening, though. It's not what I expected based on what I've seen or what Joshua said I'd find.

The girls are topless, and most are wearing thongs or lace boyshorts and heels... but I don't see Brittanie anywhere. The women are my age, and the men are bound. They're clearly getting off on this, moaning and begging... but it's more of a dominatrix scene.

One man is handcuffed to a chair with a black leather mask over his eyes. A topless woman is on her knees in front of him massaging his dick aggressively fast. Her large breasts sway over his come-covered thighs and lower stomach. He's moaning and writhing, begging her to stop... then he comes again.

I'm relieved most of the participants are already paired, because I don't know what the fuck I'm supposed to do. It's some kind of sex-torture. Not wasting time trying to figure it out, I drift through the room looking for Molly, looking for a way to get out— or a way to let Mark in.

Low grunts turn to loud moans, and the women actually seem to be enjoying this experience. I don't relate to the exhibitionism—it's not my style. Still... I suppose if what is happening here is legal, if people are into it, I'll walk away and never think about it again.

Only, that's not what we know happens in this place. There's got to be another room, somewhere where...

"Come with us."

I recognize that voice.

"Are you ready, Daddy? We want to share."

Her breathy sighs, her soft voice. It's the same sickly sweet Marilyn she uses when she's luring them to their deaths. I freeze at the back of the room watching.

Molly isn't a teen.

She's no virgin.

She knows exactly what she's doing, and she'll lull them into a dream state, a false sense of security. I search her barely clothed body for signs of a weapon. She's nude except for the red satin boyshorts and black, opera-length gloves.

"Massage or mouth?" She drops to her knees looking up.

The man in front of her is older. He's not fat like the other ones. He's lean, a silver fox. "Suck me, and after I come, use your hands."

"My favorite." Her voice is playful, and my stomach turns.

Her hands trail up his thighs, and I do my best to stay back, still as a statue. I'm not sure how I'll get her out of here. I'm not sure what she's planning to do. Will it be a bloodbath? Does she think she can get away with it?

"I'm so happy it's our turn to play." She's between his legs, getting into position. "What changed?"

She's fishing. "Brisbee's coming tonight."

Ice filters through my veins.

"Just like you're about to?" She grins, leaning forward to lick her tongue up the shaft of his erection.

Her redheaded partner clicks the handcuffs to the legs of the chair, and slides her fingers down the man's hairy chest, tweaking his nipples.

He lets out a low groan, adjusting in his seat. "He prefers torture to teenage virgins."

A younger man passes behind them. His erection wags as his female partner pushes him down on the couch.

"I hate this night," he groans as she ties his wrists behind him. "I want tight, thirteen-year-old pussy."

His tone is teasing, and my stomach roils.

Fire sparks in Molly's eyes, but she emits one of those fake, insipid giggles. "You won't see me next time. I'm not thirteen."

"Or a virgin." Her client leans back against the wall as if succumbing to her spell. "Do it."

I turn my face. I can't watch her suck him off. It's like watching my own child, which I know is ridiculous. I'm only six years older than Molly, but I rescued her from the street when she was only twelve. I took care of her when she was afraid, when she was sick. I can't look at this, even if I know it's a means to an end for her.

Loud groans, moans, the creak of furniture as another man cries out. His cock is long and veiny, and he comes hard, coating his legs and his kneeling partner's breasts. When he's done, she really gets to work, holding his still-hard dick in one hand and circling her fist fast and tight around his bright pink tip.

His face contorts and he bucks and writhes in the chair, crying for her to stop. She only laughs like a witch in a Halloween show. He keeps struggling and begging, and she keeps going until he comes again.

Their noises coat my skin like fingers. I'm swept up in a cyclone of sex and sweat and torture. Groaning and moaning, their breath is in my ears, their heat blankets my skin like the humidity in the room.

Brittanie isn't participating tonight. What happens now? How do I get out of here? I'm not going to join, but if I run, I'll be caught. Who knows what happens then.

The back door I'd been searching for opens, and it doesn't fucking matter anymore. Gavin walks into the middle of the orgy and crosses his arms, looking around like he's the Emperor of Madness.

A knot chokes my throat, and I try to disappear behind the curtain. The loud moans, the groans, the post-orgasmic torture continues without pause. He's not looking for me, and he's not looking at me. Molly sees him, though. Her lips are smeared and swollen, and she stands slowly, turning to face him.

That's when he sees her. "Well, who do we have here?"

"Hello, Gavin. Remember me?"

"Molly." The warmth in his voice makes my skin crawl. "I do… but you've changed."

Molly's redheaded partner takes her spot, hastily pulling the restrained man's throbbing cock into her mouth. Molly steps slowly toward Gavin, their eyes locked in what I know is a deadly faceoff.

I'm afraid to move in case one of them sees me. My only hope is the back door isn't bolted. Would Gavin be that careless? Mark said cocky is a good thing. Cocky means careless.

I pray Gavin has gotten cocky and careless.

Molly's fingers go to the top of one of her gloves, and she slowly rolls it down. Her bare breasts are round and high on her chest.

"My God," Gavin hisses. "You are beautiful."

I have to blink twice, because she is. She's more mature than I remember, slim body, full breasts, long silver hair curling around her shoulders. She's sexier than I ever was at her age.

As she walks, her ankles cross, tossing her hips with every step. She moves like a supermodel, until she's in front of him, blinking and smiling.

"You like what you see, Daddy?" It's a hushed whisper. "Want me to suck you off then make you come again?"

The man whose dick she was just sucking watches them, his erection deep in the redhead's throat, and I can tell he's about to blow.

Gavin cups Molly's heavy breast, rolling a tight nipple between his fingers. "Amazing," he muses.

"Will you beg?" Her voice is now a purr. "Will you cry for me to stop?"

"I'll do more than that." Gavin's eyes lock on hers. "If you're good, I'll make you a star. You'll have all the money, the fame. Anything you want will be yours."

Standing at the back wall, I can't move. It's the same promise he made me all those years ago. It's how he got me to stay at that theater. It's how he lied to me and ultimately sold me to Guy.

Will she fall for it like I did?

Has she learned? Is she smarter than I was?

She blinks curiously. "If you can do all that, why do this?"

"What can I say?" His lips curl into a smile, eyes shimmering with lust. "I'm just a freak with a fetish."

The glove is off.

The gun is in her hand.

Her voice is steel. "I'm just a victim seeking vengeance. Time to pay."

It all happens at once.

Gavin strikes her wrist.

The tiny gun explodes with a staccato *pop!*

My knees buckle, and I hit the floor as the room erupts into chaos. Women are screaming and running. Men with massive erections are fighting against their restraints, yelling to be untied. A lamp hits the floor with a loud crash, then another one. The room is plunged into half-darkness. It's chaos, and we've got seconds before cops raid this place.

Molly... I have to find Molly.

Gavin is gone, running out the way he came in, and Molly's man in the chair jerks against his handcuffs, his dick waving like a flagpole.

"Unlock me!" He yells.

The girl who was sucking him off ran after Gavin, out the back door.

"Molly!" I yell through the noise and panic.

I'm on my feet trying to find her.

Through the din, I see her fling open the door of a small closet and rip out a brown trench coat. She jerks it over her shoulders and ties the belt fast before dashing full speed out the door after Gavin.

I scan the rug, looking all around, but I don't see her gun. I don't know if she has it or if it was kicked under the furniture in the confusion.

All I know is I've got to go after her.

He'll kill her if she's not prepared.

CHAPTER 20

Don't cry because it's over. Smile because it happened.

Mark

My life has been some tough shit up to now.
My dad killed himself. Rick was murdered.
Then I fell in love and almost died.

But watching Lara walk into that place dressed like a hooker is the hardest thing I've ever done.

Joshua and I back away, trusting she'll get through the door without any problems. We can't risk the doorman—a job that once was mine—seeing us and knowing she isn't supposed to be there.

With my guts ripped out of me, trailing down the street behind her, I let her go, to enter that fucking orgy and blend in, to find Molly, and to find a way to open the back door.

I force my feet to move, to follow Joshua to the space behind the building where we'll search for the door. Only, once we get there, it's cold, wet, and four doors line the wall. All of them are covered in burglar bars, and we have no idea which leads to where we need to be.

"Fuck!" I shout, spinning in place and shoving my hands in my hair.

"Keep it down," Joshua hisses. "We'll know which one when she opens it."

He pulls a beanie out of nowhere and puts it over his silver hair. The black hoodie covers his slim body, but he's still dressed in those gray slacks.

"I can't take much more of this." I start to pace.

My gun is in the holster at my side, and I go to each door, pulling on them one by one to be sure they're locked. They're all bolted.

Be safe, Lara.

She's done this before. She and Molly were doing this when our paths crossed in Canada. She's put herself in harm's way more times than I care to know.

All of that was supposed to end when I put that ring on her finger.

"Fuck," I grumble again.

We've been out here in this cold-assed alley for coming up on thirty minutes. I feel like a fucking amateur. She went in there, and we have no plan for getting her out. We let her walk in that lion's den with no phone, no weapon of any kind. I'm going to have to fight that doorman to get to her.

He's probably twice as tall as me and three times as wide.

We're counting the minutes. I'm mentally revving up my muscles, pumping up my adrenaline to face the guy, when I see something that stops my heart. Reaching out, I slam my hand against Joshua's chest, pulling him against the brick wall beside me, shoving him down a ways so we're hidden by the large blue dumpster.

"What—"

My hand clamps over his mouth, stopping his speech.

Heavy footsteps stop at one of the four burglar-bar covered doors, and I keep my head down, waiting as Gavin fights with the deadbolt, giving us the answer we've been waiting for.

"Motherfucking   piece   of   goddamned

motherfucking shit," he growls until the lock turns with a loud squeak.

I hope my body covering Josh's is commonplace enough in this locale for Gavin not to care. So far, he's unaffected. I'm just another daddy claiming a twink to him.

Joshua's eyes are round as he looks past my shoulder, watching the man disappear through the doorway. We both hold our breath, and I won't lie. I'm praying.

God, please make him forget to lock that door.

In all the history of breaks we've never gotten, please let us get this one lucky break…

The door slams, and I wait a moment before pushing off Josh and running to the entrance.

"Yes!" I open the heavy metal outer door.

"Wait." Josh grabs my arm. "What's the plan?"

"Get in there and get them out." I grasp the bronze-colored knob of the wooden door… and it's locked. "God dammit," I growl.

It's an obstacle, but not nearly as much as those iron bars.

"Stand back," I say.

Joshua moves away, and I reach out to brace my body with the burglar door and the doorjamb. I take a deep breath, ready to throw all my weight behind my leg against this door when everything changes.

A sharp *pop!* of gunfire sounds from the other side. Screams, crashes, and noises like furniture breaking erupt from the other side of the door. The knob turns, and I look to Joshua. We both are thrown behind the reinforced black outer door as the one I was about to kick in flies open.

Gavin charges past us without even looking, leaving the door open behind him. It takes us a second to get from behind the fucking barred door, but two half-naked women run out behind him, eyes wild and arms covering their tits.

They push past me, knocking me off balance.

"Shit!" I yell, turning to Joshua. "Call 911, report a shooting at this address. Now!"

Joshua's on his phone, and I'm about to head inside to find Lara when a streak of silver hair slams into me. I grab her arms, and our eyes lock.

"Molly!"

Her blue eyes are wild, fierce and determined. "Let me go!"

"Where's Lara?"

Her brow furrows, and she shakes her head. "She's supposed to be with you. Let me go—he's getting away!"

I move her to the side, pushing her in the direction of our friend. "Joshua, keep an eye on her." Then I'm running down the hall, taking the short flight of stairs at the bottom.

Just as I round the corner, I'm body-slammed by the woman I've been panicking over for the last half hour.

"Mark!" Lara grabs my arms. Joshua's gray blazer is over her body, but she's still in her costume. "We've got to hurry! Gavin, Molly—"

"I saw them. Gavin got away, but I left Molly with Joshua."

We hurry up the steps and then the hall. Lara leans heavily on my arm, trying not to fall as she runs in needle-thin heels.

Outside, the entire alley is empty.

It's quiet and damp, like we've stepped into another world.

"What…" I look all around. "Where did they go?"

"Where is she?" Lara's voice is a gasp. "We've got to find her. She's determined to finish this."

The noise of sirens growing louder tells me we don't have time to figure it out in this location. Cops will be flooding into this place in less than two minutes, and the last thing we need is for Lara to be implicated in an underground sex-trafficking ring. She's dressed for the part, and it would take too long to explain.

"Come on." I pull Lara to me, and we run down the alley, searching for another passage to the street. Digging in my jacket pocket, I pull out her phone. "Text Joshua. See if he'll respond."

I stop when we round a corner, and she rips off the pink wig followed quickly by the stocking cap over her dark hair. They fall to the ground, and her dark hair spills in waves around her shoulders. Still, her face is garishly made up, and she's only wearing panties under that blazer.

"I need to get some clothes," she says.

Looking back over my shoulder, I realize we left the plastic bag with her jeans and sweater in the alley behind the dumpster.

"That place is swarming with cops by now."

"Good. I hope they arrest every one of those men." Her jaw is tight. "I only wish they knew everything."

"Hang on." We step into the alley again, and I pull off my jacket and my shirt. Handing them to her, I pull off my white tank and hold it out as she hands me back my clothes. "At least you'll have a shirt."

"Panties and your undershirt." She shakes her head. "Thigh high fishnets and stilettos. I still look like a hooker."

"First souvenir shop we pass, I'll grab you a Seattle sweatshirt." We're still breathless, making our way up the sidewalk toward Joshua's apartment. Lara leans heavily on my arm, doing her best to stay upright in those shoes.

"Joshua hasn't texted me back," she says, looking at her phone.

"What do you think?"

"We could go to Montage..." Her blue eyes meet mine, and I nod.

"Here."

We step into a small drugstore, and Lara opts for black leggings and flip flops instead of a sweatshirt. It's not ideal, but we're moving faster now.

Two more blocks, two corners, another street, and we reach the club. It's lit up like a rave, and music blares from inside every time the door opens. A crowd of club kids congregates on the street and into the alley like every other night. The scent of pot is thick around them, and as far as they know, nothing happens outside these four corners. It reminds me of theater life in New Orleans.

"I know where he is," she says, darting out ahead of me.

I lunge behind her, grabbing her arm. "Stop. You can't charge in there. We don't know if he's armed—"

"Molly is in there!" Her blue eyes are wide.

"Let me go first."

We go to the door, I show my ID, but Lara's is in the black hoodie she gave to Joshua. Exchanging a glance, I'm not sure what to do.

The doorman doesn't even hesitate. "No ID, no entry."

"Joshua has it—it's in my wallet in his pocket," she says, clasping her hands like she's begging the guy. "You're his uncle, right? I'm Lara... Molly's sister."

He does a double take, brow furrowed. "Haven't seen you in a while."

"Are Joshua and Molly inside? I could go and find them—"

Lara cuts me off with a glare. I know she doesn't want me to go without her. Still, we're running out of time.

"They just ran in." Another group of people crowds up behind us, and the guy waves us in. "Hurry up and come back as soon as you have it. Don't make me come looking for you."

I doubt he'll leave this spot, but Lara thanks him. I give him a twenty for the cover charge, and we pull the door open. Electric guitar chords blast us in the face, and we push inside, making our way to the center, around to the staircase leading to the small booth overlooking the dance floor.

"Think he's up there?" I'm right in Lara's ear doing my best not to blast her eardrum.

Still, she pulls back and rubs her ear. "It's so loud!"

We both look up, and I see a flash of light behind the closed blinds. Our eyes meet, and we run to the steps. A velvet rope is stretched across the bottom, but we push it aside. A male voice shouts behind us as we run up to Gavin's office, and I'm digging in my pocket for my badge. It's no good here. I'm out of district, but they don't know that.

Catching Lara's shoulder, I hold her behind me as I reach for the door handle, crouching as I push it open and run inside. It's a small space, but it still takes me a second to register what's happening on the other side of the door.

Joshua is on the floor, his head bleeding. Gavin's back is to me, and against the wall, lifted by one of his meaty fists is Molly. Her face is purple, and her eyes are closed. He's strangling her, and from the looks of it, she's almost gone.

"NO!"

It's the last thing I hear before another sharp *pop*!

Blood splatters against the wall in a flash, like someone threw a balloon full of red paint.

Gavin's body flies forward as his grip on Molly releases.

I dash forward to catch her falling body, dropping to my knees and holding her up as she gasps for breath.

I look over my shoulder, and Lara stands with her arm still raised.

Molly's small pink gun is in her hand.

CHAPTER 21

She built the kingdom she wanted.

Lara

The gun in my hand feels too small to have taken down the man who was such an enormous presence in my life for so long.

The shot felt too quiet.

The room feels so still.

Like the calm when low tide is pulled out by a storm.

Just as fast, it all comes rushing back. I'm across the room, on my knees beside Mark when the men storm into Gavin's office.

"Molly?" Tears blur my vision as I stroke her hair away from her face.

She's not okay. Her eyes are bloodshot, and she can't speak. Closing her eyes again, she seems to go to sleep.

"What's going on in here? Bris?" One of the men goes to Gavin lying on the floor. "He's dead!"

They turn on us, but Mark stops them by holding up his badge. "Mark Fitzhugh, detective. Call 911,"

Without hesitation, one of them grabs the phone off Gavin's desk.

"Molly, please..." I'm holding her hand, not even caring what's happening around us, not looking at Gavin's body dead on the floor. "Please wake up."

Mark's arm goes around my shoulder, and he pulls me close, speaking low. "She needs to be checked for internal injuries, but she's strong."

Still holding her hand, I look over my shoulder to Joshua. He's sitting up, but he's holding his head, seeming dazed.

"What happened to you?" The bartender asks him. "I'll get your uncle."

"It's okay," Joshua says, looking around the room. His eyes land on Molly, and he pushes off the floor, crawling to where she lies. "Did he hurt her?"

"He was choking her, but Lara stopped him," Mark says quietly. "Gavin is dead. I need you to tell me exactly what happened here."

Their eyes meet, but we're interrupted by the arrival of EMS. They push us aside, telling us to leave the room while they take Molly's vitals and then load her onto a stretcher. Joshua quickly stands and falls back, avoiding their notice, but I rush forward.

"Please…" I touch the paramedic's arm. "Is she going to be okay?"

"Are you a relative?"

"I'm her sister." The lie has become so common, it feels like the truth.

"Her pulse is strong. If you'd like to meet us at the hospital, here's the card."

I take the white slip of paper, and they carry her out. The music downstairs has stopped, and all the house lights are on. Bouncers are clearing the bar, and I look over at Joshua.

"Do you still have my wallet? In your pocket?"

He reaches in the hoodie pocket and pulls out a small leather case. "Sorry." He hands it to me. "Didn't know that was in there."

We make our way down the stairs and out to the street. Mark slips his phone into his coat pocket.

"I called a Lyft to take you to the hospital," he says. "Tell me what happened so I can give a report."

"It was all pretty fast." Joshua touches the cut on his head. It's already starting to bruise. "She was ahead of me, running after him. I don't know why he was on foot, but we followed him here. He went into his office first… Molly was right behind him. When I went in, something slammed into my head. There was a gunshot. That's all I remember."

A silver car pulls up at the curb.

"You need to get that checked at the hospital." Mark points to Josh's head before pulling me to his chest. "Look at me." Our eyes meet, and warmth floods my chest. "It's over. Don't think about it any more. Stay with Molly, and I'll meet you there."

Leaning down, he kisses me gently, pushing my lips apart and sweeping his tongue into mine. My entire body relaxes against his, and I believe him.

"You okay?"

Reaching up, I touch his cheek. "Is he really dead?"

"He's dead."

For the first time in my life, I feel an enormous weight lifting off my shoulders. Is it possible they're all dead? The list is clear?

Climbing into the backseat of the car beside Joshua, I'm still internalizing the meaning of what happened.

They're all gone.

Several hours later we're back at Joshua's apartment. Molly is lying on the bed, and Joshua has a bandage on his forehead. He's boiling water for hot tea, and he keeps telling me she's going to be okay. I'm trying not to hover, because I know she hates that.

I can't believe they let her come home, but apparently, being stubborn works in hospitals as well.

Mark is on the phone with the charter plane, and I'm putting the last of my things in my small bag.

Going to the bedside, I sit on the edge. "The doctor said your voice should be back to normal in a few days." Her hand is on top of the blankets, so I cover it with mine. "You want to stay here?"

She nods, her eyes fixed on the place where my hand touches hers. "Joshua wants me to stay." Her voice is a husky whisper. "He says it's easy to find work, and... I don't know."

Her hesitation makes me smile. "You like him."

A frown wrinkles her forehead, and she doesn't meet my gaze. "I like being here. I've met people, made friends."

"Will you come to New Orleans for the wedding?"

That question does lift her eyes to mine. "You're going to live there?"

I shrug. "Maybe. Mark wants to apply to the department there. He'd like to try and do some good in the city."

"Still trying to be a hero," she rasps.

"He is a hero."

"You're the hero." Determination flickers in her eyes like anger. "You always were. I just never knew it."

My chest fills, but I swallow the tears. "If there can be heroes in this twisted game we were forced to play, we're all heroes. We did this together."

"But you killed Guy. Then you killed Gavin."

"To protect you."

She studies our hands, then she turns hers so our palms meet, our fingers twine. "You're not my mother." It's not a jab, merely a neutral statement of fact.

"No, but I promised to take care of you. Then I promised to help you see this through."

"You have your own daughter now."

"Still, a promise is a promise."

I can't begin to tell her how rescuing her from the street, sharing my bed and my food, taking care of her all those nights made her as much a part of my life as any family member.

As I think about it, sister seems right.

"So I'll see you in a few weeks?"

"Is that all it's going to take?"

Mark joins us at the bed, and I grin as I stand. "If it were up to him, we'd have done it the day we got here… while we were waiting on you."

"Pilot's waiting on us. Says we can fly all night, sleep on the plane."

Leaning forward, I kiss her forehead. "I'll keep you posted on everything. You keep in touch."

She nods and looks down at her hands. Joshua steps up and holds out a hand. His other is in the back pocket of his dark jeans.

"Safe flight." That signature easy grin is back.

I bypass the handshake and give him a hug. "Thank you so much for everything. Giving us a place to crash, taking care of Molly…"

He hugs me back. "Happy to help. And we'll be at the wedding." I get a wink, and it makes me smile.

Mark takes my hand, and as much as I'm ready to be back with Jillian, my feet are slow to walk away from Molly. It's so hard.

"Just… be safe."

"It'll be a lot easier to do that now," Josh says.

Molly doesn't answer, and somehow, it's hard to believe him.

* * *

Mark

Three thousand feet above the surface of the earth, my mind slips away on a mind-blowing orgasm, my cock buried in Lara's luscious depths.

She's facing me, sitting on my lap in the bed. My back is propped against several pillows on the headboard, and her breasts are at my mouth. I pull a tight nipple between my lips, and I'm rewarded with an internal clench, a hit of ecstasy.

"Yeah," I groan. "Welcome to the mile-high club."

She laughs, kissing my lips. "Much better to join it in a bed, I think. Rather than a cramped little bathroom."

My arms are tight around her waist, and her dark hair falls over my shoulders, all around us. It's so good to be flying back to our baby, the nightmare of our past effectively ended.

While she was at the hospital with Molly, I visited the Seattle police department, where I learned six members of the sex ring were arrested. Several were wanted on previous assault and trafficking charges. Donovan confirmed my efforts in Juneau, tracking men crossing the boarder, and by putting it together with what we'd done here, it got us to ten either dead or in jail.

Police aren't convinced we've captured every member of the international club, but we crippled the group's Pacific Northwest base.

Gavin and his threats against Lara are over, and I'd been able to explain his shooting as self-defense. Molly's injuries reinforced my statement. It took a little work, but Donovan's good relations with the SPD chief helped.

I agreed to write a report once we get back to New Orleans and fax it to them. Since Gavin has no living family, they don't expect any questions other than possible insurance interests.

The only outstanding variable is Landry, but with Gavin gone, I don't see why he'd bother us. If he's even still alive.

Lara's mouth tracing a line from my ear to my temple pulls me back to the beautiful woman straddling my lap. Holding her steady, I ease us down into the bed, turning her body so I can spoon her against my chest.

"So a couple of weeks?" I kiss the side of her neck and she does a little sigh.

"I figured if you were ready in Seattle, you'd be ready in a month?"

"I'm ready now."

Her hands move down my forearms. She traces the lines on my skin with her fingers before threading them through mine.

"Roland will help me. I kind of hoped we might be able to have the reception at Preservation Hall. Will they let us do that?"

"I bet they will."

Her body is relaxing, her voice taking on the sound of sleep. "I want to dance with you under the stars. No more fear of the dark."

"Just tell me where to be, and I'm there." I kiss her hair behind her ear. "In the meantime, I'll find us a place to live."

She exhales a hum, and I listen to the sound of the jets taking us home to our daughter. The shade over the little round window is raised, and I look out at the streaks of the dawn we're chasing.

The sun is just at the edge of the horizon, and long white clouds stretch along the clear blue sky. Only they're not white. They're neon pink, lavender blue, deep red-orange lightening to yellow.

I think about my dad, and I think about my uncle. They'll never see the sunrise in all its splendid glory again. They're in boxes underground. Their eyes are gone, and their bodies are gone as well.

Did they gaze in awe of it like I'm doing now?

Did they cherish the love of a beautiful woman, the touch of her soft body, and the kiss of her lips?

Just like my family, Gavin and Guy, the men who chased her, who tormented her, are also gone.

As the sunrise grows less pinkish-blue and more yellow, I try to sort these ideas in my mind, to understand what they mean.

No matter who you are or what you do, the moment you die, it's over. The clock stops, time is up. No more chances to change your path or make amends, no more chances to make things right...

Or wrong.

Everything up to that moment is frozen in time.

Lara's breath is a gentle whisper in the room. Sliding my palm along the smooth skin of her arm, holding her against me, I dip my chin to kiss her neck. She makes a happy sound, and warmth moves through my stomach.

I left home all those years ago wanting to be one of the good guys. I met her, and I found a way to be a hero. The chapter is closed, and we've gotten a lot of answers. We can put that book on the shelf.

Still, our time isn't over.

We'll be married, join our lives, take care of Jillian, and hopefully have more children... The clock is still going, still time to do good, to make a difference, to be heroes.

CHAPTER 22

Don't let the bitter steal your sweet.

Lara

A light mist shrouds the enormous black iron planter at the entrance to the square. It's early and the green space is empty, the curved walkways leading to the front of the cathedral quiet and touched with dew.

Another hour, and it will be flooded with street vendors and tourists, but for these magical minutes, it's deserted, serene.

Burning yellow sunlight filters through the dark spires high above, causing the gray slate tiles to shimmer. Crosses stand like beacons between each, and like everything since we returned to the city, the edifice doesn't feel ominous anymore. It feels hopeful.

The large gas lanterns at the entrance on Decatur Street are still lit, and dawn is just touching the glossy green leaves of the banana trees clustered along the wrought iron fence.

It rained earlier, but humidity still hangs heavy in the air. The flagstone sidewalks are glassy, and Molly steps up to me holding a bouquet of deep blue iris flowers mixed with moonflowers and white roses.

My dress is ivory gossamer fabric over a light sheath. Lace patterns cover the bodice over flesh-toned fabric, and my hair is smoothed into a bun at the nape of my neck. I'm not wearing a veil. We decided to forego such traditions, since Evie is down front holding our daughter.

"You look beautiful," Molly says quietly.

"So do you."

She's wearing a short gray dress made of flowing silk held up by spaghetti straps. A silk sash is around her waist, and her long hair falls over her shoulders.

"I wanted to give you this." She holds out her palm, and a rectangular piece of plastic sits in it.

"What is it?"

"He had them all on his computer. Probably watched them, the perv."

My brow furrows, and I realize she means Gavin. "These are the videos?"

"Yeah. I made sure they're all there then I wiped his hard drive." Her lips tighten, and she lifts her chin to look up at the spires. "I don't recommend watching them... unless you have to."

"But... how?"

"I went back after they sent me home." She blinks back to me. "I had a hunch. It didn't take long to find them."

Roland appears, walking quickly toward us from the direction of the cathedral doors. "We should probably get moving if we're going to beat the crowds."

A noise to the right makes us all look to see a street vendor opening a large yellow umbrella lined with feathers.

"You're right," I say, gathering the train of my dress and turning to follow him, the thumb drive hidden in my palm against the flowers.

He's wearing a light gray, three-piece suit, and he holds out an arm. I take it, and Molly follows behind us. We don't have permission to be here doing this, so we're not only hoping to beat the crowds, we're hoping to beat the constable, too.

A friend of Roland's who was a minister in a former life waits at the fountain on the other side of the iron monument, and another of Roland's friends plays Pachelbel's Canon on the accordion. We walk past the ancient, oversized palms clustered beneath the sweeping live oak trees with their dark branches hanging low.

Like everything we've done, it's exciting and clandestine and perfect, and when I finally see my future husband, my breath catches. He's gorgeous standing by the small fountain waiting for me. He's wearing a dark suit, and his hair is pushed back from his face. His blue silk tie makes his blue eyes glow, and I can see the dimple in his cheek despite the light scruff of beard.

A small crescent of pink petals and two white pillar candles in jars form the staging area where we'll say our vows. Roland passes me to Mark before stepping aside next to Armand, Phillip, and Evie.

Evie's wearing a long, pale pink dress, and Jillian is in her arms. Our baby is all in white with a bow in her thickening hair, and she lets out a little squeal when she sees me. We laugh softly, and once the music ends, we draw closer in a group to begin the ceremony.

I hand the bouquet to Molly, and just before taking Mark's hands, I slip the thumb drive into his breast pocket

"I'll explain later," I whisper.

Naturally, that provokes a murmur from our friends. Mark only grins and covers my hands with his larger ones. He lifts my fingers and kisses the backs of them as the minister begins.

Another gentle breeze swirls around us as we recite the traditional vows and exchange our rings. My wedding band has three small, emerald-cut diamonds along the front. It's my compromise with Mark, and after we've promised to love, honor, and protect, the minister falls silent for us to say our own thoughts.

"Lara." Mark reaches for my waist, pulling me closer to his body. "The first time I saw you, I dreamed of making you mine. Despite all the forces pulling us apart, I never gave up on that dream. I promise always to catch you when you fall, protect you from the darkness, and hold your hand in the light." My eyes heat as he says the final words. "Thank you for my beautiful little girl and for making my dream come true. I'll love you all my life."

Smiling, I reach up to touch the tears away. Jillian makes a noise that sounds like *Mama*, and I look over my shoulder. Evie is right there, and I reach out for the baby, taking her in my arms. Mark smiles, and puts a hand on her little arm.

Noises of the street vendors setting up grows louder around us, and I hear the clip-clop of the horse-drawn carriages taking their spots to wait along Decatur Street.

Clearing my throat, I begin. "Mark, you saved my life, you made me laugh, and you gave me this beautiful little girl." Pausing, I inhale a shaky breath. "You're my hero and my handsome prince all in one gorgeous package." I look down, shaking my head. "I'm sorry I ran from you... I'm sorry I was afraid. I promise, from now on, I'll only ever run toward you, into your arms. You've proven you're strong enough to face anything that might chase us. Thank you for loving me, for giving me hope, and for rescuing me from the darkness. I'll love you forever."

A loud sniffle from Evie makes us laugh, and the minister cuts in. "I now pronounce you man and wife, you may kiss the bride."

Mark pulls me to him, covering my mouth with his. I reach up to hold the back of his neck, and as our lips part, a loud cheer erupts around us. Our kiss transforms into a laugh as a brass band starts playing "Tootie Ma" behind us.

Mark gives me another quick kiss before turning to our clapping, smiling friends.

"Let's get out of here," he says, and we blow out the candles and take off down the sidewalk in the direction of Preservation Hall.

Our reception is set up inside, with two tables holding assorted breakfast foods from scrambled eggs to fresh beignets and a huge bowl of grits. Another table holds Mimosas and a station for Bloody Marys. Small bouquets of flowers are in Mason jars and tied to the iron gates at the entrance.

Mark and I have our first dance as husband and wife to "I Think I Love You." From there, the playlist continues with New Orleans standards and newer favorites from "Santiago" to "That's It," while we mingle with our friends in the growing crowd, sip drinks, and have breakfast.

"This is amazing," Joshua says, sliding up beside Molly, a Mimosa in his hand.

Roland bounces Jillian on his hip, and she smiles, clapping to the music. Mark's hands grip my waist, and he holds my back to his chest.

The weathered grey interior blends with the flowers, the food, and the music in an inviting scene of family and home. I'm tapping in time with the music when it suddenly stops.

The fellow on the piano holds out a hand to me, and shouts, "Time for cake!"

The music changes into Mardi Gras, and two ladies walk out. One holds a cake decorated with a white basket-weave frosting and littered with purple irises, yellow roses, and green carnations. The other has an enormous king cake with beads and purple, green, and yellow sugar-covered icing.

Stepping out of Mark's embrace, I lead him to the table where we pose for pictures as we cut the cakes and give each other small bites. He leans in and kisses me sugary sweet as the room bursts into cheers and applause.

"Happy?" He holds my waist, and rubs his nose against mine.

"Ecstatic." I kiss his lips again. "I've wanted to be here with you again so long."

The band takes a break as the cake is cut and handed out to all the guests and visitors. Coffee is served, and Evie stands with her head on Armand's shoulder. Their hands are clasped, and Phillip sits in a nearby chair, holding a coffee.

"Armand." I go to him and taking his hands. "Finally, I can thank you for how you helped us with Seattle."

He smiles and kisses my cheek. "I was glad to do it, and Evie was glad to have the baby all to herself for a few days."

"Still, it would have been a lot harder and taken a lot longer. I would have been frantic worrying about her—"

"I'm sorry I had to leave before you returned, but I visited with your friend Mr. Lovel while I was in Paris. He sends you his best wishes... and a gift."

Armand takes a narrow white box from his breast pocket and hands it to me.

"Oh!" I take it. A folded note is inside, and I read the inscription.

Wishing you a lifetime of happiness, and if you ever decide to sing again...

-Freddie

I take out a beautiful gold necklace with a delicate gold treble clef charm.

"It's gorgeous. But I didn't know you and Freddie—"

"He's a business partner. We've actually worked together for years."

Glancing over at Roland, I notice he's drifted closer to where the band is playing. Jillian is on his arm, and I feel a mixture of regret and gratitude. As long as I've known him, he was always looking for ways to take care of us.

All of us.

I feel bad for the times I doubted him, was cross with him. The night I threatened to take Jilly and leave.

"What's wrong?" Molly appears at my side.

"Just thinking about Roland. How much he helped us."

"Armand gave you a gift?" She frowns looking at the necklace.

"It's actually from Freddie. They know each other."

"Small world," she says, tracing her finger over the gold charm. "It's pretty."

Joshua is at her side, and I reach out to grasp his hand. "I'm so glad you could come."

He gives me that signature smile. "Me too. I've never been to New Orleans. It's just like everyone

275

says."

"How's that?"

"Good food, great music, sticky..." I start to laugh, and he pulls Molly onto the dance floor.

She tries to complain, but he manages to get her dancing anyway. My heart is full seeing her happy with him.

Roland walks up to me still carrying Jillian. I put my arm around his waist and a hand on my daughter's back as the music transforms into a slow waltz.

"It's perfect," I say, moving side to side.

He nods. "Everyone seems happy, settled." A little sigh. "Your mother would have loved all this. She loved everything about the city."

"I wish I'd known her." The words are out before I can stop them.

My lips tighten and I blame the mimosas.

"You don't have to look ashamed," Roland says. "It's okay to miss her."

"I don't want to miss her."

"Why not?" Jillian puts her head on his shoulder, and he kisses her hair.

I stroke her baby back. "Because she left me here... with Gavin."

"She left you with the sisters in an orphanage." We sway side to side as the piano takes over the melody. He hesitates, thinking. "But you're right, you ended up with Gavin. Because he loved her. As sick as she was, she was still so beautiful, and when she died, he promised to take care of you."

"A promise he did not keep."

"Maybe... he gave us a place to live, food, work."

My eyes widen, and my voice rises. "He was a pervert and a criminal."

Mark appears almost immediately, putting his hand on my back and touching my cheek. "You okay?"

I give him a nod, calming my breathing.

"Let me have her." He lifts our sleepy daughter out of Roland's arms and carries her to the courtyard.

"Shh…" Roland puts his hand on my waist, finishing the dance. "You misunderstood. I'm not defending him. I'm defending her. Those days were difficult, especially living on the street. You were a little girl, and your mother had to do what she could to survive, to feed you."

My teeth clench, and I shake my head. "I don't want to think about the past today."

"I understand. When you do, I'm here."

The song ends and we break apart. Just before he drifts away, I catch his hand again. "Wait. I wanted to thank you. For everything."

He touches my chin and smiles. "It's what I do."

Walking away, I imagine he'll be looking for any chance to sit in with the band before long. I feel our early morning wakeup combined with mimosas and good food catching up with me. I wander out to the courtyard where my husband swaying side to side, our little girl asleep on his shoulder.

My chest fills at the sight. "Shall we head home, Mr. Fitzhugh?"

I lean my head against Mark's shoulder.

"As beautiful as that dress is, I'm ready to get you out of it," he says, and the rumble in his voice heats my panties.

"I'm ready for you to take me out of it."

His blue eyes darken. "I'll get the car."

CHAPTER 23

Love is a verb.

Mark

We found our uptown cottage less than a week after returning from Seattle.

It's actually a converted duplex tucked behind a large garden district home facing St. Charles Avenue. We're close to the river and the streetcar lines — as well as two universities. Lara has sent applications to both, and while she still wants to sing with Roland, she's going to get a degree in the meantime.

My application to join the NOPD was quickly approved, thanks to a glowing referral from my senior officer in Alaska. My rank and status increased swiftly as I discussed my experience, and I was added to the mayor's special task force on drug and sex trafficking.

Being familiar with the underworld gives me special insight when following leads and tracking down criminals. In my first month on the job I've been able to shut down a number of storefronts running drug rings and money laundering operations.

The only case I haven't closed is the disappearance of Reese Landry. We never found a body, but we also never heard from him again. Armand and Roland are convinced he wandered out into the night, got lost in the delta, and died from his wound or blood loss.

I'll probably never stop searching for the truth.

Today, all that is pushed aside. Not wanting to wait any longer, Lara enlisted Roland's help, and the two of them put together a simple New Orleans wedding that took us to all the places we know and love.

From our six a.m. start time to now, I think it was a pretty perfect day, and now I'm driving my wife and daughter home.

I park my Acura on the street and place my hand on Lara's knee as I open my door. "Wait here."

I quickly take sleeping Jillian out of her car seat and jog her inside, tucking her in her crib and making sure she drifts to sleep again. Then I'm back at the car, where my always-stubborn wife has stepped out and is standing with her arms crossed, her back against the door.

Pausing at the front steps, I drink in her sexy body loosely covered in lace. "I love that dress."

Her cheeks flush pretty pink, and she lifts the side of the almost-sheer skirt. "It was my one splurge. Designer from Barcelona."

I take a slower pace, returning to her at the car. The way the delicate top is designed, the lace appears to be falling off her shoulders, dipping low around her breasts. It's incredibly sexy and has my semi rising in my slacks.

"I'm not complaining. You're gorgeous in it." Stopping in front of her, I reach down to lift her in my arms. "Time to get across that threshold and get naked."

She laughs, rolling her eyes, which immediately widen. "I forgot to toss my bouquet!"

"We'll put it in a vase on the table instead."

Her lips twist to the side. "I guess we're not very traditional."

"Traditional is for boring people. We can start being traditional after today if you want."

She leans forward and kisses my cheek. "As long as we're together."

We're across the threshold, but I keep going until we're in our bedroom at the back of the house. It has a large master bathroom attached with a jetted, garden tub. I put my wife's feet on the carpet and go to it, switching on the hot water.

"Hm," she sighs. "I like where your head's at."

"You're going to like where it's about to be even more."

She really laughs, then squeals when I lift her off her feet and drop her flat on her back on our king-sized bed. Her breasts rise and fall rapidly, creating those sexy little peaks at the top of her bra, and my semi is fully erect.

Dropping to my knees, I slide my hands under her skirt, moving them higher up her thighs along with her dress, and she lets out a low moan. I don't stop, bunching the soft silk around her waist as I kiss the line of her lacy panties from her hip to the center below her navel.

Catching the sides with my fingers, I drag them away so I can sink my tongue over her clit and circle it fast and hard.

"Oh, God... Mark!" Her hips jump, and I give her a suck.

She's fresh and sweet like the ocean, and I want her to come hard so I can flip her over and fuck her good.

"I've been dreaming of this since you stepped around that statue this morning." I speak against her thigh, letting my beard tickle her sensitive skin. Chill bumps break out across her skin.

"Please…" she whimpers, and I'm back on her clit, sinking two fingers deep in her clenching core while I lick and pull that little bud.

Her hands slap the mattress, and her body writhes. I can feel she's starting to come around my fingers.

"Mark —" Her voice breaks as her back arches off the bed. "Oh, God!"

She jerks as if electricity is running through her, and I slide my fingers out, ripping those panties away. I quickly turn her onto her stomach and push the dress up so her smooth ass is exposed.

Unfastening my slacks, I let them fall to the floor as I scoop her up by her hips and guide my cock to her entrance. She's clenching and wet and I thrust balls deep, groaning loudly as her breathy cry fills the room. Catching both her hips, I pull her against me, fucking her hard as she begs me for more.

Her palms are flat on the mattress and she pushes against it, bucking her ass against my pelvis, riding out the waves of her orgasm as I climb. Deep inside, her pussy spasms and pulls me, and my eyes close as my orgasm spreads through my torso.

"Fuck yeah," I hiss, holding her stomach as I brace my hand beside hers on the mattress.

I'm leaning forward, thrusting harder, driven by the waves of pleasure radiating through me. I'm on one knee and it's growing tighter, tighter until…

"Lara… yes…" I groan as I shoot deep inside her, pulsing and filling her, flying through the stars as I jerk once, twice, holding her body to mine.

She arches up, pressing her back to my chest and threading her fingers in the back of my hair. Her head turns, searching for my mouth, and I kiss her good, tongues curling, tasting, lips pulling ravenously as the waves subside around us.

Another kiss, another taste…

"Shit!" I scoop her up and carry her to the almost-full tub.

I pull the stopper to allow some of the water to drain as we discard our remaining clothes.

"It's so nice." She sprinkles something that smells amazing into the warm water, and I kiss the top of her shoulder.

The back of her dress is a pattern of lace that wraps around her upper arms along a sheer panel. She drapes it over the door, and when I turn again, she's walking to me wearing nothing but a garter around her right thigh.

Her bare pussy is pink and tempting between her thighs, and my dick is perking up again.

"You're going to kill me," I groan, and she smiles.

"Touch me," she whispers, placing her palms on my chest and pushing my dress shirt and jacket off my shoulders.

I toss my clothes over a chair and cup her beautiful breasts, sliding my thumbs back and forth over her hardening nipples. Then I reach lower, running two fingers back and forth between her legs. Her eyes close, and she licks her lips.

Leaning down, I kiss her again, parting those lips and tracing her tongue with mine. She lifts her chin to kiss me deeper, and I hold her as we both step into the warm water, sliding lower, skin against skin.

"I love you," she whispers.

"I love you," I say, cupping her ass before sliding my fingers over her clit, slow and lingering, in a rhythm.

"I've loved you since the day you told me to trust you." Her voice is thick with desire.

"I've loved you since the day you laughed." I pull the back of her hair to tip her chin higher.

Our mouths unite again, and we're lost in a wave of pleasure and union, husband and wife, deeply in love.

Her thighs tighten and she begins to ride my hand, sucking my tongue and whimpering as she chases her release.

Her eyes are closed, her head tilts back as she moans and begs. I lean forward and pull the skin of her neck between my teeth, sucking and kissing her as she vibrates with need.

She's so gorgeous coming for me. I rotate my hand so I can plunge two fingers deep inside, curling them as I rub her clit with my thumb until her mouth breaks away with a cry. She pulls straight up and moans, but I don't stop until she begs.

Catching her under the ass again, she collapses on my chest, her cheek on my shoulder as I hold her.

Pressing my lips to her ear, I whisper in a teasing voice. "My favorite erogenous zone."

She starts to giggle, pressing the button for the jets. The water fizzes into a swirling spa, and she turns in my arms to face me, slippery as a bar of soap.

"You are very sexy," she says, wrinkling her nose and putting her hands on my cheeks.

"Right back atcha, gorgeous."

She pulls me closer, her mouth covers mine, and we kiss slowly, tangling our tongues and pulling with our lips. It's lush and consuming and perfect... Then a baby squeal cuts through our moment.

Lara pulls back, eyes wide. "I'm going to get her."

She stands, and I run my hand down her leg, watching as she disappears down the short hall completely naked. Just as fast, she's back carrying our daughter, and I grab a washcloth, pushing it down into the water over my junk.

"Is it okay for her to be in here with me naked?"

"She's just a baby, Mark." Lara takes off Jilly's diaper and drops it in the twisty diaper pail.

Then my naked wife and naked baby are both in the tub with me. Lara turns to lean against my chest, and Jilly is on her stomach smiling up at me and slapping the water. We both spit and laugh.

"No, Jilly," Lara says softly. "Don't splash Mommy and Daddy."

That only makes her squeal and slap the water more.

"Here." I pass her a rubber duck, and she puts it in her little mouth.

"I think she's teething," Lara says, watching her chew on the duck's beak.

So much love blooms in my chest as I hold Lara against me and she holds my daughter in her arms, I almost can't believe it.

I watch my wife smooth baby wash over my daughter's soft skin in her hair, relishing the feel of her body against mine. I reach up and wipe a blob of foam off Jillian's eyebrow.

"She's so comfortable here. Like this is how her life has always been," I say, watching them.

"She doesn't remember it any other way."

I think of a life always surrounded by love. It's something I never had. I know it's something Lara never had.

"I don't want her to know anything else."

Lara leans back to kiss me. "Then she won't."

It's a promise. I made it to her mother years ago, and I made it legal today. I make it to my daughter as well. As long as we're together, as long as I'm living, this will be her life. It will be our life.

We survived the darkness.

Now we're standing in the sun.

THE END.

EPILOGUE

The bravest thing you will ever do is love again.

Molly

Joshua's arm is across my bare stomach, and I watch the blades of the ceiling fan turn slowly above our heads. It's been six weeks since we brought down Gavin, since Lara shot him in the back of the head as he tried to choke me to death.

We spent years sneaking in and out of hotel rooms, on and off of trains, going back and forth from France to the U.S. and Canada.

The list is complete.

They're all dead.

But I'm not satisfied.

It's not enough.

"You're awake?" Joshua rises up beside me, that irresistible smile on his face.

Silver hair flops over gray eyes, square chin, square jaw, and full lips.

I love kissing those lips.

I love when they part and show off his straight, white teeth.

I can't be in love with Joshua.

People like me aren't allowed to love.

"I was thinking about the wedding."

"Yeah?" He leans that handsome head on his hand and traces a finger lightly down the center of my forehead. "Give you any ideas?"

I reach up and grip his finger in my fist. "We stood in the shadow of the cathedral, steps away from where the theater used to stand."

Lara told me as soon as Mark verified both Hudsons were dead, he had the old burned-out husk torn down.

"Okay." Josh pulls my fist to his lips and kisses it. "But it's gone. Those days are over."

"It's still happening, though. It's happening here."

"In this bedroom?" His warm hand covers my breast, and I love the feel of him touching me. It sends heat blazing between my thighs.

I've never had a real boyfriend. I've never had sex because I cared about someone... Until this happy boy singled me out on the street and decided to pursue me. I don't even remember when I surrendered. Lara left, and I had to stay with him. One night he asked if he could kiss me, and that kiss blazed into a wildfire.

We stayed in bed making love for two days.

It scared the shit out of me.

I've never lost control that way.

Now he plays with me. He knows how to touch me to have me melting into his arms, giving in to the pleasure we find together.

Then he told me his dad was some tech billionaire, and I almost left him.

"Don't distract me," I say, catching his hand and threading our fingers together.

He blows air through his lips and sits up in the bed. In this enormous loft apartment that probably costs thousands of dollars a month to rent.

I don't deserve him.

"Do you know how lucky you are?" He looks down at me, brow furrowed.

"Excuse me?" I sit up, eyes blazing. "What makes me so lucky?"

"You're lucky Lara got you out of there, took you to France and helped you find a new life. A lot of girls are trapped in the cycle. They never break free, or they end up dead."

Now he's talking. "That's why I have to do this. I escaped. I have to help them escape—all of them."

He nods. "I can help you. My dad sent me here to find what inspires me." He grins, and that absolutely unfair dimple pierces his left cheek. "You definitely inspire me."

My stomach flutters. "What does that mean?"

"It means I want between those sexy legs again." He rolls forward, dragging me down the mattress and beneath him as his expert mouth covers mine.

I'm wet, and my thighs are already parting. "Wait," I gasp, lifting my chin. "We can't have sex again."

His head pops up, and he frowns. "Why not?"

"Because I wasn't finished."

He doesn't get off me, but he does stop kissing me. Bracing his arms on both side of my face, he watches my mouth. I run my eyes quickly up and down the lines of muscles on his lean arms. Joshua is all lean muscle.

"Well?" He nods briefly. "What else? I'm trying to be patient, but it's hard. Have you seen your breasts?"

My cheeks grow hot, and I blink down to where his stomach touches mine. "You said you could help me."

It's a quiet reminder. I'm not sure I want his help, but I am curious.

"We'll start a foundation, a safe house. I'll get dad to fund it, you can run it. We can do community outreach, work with the police and social workers."

He rattles it off so fast, my head spins.

At the same time, my stomach turns.

Outreach is not what I have in mind.

Still…

"That's a good place to start." I nod, thinking. "We'll need a way to get them on their feet after—"

"After what?"

Shit. I can't say after I kill the abusers, the pedophiles…

After I cut off their balls and shove them down their throats.

I haven't been able to shake the asshole on the couch's words since that night below the tattoo shop. *I want tight, thirteen-year-old pussy…*

The words have haunted me, plagued me, driven me.

They set my teeth on edge.

They clench my jaw so tight, red floods my vision.

"Where did my girl go? he says softly, leaning down to nuzzle my jaw with his full lips.

Three deep breaths.

Inhale, exhale.
Inhale, exhale.
Inhale, exhale.

It's how I come back. I learned it when I would kill them with Lara. I had to have a way back to the light. I come back on the last breath.

"I'm here," I say, exhaling slowly. "I like your idea. I have an idea of my own, but I like yours. It's good. Like you."

He smiles and kisses the top of my chest. "Like you," he says.

It's his sheltered view of the world.

I'm not good.

And this isn't over.

* * *

HIT GIRL is Molly's story, coming March 19, 2018!

Want more second-chance romance?

Try **When We Touch,** *a sexy <u>stand-alone</u> romance!*

Keep turning for a special sneak peek...

* * *

Want more action and suspense?

The Prince & The Player *is Book #1 of my sexy, action-packed "Dirty Players" series.*

Keep turning for a special sneak peek...

See the inspiration board for *Under the Stars* on Pinterest: http://smarturl.it/WWTpin

Check out the Book Trailer on YouTube:

* * *

Never miss a new release!

Sign up for my New Release newsletter, and get a **FREE Subscriber-only story bundle!** (http://smarturl.it/TLMnews)

Join **"Tia's Books, Babes & Mermaids"** on Facebook and chat about the books, post images of your favorite characters, get EARLY exclusive sneak peeks, and MORE! (*www.Facebook.com/groups/TiasBooksandBabes*)

* * *

Get Exclusive Text Alerts and never miss a SALE or NEW RELEASE by Tia Louise! Text "TiaLouise" to 64600 Now!* (U.S. only.)

YOUR OPINION COUNTS!

If you enjoyed *Under the Stars*, please leave a short, sweet review where you purchased your copy.

Reviews help your favorite authors more than you know.

Thank you so much!

* * *

BOOKS BY TIA LOUISE

Stand-Alone Romances:
When We Touch, 2017
The Last Guy, 2017*
(*co-written with Ilsa Madden-Mills)

The Bright Lights Duet:
Under the Lights, 2018
Under the Stars, 2018

"Sundown" (*A Bright Lights novella*), 2017
Hit Girl (*A Bright Lights VAULT novel*), 2018

Paranormal Romances:
One Immortal, 2015
One Insatiable, 2015

The Dirty Players Series:
The Prince & The Player, 2016
A Player for A Princess, 2016
Dirty Dealers, 2017
Dirty Thief, 2017

The One to Hold Series:
One to Hold (Derek & Melissa), 2013
One to Keep (Patrick & Elaine), 2014
One to Protect (Derek & Melissa), 2014
One to Love (Kenny & Slayde), 2014
One to Leave (Stuart & Mariska), 2014
One to Save (Derek & Melissa), 2015
One to Chase (Amy & Marcus), 2015
One to Take (Stuart & Mariska), 2016

EXCLUSIVE SNEAK PEEK

When We Touch
(A stand-alone, second-chance romance.)
© TLM Productions LLC, 2017

Prologue: Where it begins

Ember

Jackson Cane tastes like red-hot cinnamon, salt water, and sin.

When he concentrates, his long fingers twist in the back of his dark hair, right at the base of his neck, and he tugs.

Tugs…

Tugs…

I like to weave my fingers between his and pull.

Then ocean-blue eyes blink up to mine, sending electricity humming in my veins. He smiles. I smile, and it isn't long before our lips touch. I straddle his lap as I open my mouth, and his delicious tongue finds mine, heating every part of my body.

Our kisses are languid and deep, chasing and tasting.

We sizzle like fireworks on a hot summer night.

Eventually, with a heavy sigh, I pull away, but hours later my mouth is still burning. I taste him everywhere I go.

Lying in my bed in the dark room, my heart aches, heavy and painful in my chest. Every breath is a burden. I blink slowly at the ceiling and slide my tongue against the backs of my teeth thinking about hot cinnamon, tangy salt, caramel and sugar, sunshine, and the best summer of my life.

The instant I hear it, I'm on my feet, tiptoeing to my open window. The low growl of an engine tells me he's there in the darkness, out on the street in the shadows just past the streetlight.

The late summer humidity hangs heavy in the air. Cicadas *scree* from the limbs of the mighty oak tree beside the house. Their damp wings make them too heavy to fly, and the sadness in my chest is replaced with breathless anticipation.

I'm panting. I've never felt this way for anyone, and I'm desperate to hold onto it. Somehow I know I'll never feel this way for anyone ever again.

Quiet as a mouse I scamper to my door and listen. The only sound is the hum of Momma's oscillating fan pushing the warm air around her room. I can't hear her breathing. I can't hear anything... except the noise of Jackson's engine on the street below, waiting.

Red-hot cinnamon.

Salt water.

Sin.

Pressure tingles around the edges of my skull, and a bead of sweat tickles down the side of my neck, dropping past my shoulder, slipping between my breasts.

I'm at the window slowly lifting the glass, and I don't care if she hears me. I dive through the space, out onto the cedar shake roof in my bare feet. I'll get a splinter if I'm not careful...

So many reasons to be careful...

I ignore them all.

I'm going to him like a siren's call in the ocean, like the mermaid story in reverse. I'm the hypnotized sailor. He's the promise of so many wicked pleasures.

Reaching for the tree limb, I swing my body across the narrow gap two stories high, gliding down the trunk as the skirt of my dress rises to my hips. My bike sits where I left it at the side of the house, and I carefully pull it away, holding it as I tiptoe down the gravel driveway to the street.

I can't take a chance on anyone seeing us together and telling my mother. Instead, I dash across the street between the thick beams of his headlights. He flickers them to let me know he sees me, and I plunge into the dark woods, pedaling fast.

Tires crunch on gravel, and I shoot down the pine needle path leading away from this place, through the tall, skinny trees, all the way out to the barren jetty of sand stretching under the moonlit sky filled with stars, surrounded by the clear blue waters of the ocean.

It's our place.

The place where we're the only two people on Earth.

In the summertime, the visitors to our sleepy little town use it to spend the day sunbathing and playing on the wide stretch of undeveloped sand. Now, on the edge of fall, with all the children back in school and Jackson leaving for college tomorrow, we have it to ourselves.

His engine roars on the road above, and I stand in the pedals to push harder, fueled by the burning desire twisting in my lower pelvis. I want to be with him now. I don't want to waste a moment.

I go even faster as the trail slopes downhill. A narrow wooden bridge *thump… thump… thumps* with the pressure of my tires distressing the aging slats.

The instant the trees part, I toss my bike aside and run out of the darkness onto the glowing white sand. The sizzle of waves crashing on the shore fills the night, and the black ripples are tipped with silver light.

Jackson stands in his canvas shorts, his hands in his pockets, and a thin white tee rippling across his back in the slight breeze.

I'm breathing hard when I finally reach him, and he turns. White teeth in a full-moon night, deep dimples in both cheeks, he smiles down at me, and I feel so small. A lock of too-long dark hair falls over his blue eyes, and my breath catches. He's so beautiful.

I swallow the knot in my throat as I gaze at him. What star crossed what planet in what solar system and said I could have him, even if it's only for a little while?

"You made good time tonight." His voice vibrates the warm air between us.

I force a laugh, moving to him until my hands are around his waist. My forehead rests on his chest, and I inhale deeply. He's leather and soap and a deeper, spicier scent that's pure Jackson Cane.

He feels so good in my arms.

His mouth presses against my head, and I lift my chin, reaching for his face. He leans down and claims my mouth, warm lips pushing mine open. I kiss him eagerly, curling my tongue with his, threading my fingers into the soft, dark hair falling around his cheeks, tugging.

An aching moan rises in my chest as he lifts me off my feet. Chasing his kisses, my mouth burns with cinnamon, my core tingles with need. He carries me to our place, a little shelter near the water's edge where an enormous log is slowly turning to driftwood. We lower to the sand, me on my back, him on his knees looking down at me.

My dark hair is all around us, my skirt is up around my waist. My panties are far away on my bedroom floor. A soft hiss comes from his lips, and he slides a finger down my center. My eyes flutter shut.

"Jackson..." I whisper. *I love you I love you I love you...*

He leans down to taste me, his tongue lightly tracing the line between my thighs, and my back arches off the soft sand. My body takes flight on the motion of his mouth, kissing me so deeply, tracing a pattern over my most sensitive parts.

The first time he did this to me, I didn't understand. I'd been embarrassed by how fast my body responded, the way I shook, how wet it was between my legs when the shudders subsided.

Then I was afraid of how I tasted. I was afraid it was dirty and wrong like my momma would say. *Sin...*

Then he kissed me, and my mouth filled with a delicate, clean ocean flavor, like the air after a storm. It was our first time, and when he pushed inside me, my mind came apart. My soul shifted, and I was forever changed.

I was forever his.

The flutters begin in the arches of my feet, and he kisses his way up my stomach.

"Jackson... Jackson..." I can't stop chanting his name as I thread my fingers in his soft hair.

At last his mouth covers mine. At last we're one.

"Ember..." His mouth breaks away with a groan, and I lean up to run my tongue along the ridges of his neck. *Salt water...*

I lick his Adam's apple up to his square jaw.

Rough stubble scratches my tongue.

My legs are around his waist and we're working together, chasing that glorious release. He stretches me and fills me, massages me so deeply, I feel it the moment I start to break apart.

"Oh!" My fingers tighten on his back as every muscle in my body clenches...

Tighter...

Tighter...

Then *Yes!*

Glitter gun showers of pleasure flooding my insides.

"Yes," he groans, and I feel him finish deep inside of me.

Our bodies unite, but at the same time we're flying apart as waves of ecstasy fill our veins. It's magical like the ocean, silvery water tipped in moonlight.

We kiss softly now, rich and gentle, over and over. His tongue touches my upper lip, and he pulls the bottom one between his teeth. *Red-hot cinnamon...*

We're breathing hard, and he slides a hand under my ass, turning us without ever losing contact, so I'm sitting in a straddle across his lap.

My dress is around my waist, and moonlight touches the tips of my breasts. We hold each other, skin against skin.

A hot tear spills down my cheek.

I'm not full-on crying. I'll save the ugly tears for tomorrow when he's gone. Instead, I find his blue eyes.

Dark brows quirk together, and he kisses my nose. "You're crying?"

My voice cracks with a whisper. "Aren't you sad?"

"I'm only going to college, Em. I'm not going to war."

"But we won't see each other for months."

I don't say what's truly scaring me. I don't voice the fear that I, a mere high schooler, couldn't possibly hold onto him.

He's traveling far away to where the girls are more mature, more experienced, more sophisticated.

"You're right," he nods. "It's going to suck. Especially when I want to kiss you."

He pulls me flush against his chest and groans deeply. Strong arms circle my shoulders, and I cling to him.

"But it's not something to cry about," he argues. "You're my girl, Em. That's never going to change."

My eyes squeeze shut, and I inhale his scent, doing my best to hold it in my memory, trying to absorb every part of him.

There's no way in hell I could even begin to argue. I am his, and he's... my everything. Jackson Cane is every first I've ever had. My first real kiss, my first real boyfriend, the first time I had sex... made love...

"Hey." He pulls back, blue eyes full of concern. "I'm right, aren't I?"

Blinking quickly, I try to find my bearings. "What?" I don't know why he looks so worried.

"You are my girl, right?"

My chin jerks forward, and I have to cover my mouth. "You have to ask?"

Warm hands cup my cheeks, and he trails his thumbs lightly along my cheekbones. "So beautiful," he murmurs. "My Ember Rose."

His eyes move around my face, along my hair, down the side of my jaw like a caress.

"I'll never forget this." I'm ashamed at how desperate my voice sounds. "I mean... I just..." I'm such a baby.

He blinks a few times, and a smile curls his lips. With a nod, he pulls me against his chest, strong arms surrounding me. We stay that way a long time, listening to the crashing of the surf, the beat of our hearts. The seagulls cry, and the moon climbs higher. It's all so perfect, but it's all at an end.

Finally, with a sigh, he lifts me, helping me stand. We hold hands as he takes me into the gentle waves to clean up. I slowly restore my dress.

I feel so stupid. College girls don't need to be cared for like babies. They don't whine and cry about being left behind. They blow kisses and wink over their sunglasses. They sway their hips and turn the tables on saying goodbye.

My best friend Tabby is already one of those girls, and she's my age.

I'll never be one of those girls.

"Don't cry, Ember Rose," he says in a low whisper. "I never want to see you cry."

I hold him a while longer, listening to the steady rhythm of his heart. His hands slide up and down my back in a soothing motion.

After a while, they slide down my forearms to lace with my fingers. He steps back and leads me the way we came, stopping at the edge of the woods where I left my bike.

"Get on home before your momma wakes up."

That sexy smile curls his lips. He shoves his hair behind his ears, and I step forward again, clutching the front of his shirt before I press my lips one last time to his.

Red-hot cinnamon.
Sparkling blue sin.
Salt rocks breaking my heart.

* * *

Chapter 1

Ten years and eleven months later...

Jack

"Last one in has to ride home naked!" Tiffany hurls her silky red dress over her head and runs through the trees headed for the lake.

The wheels on my black Audi R8 have barely stopped moving. I haven't even killed the engine. An empty wine bottle clatters against an empty tequila bottle rolling around on the floorboards, and I briefly think I should toss them in a nearby trashcan.

Propping my elbow on the steering wheel, I scrub the back of my neck with my fingers. My hair is so short now, it's the best I can do.

I haven't had a drink in almost an hour. I'd finished a bottle of scotch in my office, standing in front of my floor to ceiling glass windows looking down on the city, disbelief vibrating in my chest.

My career...

My reputation...

It's over.

All of it.

File after file, telling me my win, my multi-million dollar defense... all of it is based on lies.

"Fuck!" I shout, slamming my palm against the wheel.

The buzzing in my head is gone along with the numbness in my chest, and all the shock and pain and pure, unadulterated outrage rush back like a wall of water before a hurricane.

A hurricane that will send everything I've worked for these last ten years crashing down around me.

Pulling the handle on the door, I push it open and step out into the darkness. The ground is covered in moldering leaves, and it smells like faintly mildewed canvas, damp lichens, and dirt.

"Jackson! What are you doing?" Tiffany shrieks between splashes out in the black water of the lake.

Exactly. "What the fuck am I doing here?"

My chest is tight, and each inhale is like claws ripping my lungs from the inside.

It took an hour to drive from my Eighth Avenue high-rise corner office building to this lonely, two-lane highway leading to the lake. Somewhere along the way, I realized I didn't know what the fuck Tiffany was talking about or why she was even in my car. She followed me down the elevator, into the parking garage, laughing and pouring another shot of tequila on the way.

I've got the fucking receptionist with me.

I need to get her back to the city.

Digging in the pocket of my blazer, I pull out my phone and stare at the face. My lock screen is a photo of crystal blue waters, and for a moment, my thoughts blur. I left my home near the ocean with big dreams.

Half of them came true.

I finished undergrad at the top of my class, went to law school on a free-ride, headed straight into a Top

Five firm when I graduated, and now I'm one of the highest-paid litigators handling mostly corporate corruption with the occasional car crash thrown in for variety.

My face is in every "Top Thirty under Thirty" feature in the city and online. My phone never stops ringing.

My fucking dad is so fucking proud.

I've done it all.

And I'm all alone.

"I've got to get out of here." Dropping my chin, I rub my eyes.

The *shush* of feet running through the leaves is punctuated with high giggles breaking the silence. My eyes have adjusted to the semi-darkness, and I see Tiffany coming back, completely naked, blonde hair glistening with water, tits bouncing with every step.

"What are you doing back here?" Her voice is thick, and she curves into my chest, holding my neck and trying to kiss me.

She's slippery and loose. Her kiss is easy to dodge, but not her wet body pressing against my dress shirt.

"I was just thinking the same thing," My jaw tightens, and I lift my chin away from her face.

"God, you're so hard," she giggles. My brow furrows. I'm not the least bit aroused. "Like a wall of granite."

"Look, Tiff, I'm calling you a Lyft." I'm back to tapping my phone. "What's your address?"

"What?" she whisper-shrieks. "Wait a second—"

"Never mind." I bring up the firm directory, and she's gone from my chest. It takes me a second to realize she's dropped to her knees in front of me and her hands are on my belt.

"Stop…" I tap the buttons on the app faster, using my free hand to sweep her away from my fly.

"Stop, stop…" She laughs, her voice high and teasing. "What guy doesn't want a blow job?"

"Stop!" I've managed to book her a ride, but she's got my pants open and is handling my dick.

"Fuck me," she moans. I look down, and she looks up. The whites of her eyes are visible, and her mouth is a delighted O. "The rumors are true!"

"Get up." Shoving my phone in my pocket, I grasp under her arms, pulling her to her feet.

"Oh, Jackson!" She pokes her lips out, face pouty. "Let me ride your big… huge… cock!"

"Where's your dress?"

Moving fast, I refasten my pants with one hand. I'm still holding her by the upper arm, keeping her with me as I circle, looking for where I saw red silk fly over her head.

"There it is." I take her to where the dress is laying discarded on the path.

"You're always alone," she sulks, stomping beside me as I lead her to the car and hold her against it. I brace her with one leg so she can't wiggle away, while I fumble with the fabric, searching for the neck hole.

"Are you gay?" Her voice sounds like every drunk college girl I ever turned away.

"No," I answer flatly.

"When's the last time you got laid?"

Her blonde hair catches in the fabric, and I untwist it, pulling the material down her sticky body as best as I can.

"I get laid," I growl, considering it has been a while.

306

I've been so focused on my work, this case... Now the last thing on my mind is fucking some drunk girl. First, her consent is dubious. Second, she's our receptionist and could yell sexual harassment or worse.

"I'm not dipping my pen in the company ink."

"I'll quit my job!" she cries, still holding onto me. "Just kiss me once."

"Where is that fucking Lyft?" I reach into my jacket again. "He's here!"

Sure enough, high beams cut through the woods, curving around the black trees. I start up the lane in the direction of the road.

"My shoes!" she shrieks, trying to run back the way she came. "They're Louboutins!"

My grip tightens on her arm, until I'm practically carrying her to the waiting car. "I'll ship them to you at the office."

"You're not coming back to work? What are you going to do?"

Hesitating a moment, I realize it's a good question. I know what I want to do—what's nudging at my brain. What I've wanted to do for so long...

I'm tired and my thoughts are twisted and cloudy, but I know what I want more than anything. "I have a meeting to attend."

"Now?"

"Right now."

The Lyft pulls away, taking Tiffany back home. I head straight to my car, pulling out my phone as I walk. My disbelief is gone, my head is clear, and I have to face this.

* * *

"Jackson." Brice Wagner's low voice is laced with condescension as he ushers me into his enormous wood-paneled study. "What brings you all the way out here at this hour?"

It took me two hours to drive to my elder partner's ocean front estate north of the city. From the smell of his breath, he's been working on his own scotch, luxuriating in the close of our case, no doubt.

Thinking how much we could have lost...

How much I saved.

How much he covered up.

"I was doing some housekeeping before I shut down tonight."

"You young bucks." He slaps my back, barking out a laugh as he rounds his desk. "After today's win, at your age, I'd be out on the town, a bottle in each hand and a blonde on each arm."

"No doubt," I say, placing a hand on the stiff leather wingback across the massive mahogany desk from my partner. "I had something like that in mind."

It's true. I'd been finishing up, pulling all the files together ahead of what I hoped would be a long weekend.

Until I opened the office intranet we shared on the case.

Until I discovered the hidden folder labeled "Disposed documents."

The folder password protected with a dead child's name.

"Well?" He pours a crystal tumbler of amber liquid and holds it out to me. "What stopped you?"

I take the crystal and tilt it side to side, studying the trail of the liquid as it moves. The room smells of antique furniture and oiled leather. It's moneyed and ancient, and knowing what I know now, it's all the rotten stench of corruption.

A strange calm filters through my chest as I say my next words. "I had in mind a long weekend, possibly a week off. We put in a lot of hours on this one."

"You're right." He rocks back in his desk chair and props a foot on the corner. I watch as he pulls out a fat cigar and clips the end. He doesn't offer me one, not that I'd take it.

Eventually, the pungent scent of cigar smoke drifts across to me as I continue. "But the settlement agreement and release need to go out. I had to be sure Lori could find what she needed to get it done..."

"Okay."

I've reached the end of my patience, so I say what I came here to say. I speak the heart of the prosecution's case. "Johnny Mauck had been driving for thirty hours straight when he lost control of his rig and skidded across that median."

Brice lowers his foot and turns slowly to face me. Anger fires red in his watery eyes, but it's nothing compared to the fucking inferno in my chest.

"Stop right there." His voice is a calm warning.

"Big Traxx paid for the amphetamines that kept him driving. You were at the scene. You knew it all along." Every breath is hot. "I found the documents, the logs, the prescription... everything that should have been provided during litigation."

"You found nothing." He speaks the words slowly, ominously, dark eyes like stone.

My eyes are flint. "I found it all."

We're silent, sizing each other up. The brass clock on the mantle above the fireplace is the only noise, ticking louder than the beating of a drum. If I had any lingering doubts, any question of what I had to do on the long drive out here, his response put the final nail in that coffin.

Finally, he leans forward. His leather chair creaks under his weight. "So you've made your decision?"

The fist in my chest still hasn't unclenched. Perhaps it never will. Either way, the answer is yes. "I'm not doing this anymore."

He has the nerve to look smug. "Where will you go?"

"Back to the beginning."

If I've lost everything, I might as well. I'll walk away. All the way to the only place I've ever known happiness.

I'll pick up the pieces and start over.

* * *

Chapter 2

Ember

It's a penis.

I stand in front of the table looking down, and there is no mistaking what it is.

Hours of online courses, too many YouTube videos to count (so many YouTube videos), correspondence courses at the community college, and this is what it comes down to...

Penis cakes for money.

Tabby rocks forward on her stool, leaning on her elbows watching me carve the corners off the beige sheet cake. Her jet-black hair is smoothed into thick curls, and a red handkerchief is wrapped around her head. Severe bangs, arched brows, and velvet-red lips. My best friend is punk rock Bettie Page.

"How can you make these and be so unaffected?"

I continue carving two round balls at the bottom of the long, almond-colored shaft. "It's cake."

"Still… you haven't been with a guy in what? Five years?"

"Don't go there."

"I'm just saying. That's one well-constructed penis."

"Again, it's cake."

"I wish Liam was black." Instantly her green eyes go round, and she leans closer, whispering, "Is that racist?"

"Depends on what you say next. Why?"

She falls back on the stool, her eyes fluttering shut. "Because your Devil's food cake with the coconut pecan buttercream icing and dark chocolate ganache is better than sex."

"Then you're not doing it right."

"You're not doing it at all!"

Cutting my eyes at her, I set the sharp knife aside.

She sniffs. "Well, you're not."

Choosing to ignore her jab, I return to her original statement, reaching for the bowl of vanilla pastry cream. "Liam is white. His penis has to match him." Pausing in my filling, I study the bisected cake in front of me. "I was planning to use all this cream for the inside, but maybe I should save some for the tip…"

"Oh my god," Tabby snorts. "Mousey little Donna White has totally knocked my socks off. This is the tackiest order in the history of Ember Rose Cakes!"

I arch an eyebrow at her. "Donna didn't order it."

Red-velvet lips part, and Tabby's eyes sparkle with mischief. "Who did?"

"Help me."

She lifts the opposite end of the top layer, and together we slowly place it over the cream-filled bottom.

The little bell over the door rings, and I step back, crossing my arms, admiring the lifelike almond-sponge penis cake with vanilla cream filling. "She doesn't like fondant, so I'm thinking I'll cover it in beige marzipan—"

"You're working late tonight, Ember." My mother's stern voice echoes through the large, empty store (a.k.a., my future bakery-slash-home).

With a hiss, Tabby spins beside me, blocking the cake with her body. I freeze, my heart thudding frantically in my chest. *Oh, shit.*

"Uh..." Tabby walks fast to meet my mother halfway between the front door and the large table at the back wall where I do my decorating. "We got a last-minute cake order for Donna's shower."

I frantically look for anything to cover the oversized male member—as if that could possibly save us from the shit-storm about to erupt.

"That's nice." Condescension is thick in her voice. "Donna's mother has been a faithful member of the church since you were little girls. I'm sure she'll appreciate your talent..."

My mother stops, and a knot lodges in my throat. Seconds like hours tick past as she steps around my best friend, arms crossed, frowning down at the phallus. Thank God I haven't added the extra cream to the tip yet.

"What is this?" Her voice is hard, disgusted.

"Just what the doctor ordered!" Tabby calls out. "A little taste of what's to come!"

It's no use. My mother is impervious to humor.

"God gives you a talent, Emberly Rose, and this is how you thank him? By making *porn*?"

My mind drifts to a list of questions, the way it always does when her lectures start: *Would God really be angry about a cake shaped like Donna's future husband's penis? Doesn't God have bigger fish to fry? Does God even fry fish? Jesus ate fish...*

"Are you listening to me, Emberly Rose?"

I blink back to attention. "It seemed like an interesting challenge."

The sweetest little voice cuts through the tension in the air. "Mommy's cake! Mommy's cake!" Everything is forgotten as I dash forward, scooping my little girl into my arms.

"Coco bean!" I spin her around and kiss her velvety cheek. The entire world is suddenly brighter.

"The purple monster says *tres*!" she chants.

"*Tres*?" I pretend to be confused. "What is *tres*?"

"Three!" she cries holding up three small fingers.

"That's right!" I hug her body snug against mine.

All the shame and fear are gone when I hold Coco, but she starts to wiggle. She wants to get down.

"I want cake! Mommy cake!"

My mother is quick to interrupt. "Colette, come to Grandmother."

"Cake! Cake! Cake!" Her little eyes sparkle and two dimples punctuate her cheeks as she cheers for cake.

Happiness rises in my chest with every pump of her cute little fist over her head.

"How about this..." I go to her and kneel, putting my hands on her tiny waist. She puts her hands on the tops of my shoulders, her dark eyes suddenly serious. "I'll make you a special cupcake with a purple monster and a big three on it."

"I'm four now."

"This isn't a birthday cake." I smooth my fingers in her hair, moving a cluster of silky brunette curls behind her ear. "It's a special cake, and I'll give it to you tomorrow."

"You won't spend the night?"

My heart sinks with her question, but I can't spend another night in my mother's house. I just can't.

"I have to fix this house for us. Remember? We're going to live upstairs. And I'll be over first thing tomorrow with your cupcake."

I carry her to the door where my mother waits, disapproval lining her thin lips. "Church tomorrow. I expect you to be there."

"I will." I give Coco another hug, taking a deep inhale of her sweet little girl scent. "Go with Granny now."

"Grandmother." My mother corrects me. "Come, Colette."

"Let's go, Granny!" Coco wiggles out of my arms to the floor then hops out like a kangaroo.

Tabby snorts behind me, and my mother's eyes narrow. "We'll finish this tomorrow."

With that she strides out, and I push the door closed behind them, resting my forehead against the glass.

"I swear, if that little girl were any less stubborn, I'd be worried about her," Tabby says from behind me.

I watch them a few seconds longer—my mother trying unsuccessfully to hold Coco's hand while they walk the four blocks to her house, the old house where I grew up.

"She'll be okay a little while longer," I say, feeling like my heart is hopping away from me, batting at her grandmother's hand with every bounce.

"Old battle axe. I guess you survived living with her."

"She wasn't like this before Minnie died." My voice is quiet, repeating a memory.

"Says who." It's not a question. It's a skeptical retort from my bestie.

"Aunt Agnes. She said my mother used to know how to have fun."

"I don't believe it."

"To be honest, I've never believed it either." I don't even remember my older sister.

"You're too independent for her. She can't handle it. She almost lost her mind when you took up with Jackson Cane so young—"

Cutting my eyes, I stop that line of conversation. "We don't talk about him."

"We should." Tabby studies my face. "He's the only guy you were ever serious about."

He said he'd come back, and he never did...

Exhaling deeply, I return to my phallic creation. "Ancient history. Now let's finish this thing before it's too late."

I ditch the marzipan idea and opt instead for a skin-toned buttercream. Tabby starts cleaning up, and I'm almost finished frosting when the bell over the door rings again.

"What is this, Grand Central?" Tabby mutters.

"How's it hanging, girls?"

"Jesus!" Tabby jerks around with a gasp, running to meet Betty Pepper, Oceanside Village's busiest of the ancient busybodies.

315

"Hi, Miss B!" she calls too loudly, intercepting the old woman. "What brings you to the store this evening?"

Betty glances around. "You should have items to sell if it's a store."

"Soon, Miss B… Just you wait," I call out. I've finished frosting the balls, and I reach for the bowl of dark chocolate shavings to sprinkle over them.

"How's my order coming?" Betty asks, and I'm pretty sure Tabs swallows her gum.

"Just finishing now," I call over my shoulder.

"Wait!" Tabby holds out her hand. "Hold the phone. Betty Pepper ordered that?"

The squat octogenarian pushes my rockabilly roommate aside and joins me at the massive, weathered-wood table where I work.

"Oh," she gasps. "Emberly Rose!"

Tabby's right behind her. "*You* ordered the penis cake?"

"Oh, *yes!*" BP clutches her chest.

"Well, don't have a heart attack," my friend snarks.

Stepping back, I survey the raunchy masterpiece. "I think it needs a vein." I pinch a bit of fondant and roll it into a long, skinny column, laying it along the shaft.

Once it's in place, I add the last bit of vanilla cream at the tip.

Miss Betty's voice is thick with lust. "It's so *good!*"

My friend arches a perfect, black eyebrow. "How long has it been since you've seen one of these?"

"Get a life, Tabitha Green. I see what I want on the Internet," Betty says before turning to me. "I can't believe you did this without a mold."

"The frosting helps." I walk to the wall of cabinets and take down my vanilla extract and a small paintbrush. "I thought about putting a square cake around the bottom and molding jeans with the fly down… Painting it blue, like it's rising out of his pants?"

The old lady's eyes widen. "You can do that?"

Using the paintbrush, I lightly dab the dark-brown vanilla around the ridges, giving the cake more dimension. "It would take a few hours."

"Forget it, then. I need it for Donna's shower now." She carefully steps around me. "It's absolutely thrilling! Hopefully it'll loosen her up some."

Tabs and I exchange a glance. "I'm glad you like it."

"How much do I owe you?"

Tabby starts to speak, but I cut her off. "Two hundred." I don't miss my best friend's glare, but I'm not going to charge an old lady full-price, even if she is annoying as hell half the time.

I also know the old biddies gossip about how much I charge for my cakes. They might call me a genius, but they won't pay genius prices for something they think they can do at home.

"Two hundred dollars?" Her lust turns to shock.

"I'm sure you took up a collection," Tabby snaps.

She still hasn't gotten over Betty Pepper ratting her out for skinny-dipping in the Holiday Inn pool last year with Mayor Rhodes's out of town nephew. It was a pretty tame stunt for Tabs… until we found out the kid was only seventeen.

In my friend's defense, the boy had a tattoo, rode a Harley, and we all thought he was at least nineteen.

BP digs in her wallet and shows us a few twenties. "This is all I've got."

"Make it a hundred and fifty, then," I sigh.

"You can write a check," Tabby adds, irritation in her tone.

The old lady is huffy, but she pulls out her checkbook and starts to write. I lift the foil-covered cardboard tray and place it in a waiting gift box on the opposite counter. Her next words stop my breath.

"Bucky can't wait until your date next Friday."

Tabby gives me a horrified, *I smell sour-milk* face, and I cringe. "Whaaat is this about?" she asks.

"Emberly is such a dear." Betty pats my forearm. "Bucky said after that brat Cheryl Ann dumped him last week, you talked to him for an hour at the Tuna Tiki."

"How could you stand it?" my roommate says. "And what were you doing at Tuna Tiki?"

"I wanted sushi," I say.

Betty pushes on undeterred. "Then she agreed to have dinner with him."

"You did not!" Tabby grabs my arm.

"It wasn't… quite like that." I step away, untying my apron and wiping my hands with it.

"He said you were. Are you not going to dinner with Bucky on Friday?" Betty cries.

"No. You are *not* going to dinner with Bucky on Friday," Tabby says.

"Why would you say something like that, Tabitha? Just because my Bucky isn't some pot-smoking, Harley Davidson riding —"

"I'll have you know, Betty Pepper, I've only dated three guys who smoked pot —"

"You know what?" I shout before those two start throwing punches. "It's just dinner. I'm glad to do it if it helps Bucky get over Cheryl… or whatever."

"You are *not* glad to do it. Bucky Pepper is a — *Ouch!*"

I release her flesh from my sly pinch and pull the pin out of my dark hair, letting it fall down my back. "Thank you so much, Miss Betty."

"It's too bad you won't be joining us for cake." The old lady prances to the door, and I lean against the counter. The bell tinkles, and she's gone.

Tabby turns, arms crossed to glare at me. "What. The fuck. Bucky Pepper smells like formaldehyde!"

"He's a taxidermist."

"He's the shape of a coke bottle, and he'll probably give you a stuffed squirrel!"

I can't help a laugh. "It's better than herpes."

"Jesus, don't even joke about sleeping with him." Tabby does a full-body shiver. "His breath is like… like…"

I think a minute then it hits me. "Deviled eggs." Nodding, I collect my ingredients and carry them to the shelves, where I arrange them neatly in order. "I just realized it smells like deviled eggs."

"Good lord, Ember." My friend lowers her gaze. "I cannot in good faith let you go out with that… that…"

Reaching out, I squeeze her arm. "So I go out with Bucky the stinky taxidermist. He gives me stuffed road-kill. It's one night."

"I heard he tried to grab Cheryl Ann's cooch on their very first date. That's why she ditched him. She should've slapped him into next week." Tabby puts a hand on her hip and does her best Jane Russell glare. "What will you do if Bucky tries to grab you?"

"I'll throw ice water in his face and go home." Stepping forward I kiss her cheek. "See you tomorrow."

"There's no shame in pretending you don't hear him knocking."

"Goodnight, Tabs."

She grumbles as she leaves, and I walk slowly to the back of the old store where stairs lead to my loft apartment above. After my aunt died, she left this old five and dime store to me. Tabby helped me sell or trash all the shelves and retail furnishings, and I've been scrubbing and painting ever since.

Weathered wood painted white makes up the walls of shelves where I keep my meager baking ingredients. Two vintage chandeliers, fake branches, and driftwood arranged in vases are the start of my interior design. One day I imagine having a garland of multi-colored spring roses like Peggy Porschen's at the entrance.

"One day," I say softly, dreaming of the lavish London bakery and the lady who owns it.

The only piece of furniture I've been able to buy is the heavy wooden table where I do all my mixing, kneading, arranging, decorating...

I kept my aunt's register and checkout counter for front reception. Slowly, slowly I'm saving up to add a refrigerated case. Last month, I was finally able to buy a second oven so I can cook two cakes at once.

"Just keep swimming." I push open the heavy door leading to the upstairs where Coco and I will live.

When Mr. Lockwood developed that old stretch of sand, all the tourists moved away from our little village down to the beachfront property. I hope my cakes lure them back here—at least to shop—and if they do, I'll be a small-town hero pulling tourist dollars back into Our Town.

I walk over to my small table and pick up the photo of me on the beach, looking up, holding my little girl. "That's the plan, Coco Bean," I whisper.

I'll have my daughter and my cake shop, and that's all I need. One foot in front of the other, and before I know it, my dreams coming true.

* * *

Get *When We Touch* on Amazon Today!

Exclusive Sneak Peek

The Prince & The Player
(Dirty Players #1)
© TLM Productions LLC, 2016

Prologue

Zelda Wilder

My legs are wet. Thunder rolls low in a steel-grey sky, and the hiss of warm rain grows louder. I lean further sideways into the culvert, closer against my little sister Ava's body, and grit my teeth against the hunger pain twisting my stomach. There's no way in hell I'm sleeping tonight.

Reaching up, I rub my palm against the back of my neck, under the thick curtain of my blonde hair. A shudder moves at my side, and I realize Ava's crying. We're packed tight in this concrete ditch, but I twist my body around to face her.

Clearing my throat, I force my brows to unclench. I force my voice to be soothing instead of angry. "Hey," I whisper softly. "What's the matter, Ava-bug?"

Silence greets me. She's small enough to be somewhat comfortable in our hideout. Her knees are bent, but unlike me, they're not shoved up into her nose. Still, she leans forward to press her eyes against the backs of her hands. Her glossy brown hair is short around her ears and falls onto her cheeks.

Our parents were classic movie buffs, naming her after Ava Gardner and me after Scott Fitzgerald's crazy wife Zelda. We pretty much lived up to our monikers, since my little sister wound up having emerald green cat eyes and wavy dark hair. She's a showstopper whereas I'm pretty average—flat blue eyes and dishwater blonde. So far no signs of schizophrenia (*har har*), but you can bet your ass I can keep up with the boys in everything, which brings us to this lowly state.

"Come on, now," I urge. "It can't be as bad as all that."

Her dark head moves back and forth. "I'm sorry." Her soft whisper finally answers my question. "This is all my fault."

"What?" Reaching for her skinny shoulder, I pull her up. She's the only person I've ever known who looks pretty even when she's crying. "Why would you say something like that?"

"I tried cutting my hair off. I tried not brushing my teeth—"

"Don't be doing shit like that!" I snap, turning to face front. The rain keeps splashing on my side getting me even wetter. "We can't afford a dentist."

"I don't know what to do, Zee."

Pressing my lips together, I clench my fists on top of my knees. "We ain't going back into no foster home. I'll take care of us."

"But how?" Her voice breaks as it goes high in a whisper.

"Hell, I don't know, but I got all night to figure it out." I press my front teeth together and think. We're not that far from being legal. I'm seventeen, but Ava's only fifteen. Looking at the sand on my shoes, I get an idea. "We got one thing going for us."

"What's that?" My little sister sniffs, and I hear the tiniest flicker of hope in her voice. She'll trust whatever I tell her, and I take that responsibility very seriously.

"We live in the greatest state to be homeless. Sunny Florida."

"Okay?" Her slim brows wrinkle, and the tears in her eyes make them look like the ocean.

"We don't have to worry about getting cold or anything. We don't have to worry about snow…" I'm thinking hard, assembling a plan in my mind. "During the day, we fly under the radar—keep your head down, don't attract attention. I'll see what I can find us to eat. At night we can sleep on the beach. Or here, or hell, maybe one of these rich assholes forgets to lock his boathouse. Have you seen how nice some of these boathouses are? They're like regular houses!"

Her eyes go round with surprise. "Why are they like that?"

"Hell, I don't know. Rich people are crazy. Some rich men even get their nails polished, and they aren't even gay!"

Air bursts through her lips, and she starts to laugh. I smile and pull her arm so she can lie down with her face on my bony, empty stomach. "Now get some sleep."

The rain is tapering off, and my little sister is laughing instead of crying. I don't have any idea if anything I just said is possible, but I'm going to find out. I'll be damned if I let another foster asshole touch her. It's what Mom would expect me to do. I'm the biggest. I have to take care of us, and I intend to do it.

* * *

Rowan Westringham Tate

The navy fabric of my father's uniform coat stretches taut across his shoulders. It's the tangible warning sign his anger is rising, and the person addressing him would do well to *shut up*.

"Monagasco has been an independent nation for eight hundred years." His voice is a rolling growl pricking the tension in my chest.

The last time my father started on our nation's history, the offending party was thrown out of the meeting room by the neck. He's getting too old for such violent outbursts. I worry about his heart... and my future. My *freedom*, more specifically.

"I think what Hubert was trying to say—" The Grand Duke, my mother's brother Reginald Winchester, tries to intervene.

"I KNOW what Hubert is trying to say!" My father (a.k.a., The King) cuts him off. "He thinks we should cede our southwestern territory to Totrington! Even though their raiders and bandits have pillaged our farms along the border for *generations*!"

Leaning back in my heavy oak chair, I steeple my fingers before my lips and don't say what I want. As crown prince, I've attended these meetings for three years, since I turned nineteen. I've learned when to speak and when to discuss things in private with my father.

I could say I agree with Reggie, we should consider a trade agreement with our neighboring nation-state, but I'm more concerned about the King's health. I've never seen him so worked up before.

"Independence at all costs," he continues, his naturally pink cheeks even pinker. "We will not give those savages an open door to the control of Monagasco."

"No one's suggesting—"

"Shut UP, Hubert!" My father shouts, and I glance down to avoid meeting the earl's offended eyes.

Hubert's sniveling voice is like nails on a chalkboard, and I privately enjoy my father chastising him. I've always suspected him of conspiring with Wade Paxton, Totrington's newly elected Prime Minister, from the time when Wade was only a member of their parliament.

"I've had enough of this." My father walks to the window and looks out. "I'd like to speak to Rowan in private. You can all go."

"Of course." Reginald stands at once, smoothing his long hands down the front of his dark coat.

Tall and slender, with greying black hair and a trim mustache, my uncle embodies the Charmant line of our family. I inherited their height and Norman complexion. My father, by contrast, is a Tate through and through. Short, pink, and round.

As soon as the room is cleared, he stalks back to the table, still brooding like a thunderstorm. "Reggie's in league with them as well," he growls.

"Not necessarily." My voice is low and level, and I hope appeasing. "My uncle does have an idea, and of the two, it's the least offensive. Hubert would combine our countries and walk away—"

"Exactly!" Father snaps, turning to face me, blue eyes blazing. "My own cousin, born and reared in our beautiful land. He's been promised a place in the new government, I'll bet you. They'll throw the lot of us out—behead us if they can."

"I'm pretty sure beheading is no longer tolerated in western civilization."

"Harumph." He's still angry, but at least he's calmer. "It would break your mother's heart. The Charmants founded Monagasco. We can't let those Twatringtons in."

His use of the unofficial nickname for our southwest neighbor makes me grin. Rising from my chair, I brace his shoulder in a firm grasp.

"We won't let that happen." Our blue eyes meet. It's the only feature we share. He's a few inches shorter than me, but he makes up for it in stubbornness. "We're flush with reserves, and the economy can change at any time."

His thick hand covers mine. "I'm doing my best to leave you a strong country to rule. The country I inherited."

"We would do well to reduce our dependence on foreign oil reserves." He starts to argue, but I hold up a hand as I head for the door. He's finally calm, and I'm not interested in riling him up again. "In any event, you'll be around long enough to see the tides turn. Now get some rest." I'm at the enormous wooden door of the war room. "We can't solve all our problems in one day."

"Goodnight, son."

The tone in his voice causes me to look back. He's at the window, and a troubled expression mars his profile. A shimmer of concern passes through my stomach, but I dismiss it, quietly stepping into the dim hallway. It's enormous and shrouded with heavy velvet curtains and tapestries.

I grew up playing in these halls, hiding from my mother and chasing my younger brother. I'm tired and ready for bed when the sound of hushed voices stops me in my tracks.

"Pompous ass. He's going to kill himself with these outbursts. We need to be ready to move when that happens." The glee in Hubert's sniveling voice revives the anger in my chest. I step into the shadows to listen.

"By climbing into bed with Wade Paxton?"

I recognize my uncle's voice, and my jaw clenches. *Is Father right? Is Reginald conspiring with that worm against the crown?*

"Wade Paxton would unite the kingdoms and make us both leaders in the new government."

"Wade Paxton is a thug."

"Not very respectful verbiage for the Prime Minister of Totrington, also known as our future partner."

"He's no better than one of those mob bosses on American television. Savage." Reggie's voice is laced with snobbery. "He'd tax the people and change the very nature of Monagasco."

Hubert's tone is undeterred. "Some things might change, but as leaders, you and I can help maintain the best parts, the heart of the nation. Once Philip is out of the way, of course, which could be sooner than we think."

My fists tighten at my sides. I'm ready to step out of the shadows and shake Hubert's traitorous neck until his teeth rattle. The only thing stopping me is my desire to hear the extent of this treachery.

"You're right about one thing," Reggie says. "Philip's health is tenuous. We need to be prepared to act should a crisis arise."

"What about Rowan? If he's not on our side, we could end up in the same position—and with a much younger king to wait out."

"Possibly." My uncle pauses, and I feel the heat rising around my collar.

"Wade has a plan for managing such a contingency. Should Rowan prove... difficult."

"I'm sure he does," Reggie scoffs. "And Cal? Shall we wipe out the entire Tate line?"

Hubert's voice is low and wicked. "Perhaps being in league with a 'thug' as you put it has its advantages."

How dare these bastards! What they're saying is high treason! My body is poised to move when Reggie's words freeze me in place.

"I'm sure Wade's tactics won't prove necessary. When the time comes to do the right thing, we can count on Rowan."

Count on Rowan? Is it possible he thinks I would even consider a merger with Twatrington? Their voices recede down the corridor as my level of disgust and loyalty to my father rises. The king has had a difficult evening. I'll let him rest tonight, but I will present him with this conspiracy first thing tomorrow. Reggie is right. When the time comes, I will do the right thing.

Looking back, I had no idea the time would come in less than twenty-four hours...

* * *

Get The Prince & The Player *from your favorite retailer today!*

Also available in audiobook format.

ACKNOWLEDGMENTS

The few people who read *Under the Lights* in 2011, when I first wrote it, have asked me for the rest of the story ever since… To be fair, the original ending was slightly different—Mark was not beaten almost to death—but Lara still fled with Freddie.

Early readers didn't care for that ending, and to be honest, I had more exciting times, a red-hot reunion, revenge, traveling, all the things in my head.

I just wasn't sure I'd ever be able to get back to it—my writing life kept pulling me farther and farther away from here.

So I should start by thanking A.D. Justice for pulling me into the Vault anthology, making me write the novella "Sundown," which led to where we are now—the story finished and me sharing it with you all!

I hope you love this story as much as I have from the time it floated to me on a song one cool, autumn morning in 2010.

And now for the people I absolutely cannot get a book out without, Ilona Townsel, Mr. TL, Ilsa Madden-Mills, Aleatha Romig, Lisa Kuhne, all my author friends who help me spread the word, all the bloggers and early readers…

New this time, I had an incredible little band of beta readers who kept me writing chapter by chapter, every day—Lulu Dumonceaux, Tina Morgan, and Ilona. Y'all know how much I needed that push to get this finished.

So much thanks to Tamara Mataya, my amazing editor, who keeps me laughing through the pain and to Letitia Hasser for the absolutely gorgeous cover designs. You ladies ROCK!

And to Shannon and Shayna who make the most amazing little works of art... we need a better name than "teasers" for these little gems.

Enormous thanks to Brooke Nowiski, the hardest working girl in the PR business; also, Jenn Watson at Social Butterfly PR, and a special thanks to Lisa Hintz at TRSOR. I appreciate you ladies more than I can ever say.

THANKS to my MERMAIDS for loving my books and being so excited about this new release. (Special thanks to "Trixie Trixie," Angel Hollmeyer Crum, and Patricia Cordovez for donating a quote for the chapter heads — I used them!)

THANK YOU to ALL the bloggers who have made an art and a science of book loving. Sharing this book with the reading world would be impossible

To everyone who picks up this book, reads it, loves it, and tells *one* person about it, you've made my day. I'm so grateful to you all. Without readers, there would be no writers.

Keep reading,
Stay sexy,
So much love,
<3 *Tia*

ABOUT THE AUTHOR

Tia Louise is the *USA Today* best-selling, award-winning author of *When We Touch*, the "One to Hold" and "Dirty Players" series, and co-author of the #4 Amazon bestseller *The Last Guy*.

She loves all the books, all the chocolate (the darker the better), strong coffee, and sparkling wine.

After being a teacher, a book editor, a journalist, and finally a magazine editor, she started writing love stories and never stopped.

Louise lives in the Midwest with her trophy husband, two teenage geniuses, and one grumpy cat.

Keep up with Tia online:
www.AuthorTiaLouise.com

www.ingramcontent.com/pod-product-compliance
Ingram Content Group UK Ltd.
Pitfield, Milton Keynes, MK11 3LW, UK
UKHW041855161224
3699UKWH00046B/971